[Y]ou cannot help but be moved, amused, a:
teaches. You want to help them, and Clark .
impulse to generate interest in these lost kids.

— *Globe* and

Chai Tea Sunday is both heartbreaking and heartwarming. A story about love and loss, it's real, honest, and compelling. I loved it.

— Chantel Guertin, bestselling author of *Stuck in Downward Dog*

Life affirming . . . every woman will be able to relate to some part of the journey Heather A.Clark has created. Through the heartbreak and the happiness, I couldn't put it down.

— Liza Fromer, host of Global's *The Morning Show*

Clark effortlessly takes the reader to the emotional and physical places her characters go and has written a moving tale about love, loss, and caring. The story, like the land in which it takes place, is full of contradictions — both wonderfully sad and beautifully uplifting — and it breathes life into the understanding that most readers have about how people might actually live in Kenya through layers of dimension and richness.

— Julie Osborne, deputy publisher, *Maclean's* magazine

Heather has painted a picture that so many women will relate to. The main character, Nicky, became my best friend while I read the book. She had a story that I so deeply related to — I cried when she did and rejoiced in her happiness. I found myself learning lessons that I will apply to my own life. But even above these lessons, I just found myself enjoying a great story of adventure and love.

— Christina Litz, iVillage.ca

Chai Tea Sunday is a beautifully written novel about life, love, loss, and living. The characters and emotions are so real, and raw, at times I felt that I was experiencing their circumstances first hand. Clark has written an incredible first novel.

— Joanna Track, founder, eLuxe.ca

The novel tells the story of a life complicated by first-world problems that is put into the context of lives in developing and unstable cultures.

— *Waterloo Region Record*

PRAISE FOR CHAI TEA SUNDAY

Chai Tea Sunday by Heather A. Clark is a thoughtful new novel that is sure to pull at your heartstrings.

— *Haliburton County Echo* (Book of the Week)

This is a light and straightforward read that still explores the nature of true love and the delicacy of human rights. . . . This is a book you can feel good about buying, too: a portion of the proceeds from the sale will be donated to Artbound, a Canadian volunteer initiative committed to building schools in developing nations.

— *Scene* magazine

[*Chai Tea Sunday*] is a refreshing and enjoyable read.

— *The Guelph Mercury*

A week later, after reading close to half a dozen [more] books, I can't forget the lessons learned in *Chai Tea Sunday*. I loved this novel. . . . It brought tears to my eyes and was hard to put down as I turned pages waiting to see what would become of Nicky.

— *Roundtable Reviews*

I was mesmerized and read *Chai Tea Sunday* in one sitting. I just couldn't put the book down and didn't want it to end. This is one novel I won't soon forget and it has earned a spot on my permanent bookshelf! Congratulations Ms. Clark on a wonderful debut novel!

— *The Book Bag Lady*

As I started reading this book, I could not put it down. I was originally drawn to learning about the relationship of Nicky and her husband, then I was torn as they battled difficulty. As Nicky moved her life to try to regain a sense of herself, I packed my bag to join her.

— *Mother Daughter Reading Team*

In style, the writing reminds this reader of Lisa Genova, author of *Still Alice* and *Left Neglected*. Although the story presents an experience for the main character with which I cannot personally identify, I was moved nonetheless.

— *Julie's Reading Corner*

HEATHER A. CLARK

ELEPHANT
IN THE SKY

ECW PRESS

Published by ECW Press
2120 Queen Street East, Suite 200, Toronto, Ontario, Canada M4E 1E2
416-694-3348 / info@ecwpress.com

This is a work of fiction. Names, characters, places, and incidents either are the product of the author's imagination or are used fictitiously, and any resemblance to actual persons, living or dead, business establishments, events, or locales is entirely coincidental.

LIBRARY AND ARCHIVES CANADA CATALOGUING IN PUBLICATION

Clark, Heather A., 1977-, author
Elephant in the sky / Heather A. Clark.

Issued in print and electronic formats.
ISBN: 978-1-77041-083-1 (PBK) | 978-1-77090-491-0 (PDF) | 978-1-77090-492-7 (EPUB)

I. Title.

PS8605.L36225E54 2014   C813'.6   C2013-907765-0
C2013-907766-9

Editor for the press: Jennifer Hale
Cover and text design: David Gee
Cover image: © Alloy Photography/Veer
Author photo: © Negin Sairafi
Printing: Friesens 1 2 3 4 5
Printed and bound in Canada

The publication of *Elephant in the Sky* has been generously supported by the Canada Council for the Arts which last year invested $157 million to bring the arts to Canadians throughout the country, and by the Ontario Arts Council (OAC), an agency of the Government of Ontario, which last year funded 1,681 individual artists and 1,125 organizations in 216 communities across Ontario for a total of $52.8 million. We also acknowledge the financial support of the Government of Canada through the Canada Book Fund for our publishing activities, and the contribution of the Government of Ontario through the Ontario Book Publishing Tax Credit and the Ontario Media Development Corporation.

In loving memory of GAC

1
Nate

I want gum. Not the gross green kind that Mom has in her purse. I need the awesome sticky pink gum. Or the purple kind. That's good too. The yummy Hubba Bubba stuff that lets you blow a bubble so big it sticks to your whole face when it pops.

One time last summer I blew my best bubble ever. It took four pieces. And it was so amazing because it went in my eyes and all over my hair. And Mom was mad. I knew right away because her face was all blotchy and red. And she kept biting her lip when she used ice to get it all out of my hair.

"I'm going to get pink gum. No . . . I want purple. Or maybe orange. Wanna come?" I ask my best friend, Noah. He lives four doors down from me in the blue house and we do everything together. Our favourite thing is swimming. But Mom says we can't do that anymore because summer is over and the pool is closed. So instead we ride our bikes. As long as we have sweaters on because it's starting to be cold.

"Noah?" I repeat. He is ignoring me. "Do you want to come?" .

Noah shrugs. He doesn't look away from the Wii game he's playing in my bedroom. It's tennis. Our favourite. I thought I wanted to play with him but then I started and it kept hurting my eyes, so I stopped. And now I want gum, anyway.

"How are you going to get it?" Noah asks me. His eyes stay on the screen.

"There's gum at the store. Lots of it. I'll bike."

Noah shrugs. He doesn't care about my gum.

But I want it. I need to have it. Even though I know I shouldn't go to the store by myself.

I pause for a minute. I feel bubbles in my belly. The kind that come when I know Mommy will be mad. And I feel hot. I always feel hot right after the belly bubbles.

I push past Noah and the Wii remote he's still holding. I need to get to my dresser fast before I start sweating. The sweating happens after I feel hot.

I rip off my sauce-stained sweatshirt. Dad made spaghetti when he picked me up from school for lunch. It's Friday and he said we could have a special treat. So I picked spaghetti. But then I didn't feel like eating it so I used it to paint rocket ships on my belly. I thought Dad would think I was creative and smart. But Dad just seemed mad when he saw my rocket ships.

I tear open my top drawer. I pull out the first T-shirt I can find. It's red. I wish I wore that at lunch. Maybe Dad wouldn't have seen the spaghetti sauce.

I put the red T-shirt on.

I'm still hot. And I'm sweating now too. I pull off my track pants so I'm wearing just the red T-shirt and my Spider-Man underwear. They are totally my favourite underwear. They are from Santa. And I still believe in him even though everyone at school says he's not real.

I think about putting on some shorts but I am too hot. And the belly bubbles are getting bigger.

I need gum. Orange gum.

"You're going out there like that?" Noah asks. "Don't you think your mom will be mad?"

I know he is right. Mommy will be mad. But shorts will make me too hot.

Oh, I know what to do!

I will put on another pair of underwear. The blue ones. They will cover up my Spider-Man *real* underwear. I am smart for coming up with this solution. Mommy will be happy. She likes it when I think of my own ways to solve my problems.

But then something does not feel right on my insides. I don't know why.

I think it is because the red shirt is too tight and it is pressing on my belly bubbles. I yank it off and pull out all of my shirts from the drawer.

I try on a yellow one. It's scratchy.

I switch it for an orange one. Mommy says it is faded. And way too small for me and needs to be thrown out. But I will not throw it out no matter what. I love it because it says "Grandpa Loves Me" and I don't see him anymore. It was the last present he gave me. So I will wear it forever.

The orange Grandpa shirt is too tight on my arms. It hurts.

So I try every other shirt in the drawer.

Nothing works.

I am hot anyway so I decide that wearing two pairs of underwear is kind of like wearing a bathing suit. And summer wasn't that long ago. I need my gum.

I run to my door and listen. I know my big sister Grace is in her room pretending to do homework. And she will tell Dad if she knows I am going to get gum. She always tells on me.

"Dude, you gotta make a run for it if you're going to get gum. Just go already, would you?" Noah gives me a little push.

I look back at him. I am not sure I should go anymore. I don't know what to do. I cannot seem to think and my brain feels all fuzzy.

"What if they find out?" I ask Noah. I do not want Mommy or Daddy to be mad at me. But I need to get the gum. I *have* to have the gum.

"Dude, if you want the gum that bad, I'll lie for you. I'll say you're going poo in the bathroom or something. Just go."

I do not want Grace to stop me so I run down the hall. Superman fast. I pass her bedroom. I think I hear Grace humming but I am running too fast to know. She must *actually* be doing her homework because she always hums when she's doing it. It hurts my ears, but Mommy likes it.

I do not know where Dad is so I grab my bike from the garage and ride down the street very fast. I speed to the next street. Cars zoom by me. There are so many of them. One almost hits me. The guy driving the car honks his horn. But I don't care. The outside feels good. I am almost not hot anymore. But the belly bubbles will not go away.

I ride to the store. I jump off my bike and run to the fruit stands outside on the sidewalk. I smell grapes. So I stop to look at them. There are rows and rows of the dark purple kind that turn into grape jelly. I want to eat one because they remind me of my Mommy. They are her favourite.

But I need my gum. So I forget the grapes and run to the front counter. There is a skinny man in a white shirt with a green apron sitting on a stool. He does not look up from his book but waves his hand to say hello. He does not see me.

I look at the gum. I want red.

No, pink.

Purple.

Or maybe orange.

Nope. Pink. It has to be pink.

I feel hot again. I cannot decide. I do not know which one I want and my brain is buzzing.

I will buy them all with my money. Dad gave it to me as a prize after lunch because I helped him clean up and did not break one dish. I put it in the pocket of my pants to keep it safe.

I look down.

I am not wearing my pants anymore. I do not have my money. I try to figure out how to get the five-dollar bill from lunch. Dad gave me that one because he knows it is my favourite money because I love blue so much.

Oh, right! Now I know. *Blue* gum. It's my favourite colour so I know I will love it. Do they have blue gum? They must.

I keep looking but can't find it. I do not know if there is blue gum. I need to think harder. But my brain is working too fast. I cannot make it stop no matter how I try. I hit my head with my hands to try to make it work better.

And then I remember something important.

The big bubble gum machine from swimming lessons. Mommy sometimes gets gum for me if the swimming teacher does not need to "talk to her" after my lesson is over. When I am good I get to put a quarter in the bubble gum machine that has all different colours of big sticky gumballs. And it has *blue* gumballs.

I know there must be blue gum if the swimming gumball machine has it. I pull off some chocolate bars from the counter shelf to look underneath them. The chocolate hits the floor and the noise sounds kind of like the drums on my Wii Rock Band game. I like the sound. So I pull off some more. There is no blue gum under the chocolate bars.

The man in the green apron looks up from his book. He

looks really mad. He is shaking his arms and yelling at me but I cannot understand his words. His voice sounds funny to me. So I start laughing.

The man yells at me in a louder voice. And I still think it is funny. So I laugh harder. It is like a contest to see who is louder. And I want to win.

But then I stop laughing. It is not funny anymore. I hear what the man is yelling. He is telling me to get out of his store. But I cannot leave yet because I need my blue gum.

The man starts screaming the word "police." I am happy because the police help you. And I need help because the man is not funny anymore and he is scaring me. I want to go but I cannot leave without my gum. There is no blue so I get pink and purple and red and orange. Four packs.

The man comes out from behind the counter. He grabs my arm. I am really scared so I kick him in the leg and pull away.

Then I grab my bike and ride home as fast as I can so I can share my gum with Noah.

2
Ashley

Without needing to look at the clock on the wall behind me, I knew I was pushing my luck. Despite finishing my part of the presentation sixty minutes earlier, I didn't need to glance at my boss, the CEO of one of the world's largest and most successful advertising agencies, to know I wasn't going anywhere any time soon.

I stifled the sigh threatening to expose itself, plastered a smile on my face that I knew would look genuinely energetic, and forced myself to remain engaged in the creative concepts discussion — even though all I could think about was that I had promised my family that I wouldn't be late for dinner. Again.

As the creative director at AJ & Emerson, I knew how

important the meeting was that was going on around me. We had just finished our pitch presentation for one of the largest bids the industry had seen in years, and just over a hundred million dollars in yearly revenue was up for grabs. I'd had a team of twenty working on the pitch creative for weeks, and I couldn't let them — or myself — down by not remaining fully engaged in the meeting. Even though it was running over by about sixty minutes and I was once again going to miss dinner with my family.

This has to be a good sign, I could practically hear my boss, Jack, thinking. He smiled and nodded, soaking up the glory of the overly enthusiastic clients who were asking so many questions I knew we had nailed the creative.

I caught his glance and returned his smile before answering the question that had just been posed by Chelsea, the client's senior vice president of marketing. A woman in her early forties with a bright smile and a killer Dolce & Gabbana suit, I knew we'd have fun together at a business dinner with lots of wine.

"Yes, Chelsea, concept three is our official recommendation. We love all the creative we've shown you today, and we think any of them will work. They all effectively communicate the business strategy you've briefed us on. But we feel the skyline concept does the best job of showcasing your unique selling proposition. It's highly visual and we think it will immediately resonate with your consumers." I took a quick breath, pausing purposely for effect. "When we came up with the idea, I knew we had a winner."

"And how long did that take?" Chelsea asked, smiling across the boardroom table that was littered with concepts and sketches. The meeting was quickly waltzing towards the two-and-a-half-hour mark.

"Let's just say it wasn't straight out of the gate. The team has worked very hard on your business. In fact, the whole team has been, and would continue to be, extremely committed to ensuring we deliver the best creative this industry has seen." I returned Chelsea's smile. We connected, and my spidey senses told me how close we were to winning the business. "I'll be honest and tell you the creative process for this presentation took a lot of work. But of course we had fun along the way, too . . ."

"Well, we certainly like fun. As long as it accompanies great work. Which this is, by the way." Chelsea pushed her dark-rimmed glasses to the bridge of her nose and continued to examine the concept I had recommended. "In fact, it's excellent. Absolutely amazing work."

And there it was. The final confirmation that told me we had won the business. For a pitch presentation, Chelsea was much more forthcoming in her feedback than most clients would be in her shoes, which I couldn't help but notice were the hottest pair of suede Miu Miu peep-toes to hit the fall runway. The woman clearly had great taste, in both her attire and creative judgement.

"May I ask what the next steps are?" I was anxious to know what would happen next, but even more eager to wrap up the meeting, since we had pretty much secured the business. With the long hours and tough work now behind us, I wanted to get home to my family. All I could think about was sinking into my kitchen chair at our oversized harvest table and talking to my husband and children about how their days had been.

I knew that Pete, my husband of almost thirteen years, who had decided to quit his full-time job as a copywriter to stay at home with our kids, would be just finishing making dinner. I vaguely remembered him saying something about pork tenderloin as I was getting dressed that morning, but my brain had been focused on my big presentation and not on an early-morning dinner selection.

Our twelve-year-old daughter, Grace, would be setting the table for dinner, still wearing her volleyball uniform, which would likely be wrinkled and untucked. Setting the table was Grace's weekday chore that she couldn't miss — or complain about — if she expected her allowance on Saturday. She had learned her lesson the hard way when she'd complained about it every night and had to wait another week for her allowance so she could afford to buy the new shirt from Aritzia she'd wanted.

Grace was our early-marriage surprise, leaving both Pete and me completely panic-stricken at the sight of the faint double line on the pregnancy test I had peed on. We'd only been married for a few months, and were in the very early stage of our careers. Both of us still worked the incessantly long hours required by any advertising job, and we never seemed to leave the AJ & Emerson office, where we had met two years before our daughter's arrival.

Bolting through one of the speediest engagements in history, Pete and I had decided to get married after only six months of dating. With no more than a long weekend available to us, we eloped to the closest warm location that had a minimal waiting time. We were married on our second day at the only dodgy hotel we could afford in the Bahamas, with no one but a rented-by-the-hour minister and a witness from our hotel, whom Pete swears was the same person who brought our room service the next day. We flew home and returned to work on Monday morning.

Three months after we were married, I found out I was pregnant. Lucky for me, I had one of the easiest pregnancies a girl could hope for, and I breezed through the nine months with very few changes to my lifestyle or crazy workaholic ways.

Despite my immediate infatuation with our daughter, I fell victim to the pressure to return to work, and took only half of my maternity leave. To my surprise, Pete suggested that he take advantage of the recent changes that allowed fathers to stay at home with their babies, and he temporarily left his job to take paternity leave with Grace. With no family to help take care of Grace, and local daycares that all had mile-long waiting lists, we had limited options for who could stay with our daughter during the day.

Pete happily fell into the daily routine of babyland, and he and Grace quickly formed a tight-knit bond that, if I was honest with myself, I knew I didn't have with my daughter. I loved Grace more than life itself, but the monotony of diaper changes and feeding schedules drove me batty. And I wasn't prepared to return to it for many more years.

But Pete's plea for more children grew in frequency as Grace got older and when he returned to work. He'd lost both of his parents when he was in his early twenties, and the only family left was his sister, whom he rarely saw, so he'd become anxious to surround himself with a big family and lots of children.

I wasn't so ready to add to our brood. I had recently been promoted, and was thriving at work. I loved the challenges of my job, and wanted to keep climbing the AJ & Emerson creative ladder.

Pete, on the other hand, seemed more content to ride the slower track at work. But even with him coasting in his career climb, we were still struggling to achieve balance at home. The demands of an advertising agency were intense, and we bounced from job to home at lightning speed with very little room for anything else. I was convinced that adding another child would throw us even more off kilter and unhinge any sense of sanity we'd managed to hold onto.

But when I couldn't resist Pete and all of his charm a moment longer, I conceded to his insistent request and we began to try for baby number two. I convinced myself that I'd still have time because it would likely take a while for me to get pregnant again. But almost nine months to the day after I gave in, we welcomed Nate to the family. Grace had a brother, just as Pete wanted, and my husband was reunited with his glory days, and stayed at home with two kids while I went back to work. After a year, he decided he was happier at home and became a freelance writer.

"Ashley? Do you have anything more to add?" Jack asked abruptly, interrupting my thoughts as he wrapped up the meeting.

"I'd say we've covered everything," I responded, forcing my brain back into the meeting. I smiled as I stood from my seat and walked around our biggest boardroom, which also boasted impressive views of the city. I shook everyone's hands. "Thank you so much for coming in today. We're happy you could see our offices and get a sense of our working environment."

Chelsea nodded, quickly smiling before turning back to her smartphone. Using her distraction as my cue that the meeting was officially over, I said a final goodbye and excused myself from the boardroom.

Running out of the main doors of our building, I hailed the first cab I could find. The stench of body odour mixed with vomit smacked me in the face as I pulled open the door. I paused for half a second, thinking I needed to wait for the next taxi.

But my promise of getting home for a family dinner trumped the cab stink; I took a final deep breath of clean air before climbing in and giving the greasy-haired cab driver my address.

I texted Pete to let him know I was on my way home, and received a response back ten minutes later with nothing but a warning to brace myself and come home quickly. *"He's driving me nuts and he's done it again. Come home quickly, okay? I need help."*

"Thanks for the details, Pete," I mumbled under my breath. I knew he was talking about Nate, but I had no idea what had happened. Or just how bad it was.

I immediately texted Pete back, but got nothing in return. I knew if Nate was in danger Pete would have said otherwise, but I could only imagine what Nate had done this time.

3

Sitting in front of my house, I handed the cab driver forty dollars and told him to keep the rest. It had been a long ride home, filled with honking horns and commuter traffic. I didn't have time to wait for change.

I grabbed my red Prada laptop bag from the seat beside me, and rid myself of the stench that I had grown too accustomed to during the extended cab ride home. I wondered if I now smelled like it, or if my beautiful bag, a present from Pete the previous Christmas, had absorbed the stink.

I kicked the door shut with my right foot, and practically ran into the house. In the family room, I found Nate on the sofa wearing nothing but blue underwear and holding four packs of gum. Pete was standing opposite him, with his arms folded and his face the colour of my bag.

"What's going on?" I rushed into the room. "And why are you in your underwear, Nate?"

"I think the bigger question right now is where he got the gum. Or should I say *how*," Pete answered, not taking his eyes off our son for one second. Nate looked down and I could see his shoulders slump at what I could only assume was regret mixed with a bit of fear.

"Nate? *Answer* my question," Pete said harshly, trying hard to keep his voice calm.

We waited, but still Nate said nothing.

"He won't talk to me. Won't answer a thing." Pete shook his head, his fists tightly clenched.

I looked up to see a pork roast resting beside the stovetop. Grace had finished setting the table and had disappeared somewhere in the house. I grabbed a blanket to wrap around Nate. He was shivering, and still looking down.

"Will you talk to me, sweetie?" I asked. "Where'd you get the gum?"

Nate shrugged. His breathing became more rapid, just as it always did when we faced this type of situation with him.

Pete motioned for me to follow him so we could talk privately, and I was just starting to step away from my son when Nate piped up, "I, uh, I got it at the store. That one where we went for milk last week." Nate was twitching now, tears streaming down his cheeks. Beside me, Pete softened as he watched our son's confession.

"And . . . how did you pay for it?" Pete asked. I wanted to know the answer, but based on the way Pete asked it, I was also afraid of what it would be.

Nate shrugged again.

"Nate?"

"I . . . um . . . well, I . . . I took it."

"You *took* it?" I asked. My blood began to boil. Nate had done a crazy amount of frustrating things in his short lifetime, but breaking the law wasn't one of them. I glanced at Pete as he raised an eyebrow at me, and I realized he already knew this.

Nate nodded, a large tear falling into his lap. I didn't know whether to yell at him or hug him. "*Why* Nate? Why would you do something like that? You know stealing is wrong." I tipped my son's chin upwards and forced him to look at me.

Nate begrudgingly met my gaze, his blue eyes even more piercing with their tear-lined lids. "I really wanted gum. I really had to have it. And Noah said I should go."

I took a deep breath. I reminded myself that I needed to dig deep and find more patience. "Sweetie, this isn't about Noah. This is about *you*. And your actions. What *you* did. Stealing is wrong. You know that."

"Why wouldn't you just ask me to take you to the store, bud?" Pete asked gently. The calm and patient husband whom I typically knew in situations like this had returned.

"Because . . . I knew you would say dinner was almost ready . . . and I really, really wanted it." Nate was fully crying now, knowing he was about to be punished. "And my thoughts just got all jumbled in my head . . . and all I could think of is that I *really* wanted the gum. The pink kind. No, the green. Or maybe the orange. I don't know. I forget. I just wanted gum. Really bad. I *had* to have it."

"You did not *have* to have it," I responded, my voice coming too close to mimicking his. I took another deep breath. "Stealing is wrong, Nate. You can't just go and take things when you want them."

I waited for him to respond, but only silence filled the room. "Nate?"

I glanced at Pete. We were getting nowhere.

"Nathan William, what do you have to say?" Pete's voice was even, but firm.

Nate shrugged.

"Well, I'll tell you what you're going to say, then. Right after you put some clothes on, we're going back to the store you took the gum from, and you will apologize to the owner and admit what you did."

From somewhere deep within Nate's silence came rage like I'd never seen before. "No! I won't! You can't make me. He's scary and he hates me. He chased me down the street, and if I go back there he'll lock me up in a jail with no food. Or water. Then I'll die! Do you want me to die?" Nate's face was so red it looked purple, and he was punching a pillow with a force unlike any he'd shown before.

Nate jumped off the couch and stood on the coffee table. If I hadn't been so angry, I'd probably have been laughing at the sight in front of me: a nine-year-old wearing only what I could now see were *two* pairs of underwear, jumping all over our wood coffee table like a monkey. And still clutching his four packs of beloved bubble gum.

"Why are you doing this to me? You hate me, don't you? I know you do. And I hate myself. So maybe actually I *want* to go to jail. To starve. And die. Then you'll be happy. Because you hate me. And YOU want ME to die."

"Nate, please don't talk that way. You know that's not true. Please, come down from there. You'll hurt yourself." Pete's voice was calm. Somehow soft and composed. It reminded me of how he used to sound when he dealt with the tantrums of a two-year-old.

Nate kept shrieking, and Pete continued to coax him down from the table. I knew my husband was as alarmed as I was by the whole thing, but his calm and collected approach didn't falter. We had learned through the years that when Nate got into one of his moods, he often responded best to an even-keeled voice of reason. But not always.

This time, much to our luck, Nate weakened and eventually he slowly stepped down from the table. He was still shaking.

With our son now calmed down and sitting in front of us, my emotions turned from fear back to frustration, and I was torn between dishing out the world's worst punishment for a nine-year-old boy and wrapping him in my arms until he felt better.

Although the logical side of me was inclined to send him to his room to think about what he had done before coming down hard with the official punishment, my mommy instinct was to try to take away what was hurting my son, because I knew in my gut something bigger was going on.

And so I did what I had to do: I opened my arms and invited him in. Nate folded into me. Over the top of his tousled brown locks, so silky they tickled my nose, I could see Pete raise an eyebrow. He wasn't sure this was the right way to handle the situation. But he also didn't protest. Instead, he grabbed his coat and car keys.

"I'll be in the car. Get him dressed and I'll take him to the store to apologize and pay for the gum," Pete said. His voice was slightly colder than it had been when he was coaxing Nate down from the table. And I couldn't help but notice the door shut harder than usual on his way out.

"Come on, bud. Let's go get you dressed," I whispered into my son's ear. I gave him what I thought was a final squeeze, but Nate didn't let go. He held on tight, as if deathly scared of something.

I hugged him back, trying to reassure him that he would be okay. Cradled in my arms the way he was, Nate reminded me of when he was a newborn, and I was immediately taken back to a time that had happened long before . . .

Always sleep-deprived, I would become increasingly frustrated by the son Pete and I had dubbed "the baby unlike others." From the moment he was born, Nate seemed feistier in everything he did. He was punchier in his cries than any newborn

I had ever met. More sensitive to needing a diaper change. Angrier when he was hungry. And all-around more demanding.

Early one morning, when Nate was about eight months old, after I'd been up all night walking back and forth in our downstairs hall in an attempt to soothe him before he woke up anyone sleeping upstairs, he suddenly just stopped crying. I didn't know what I had done differently, but something had seemed to work. Perhaps his relentless cries, which sounded more like screams from someone hurting him, had simply exhausted him.

Whatever the reason, Nate had swiftly abandoned the angry, back-rearing screams that made his face resemble a squished tomato all night long, and collapsed into my arms. Yet he didn't fall asleep as I had been convinced he would. He simply buried himself into me, gazing at the wall.

An onlooker might have thought he was finally content, but something about the way he gripped at me with his little fingers made me think they would have been mistaken. There was something almost haunting about the way he stared at the wall. It was as though, even at eight months old, he was sad for no reason.

Deep down, I knew there was something going on with him.

Exhausted, I took my precious baby to his room, and curled up in the well-loved rocking chair that I had used so often. I fell asleep before he did, worn out from my night with him. When I woke up he was still awake. Still gazing into nowhere — just like he was doing now, eight years later.

I knew Pete, waiting in the car, would be furious that we were taking so long, but I couldn't let go. I knew Nate needed me, and my devotion prevented me from tearing myself away from him. My instinct told me to stay right where I was. To keep hugging him. To be there for him, just as I had always done, and as I'd always do. No matter what.

4
Nate

I can't sleep. I feel tired. I want to sleep. But I can't.

I don't know what time it is. I used to know. But the red glow on my clock freaked me out. So I unplugged it.

That was forever ago. Now I don't know what time it is.

Oh, I know! I will play my Wii. I'm ready to play tennis now. I love tennis. And gum.

But then I remember that Mom and Dad punished me by taking my Wii.

Shit.

Oh, crap. I'm not allowed to say shit. And I don't want to get into any more trouble. Mom and Dad were really mad. Madder than I have ever seen them.

I lie back down. I'm hot. I kick off my covers. It's still hot.

I look under my pyjamas. I'm wearing Spider-Man underwear. The ones I covered up with my blue ones to go get gum. I want that gum. I didn't even get to eat one piece. Dad made me give it all back to the mean man after I said sorry.

My heart feels like it is pounding really fast. I know it is because I want to play my Wii so bad. Mom calls it being anxious. She tells me I feel that way a lot.

Mom wouldn't want me to feel this way. And playing my Wii will make me feel better. I think she would let me play it so that I will feel better.

I quietly open my bedroom door. I tiptoe down the hall. I try to be quiet. I don't want to make the floors creak. I do not want Mom or Dad or Grace hear me.

I go down the stairs. I will look in the kitchen first. That is where Mom usually hides things. So I know it must be there.

5
Ashley

On Friday morning, just as I was wrapping up a creative brain-storming session for Pepsi, one of our longest-standing clients, Jack walked into the room.

"Can I speak to you, Ash?" He nodded his head towards the door, motioning for me to follow him. I looked at the mess around us, a team of about ten, who had spent the past two hours coming up with new ideas for Pepsi's winter campaign.

"I can clean up here," Alex, one of our youngest, yet most promising, new hires piped up. I flashed him a smile to show my thanks.

"Great work, you guys. I think we came up with some solid stuff. Lilly, if you could write all of this up into notes and distribute to the team, that would be really helpful. Juliette, can you please follow up with Pepsi and book the creative presentation meeting? Gabriela, why don't you brief the art department so they can turn these sketches into mocks?" All three nodded their heads in response, taking down their respective action items before I followed Jack out the door and to his office.

"Great work at the pitch presentation the other day. As always, you were our shining star." Jack sank into his leather chair at his oversized desk, his back to floor-to-ceiling windows that showcased the best views of the city. He smiled. "We nailed it."

"We got the business?" I was ecstatic to confirm the news I already suspected.

"Yeah, we got it. Chelsea's exact words were that it was 'the tight-knit integration between the creative and the strategy' that really impressed her. Like I said . . . we nailed it."

I smothered my impulse to point out that the "we" included the entire creative team, but not Jack. He certainly cheered on the hard work from afar, but Jack was too busy travelling and schmoozing with clients to see how late the nights truly went. Other than popping into working sessions on occasion during the day, and learning everything he needed to know at the rehearsal meeting, Jack hadn't contributed at all.

I forced the truth to the back of my mind and let my genuine grin take over. "Congratulations, Jack! This is fantastic for our business, and it will be fun to work on the account, too. We need to celebrate."

"My thoughts exactly, Carty." Jack said, calling me by the last-name nickname he had given me so many years earlier. It was a name he had christened me with as soon as Pete and I were married. "We want to start this relationship off right. Let's book a team dinner next week at The Fifth. No time to waste, after all. They want to jump right into planning for next year's fiscal."

"Sounds great. I'll let the team know."

"Bring who you want from your team, but let's keep it to about ten or so, including clients. These dinners become too impersonal if they're bigger than that. And I want you sitting beside Chelsea."

"No problem at all." I smiled at Jack. His demanding ways always settled slightly whenever his stress was eased. And I knew this was going to make his bosses very happy. Which always made him happy.

"Is that all?" I asked.

"Yep. Wanted you to be the first to know. Go spread the news internally however you'd like. I'll get the account team to write up an official press release."

I nodded, and left for my office, one floor below. Jack had insisted I sit on the executive floor with him and the other C-level management team, but I had held my ground and told him I needed to sit on the same floor as the rest of the creative department.

I motioned for my assistant, Emily, to follow me. "We need to order a huge cake, Em. One that says 'Congratulations AJ & Emerson!' And get some beer and wine, too. And lots of food. We've definitely got reason to celebrate."

Emily nodded her head, smiling as she realized exactly what celebration I was referring to. She wrote down all of my instructions for the party and left my office to start the planning.

I turned to my laptop and noted the ninety-seven emails that had come in since I'd started the Pepsi brainstorming session earlier that morning. Nine of them were from Jack.

Then, within one minute of sitting at my desk, another arrived.

Ashley:
I need you in New York the second week
of November. You need to be there for a 9
a.m. meeting on Monday morning, so leave

*Sunday night. There are top-to-top planning
meetings all week for the Amex account.
Oh, and it needs to be you so don't think
about sending one of your associate creative directors.*
~ Jack

I checked my calendar and felt my shoulders drop as I realized I would disappoint every member of my family by being
away that week; in addition to missing more family dinners, I
was going to miss Grace's volleyball game and Nate's hockey
game.

I sighed before sending Emily an email asking her to cancel
the majority of my meetings that week. I highlighted the meetings I couldn't miss, which I would join by conference call.

"Too bad I can't video conference into my kids' games,"
I mumbled under my breath, scanning my schedule. Grace's
after-school volleyball game was against the best team in the
league, and she'd already asked me to go and cheer her on.

"Ashley? Do you have a minute?" asked Ben, one of my two
associate creative directors. I bit my tongue, avoiding the temptation to ask if we could meet later. My growing list of emails
was already over a hundred deep. But when I glanced up, I knew
my emails would have to wait. The expression on Ben's face told
me it was important, and I suspected it was about the Starbucks
account.

"Sure, Ben. What's up?"

"Just wanted to show you some of the thought-starters we've
designed for the meeting tomorrow. I think they're great, but
wanted you to sign off before we present." Ben lay out the glossy
11x14 comps, and walked me through the thinking behind the
ideas.

I nodded my head, absorbing the work. "This *is* great. You
guys have done well. Good job on leading the team."

"Thanks. Any changes?"

"Nope. They're great."

"Thanks, Ash." Ben collected his work. He looked up and smiled, then hesitated slightly before leaving. "Hey, are you okay? You seem a bit tired."

"Oh . . . what? Tired? No, I'm okay. Just coming down from the pitch presentation high, I guess. And things are hectic at home, too."

Ben nodded as if to suggest he knew exactly what I was talking about, yet he didn't really understand at all. As the typical urban bachelor living in a downtown loft, Ben had no idea about trying to balance a crazy advertising schedule alongside a family with kids' schedules as nutty as your own.

I decided to change the subject. It was easier to just not talk about it. "Hey, great news: we won the business. The announcement hasn't been released yet, but I wanted you to be among the first to know since you worked so hard on the pitch."

"Wow. The verdict came quick! I remember we had to wait forever with the last big pitch . . . and it was small in comparison to this one." Ben's wide smile became even bigger with each word. I knew he shared my excitement. And rightly so. Ben had worked hard on the pitch, and had made things more reasonable for me as a result; he'd worked the majority of the late nights, including the three all-nighters, which were required to win the bid.

"You should be very proud, Ben. So much of this was you."

"Thanks, Ash. It's great to hear you say. And I won't breathe a word until I know I've got the thumbs up."

I shut the door behind him so I could dive into my email and sort through the priorities. But I couldn't seem to focus. No matter how hard I tried to respond to the urgent emails that required instant attention, all I could see in front of me was an almost naked, trembling Nate. Repeatedly, the images of my youngest child looking frail and scared popped into my mind. I couldn't seem to shake them.

I glanced at the clock on my laptop and noticed that I could be at Nate's school just in time for lunch. I texted Pete to tell him that he didn't need to pick him up, and sent an email to Emily asking her to reschedule my lunch meeting.

6
Nate

I like my teacher, but not today. Mrs. Brock is being mean to me.
I don't know why she is mean to me today. She is nice on other
days. But today she doesn't like me.

"Nate? Are you going to write in your journal?" Mrs. Brock
asks. Her voice is quiet. She is tucked down beside me. She
points to my empty page. She is smiling. Why is she smiling
when she doesn't like me?

I want to say yes, but it doesn't come out. "No."

"But, why not? You're so good at it!" Mrs. Brock smiles
again. Her teeth look different. I wonder if it's really her or if
the scary people have sent someone who only looks like her. I
know the difference. You can tell by her teeth. They look funny.

"I just don't *wanna*."

"Why not?"

"Because I only like patterning. I don't like writing in my journal. "

"You wrote in your journal the other day. You did a great job. And today we're writing in our journals again."

I shake my head.

"Maybe you could write about pizza? Do you like pizza?"

"No."

"Oh, I don't think that's true. You told us in Show & Share last week that your dad made you, your friend Noah, and Grace pizza for dinner on Saturday night. And that you loved it."

"That wasn't me."

"Yes, Nate, it was. You even made the pizza in our art time. Here, look . . ." Mrs. Brock walked to the sharing bulletin board. She pointed to something that looked like badly drawn pizza.

"It wasn't me."

Mrs. Brock gets a look I see on my mom's face and I want to stop talking. She doesn't get my talking. So I decide to make her laugh. I jump on my desk. I wiggle my bum. I make funny faces. But Mrs. Brock is not laughing.

"Nate? Get down! You'll hurt yourself."

I need to make her laugh. Then she will like me. So I jump up and down. Even harder. I try to look like a hyena. I watched hyenas in *The Lion King* with Dad and Noah. Dad showed us which ones were the hyenas. Noah and I danced around the kitchen and Dad said I looked like a hyena. And he was laughing. So jumping like a hyena will make Mrs. Brock laugh too.

I want Mrs. Brock to like me again. I want to like her. I want her to laugh. If she laughs, she will like me.

"Nate. Come down immediately."

I dance harder. So she will laugh. She will laugh if I dance better.

"Loook, Mrs. Brock. I'm a hyeeena. Isn't it funny?!"

"Nate, I am not kidding. Please, come down from there. You are scaring the other children."

But I can't come down. I need to make her laugh. I need to try harder to make her laugh.

And then I'm on the floor.

And my head hurts.

And all I see is darkness.

7
Ashley

I hailed a cab and made it to Nate's school just before the bell rang. I was tempted to go in and surprise him, hoping he'd be happy to have an unexpected lunch with his mother, but opted to wait at the usual pick-up spot for fear of upsetting him. We'd learned over the years that our son was driven by routine and consistency. He was unpredictable when things fell outside of his normal routine.

I waited and waited by the slide, glancing at the clock on my iPhone in between email replies. The agreement between Pete and Nate was to meet at the twisty yellow slide at noon, because Nate didn't like Pete going into the school to get him when he picked him up for lunch each day.

Even though all of the other kids at Nate's school stayed for lunch, we'd been given special permission to pick up our son each day and take him home to eat. There was no alternative.

At first, we'd resisted our son's requests. As big believers in social integration, we explained that it was important to stay with his friends and have fun at lunch.

"But I don't have any friends at school. They all say I'm weird," Nate had complained. "None of them like me . . ."

I thought he was being overly sensitive, and accused him of being dramatic, like his sister. But when he started coming home with scratches on his neck, and ravenous, I began to suspect he was minimizing the situation.

It was Nate's first bruised cheek that tipped us off about what was going on, and we began to pay closer attention. It was the heightened silence at home that told us Nate's repeated bruising wasn't from tripping during gym class. And when he finally came home with a swollen black eye, we permanently dismissed all of the excuses he'd been feeding us at dinnertime.

Once we raised it with the school, and the parents of the bullies were brought in, we thought the problem had been dealt with. The kids were all disciplined, and one student was even expelled, which I suspected was done not only for punishment but also to set an example.

Everything seemed better. The principal moved Nate into a new classroom, which breathed life into our son, and he was suddenly begging us to stay for lunch instead of being the only one to go home. Over and over, Nate would tell us that he wanted to be *just like the other kids*. He was desperately scared of being different — even more so than he was of being bullied.

Once Nate was settled in his new class, I became obsessed with making sure he was okay. I begged Pete to go to the school at random times to check in on what was going on at the playground. I prayed every night that the bullies from the other class would leave our son alone, that they had become scared by the doled-out punishments, or were simply bored by Nate and had decided to move on to something else.

I was also frantic for Nate to make friends in his class, and made his teacher promise me she would do everything possible to encourage other kids to hang out with him. As his mother, I simply wanted him to be given the new start he deserved.

But no names of kids in his class were ever mentioned at home. No play dates were booked. And Nate's dinnertime silence soon returned.

When the scratches reappeared, this time under his shirt, we dealt with the problem. Again. More kids were expelled. We moved Nate to a new school. But no matter how drastic our actions, or how many kids were punished, the bullying always returned, whether physical or emotional. The other kids didn't seem to like Nate because he was different.

Ultimately, we had no other choice but to bring Nate home from school for lunch. Pete picked him up every day at the same yellow slide, and took our son home to eat. It gave Pete and Nate some needed one-on-one time, and the chance for Pete to find out how Nate's morning had been. For our son's safety, we needed to be involved in each increment of Nate's day.

After lunch, Pete would bring him back exactly two minutes before the afternoon bell, and would watch from the parking lot to make sure he got into the school safely.

Lunch pick-up times weren't as precise. Depending on how much Nate dawdled while getting ready at his locker, he would sometimes be late for Pete. Or me, on the rare occasion that I could fit in lunch. I began to suspect today was going to be a late day for my son.

Tired of emailing, I threw my iPhone back in my bag, and turned my face towards the warm October sun. The day was unseasonably balmy, and I let myself enjoy a few moments of escape, knowing cooler temperatures were expected to return the following day. I was excited for my lunch with Nate, and looked forward to eliminating some of the tension we'd been feeling in our family since we'd punished him. After everything that had happened recently, I needed to spend quality time with my son.

But Nate didn't appear. He didn't come and find me. I forced myself to give him the benefit of the doubt for ten minutes. When I couldn't hold off any longer, I started walking towards the big red doors at the entrance of the school and tried to ignore the knots forming in my stomach.

8

I looked down at my hands, which were clenched together so hard there were sweaty red lines tracing my grip. Nate was sitting just outside the closed office door with an ice pack on his head, and my iPhone, still tucked into the side pocket of my bag, hadn't stopped buzzing with work emails since I had sat down with Nate's principal, Mrs. Spencer, to discuss Nate falling off the desk.

"We're concerned, Mrs. Carter. Nate seems to be getting . . . well, more extreme. We don't see behaviour this intense in our other students. To be honest, we don't quite know what to make of it. And we're worried about what has happened to Nate in the past —"

"Has Nate been bullied again?" I jumped in. My heart began to race at the thought of anyone hurting my little boy again.

"No, no. I'm sorry to alarm you. It isn't that. And we've kept a close eye on Nate since he joined us. So far none of that has happened. But we're wondering if other proactive solutions might *help* him. And perhaps mitigate any future bullying problems."

I nodded, wondering what, exactly, she was referring to. Beside me, my phone kept buzzing.

"Have you taken him to see anyone?" Mrs. Spencer asked gently. Despite her attempt to ask the question with a smooth voice that she'd purposely quieted, something bugged me about the way she said it. Her curtness, perhaps. It was as though she was pretending to care.

"I'm sorry . . . see anyone?"

"Yes, like a psychologist. Or even a family doctor. You know, just in case . . ."

Just in case? Just in case of *what*?

I shook my head and forced a smile. "No, we haven't taken him to see anyone. I know Nate is . . . well . . . he *is* sometimes more extreme, as you put it. But he's also a nine-year-old boy with a ton of energy. Boys are like that . . . right?"

"They can be, certainly. And Nate can also be a sweet boy. But he gets into these hyper moods and no one can seem to calm him down. I'm no doctor, but I do know of cases where Ritalin helps. Seems to calm the nerves. The extreme jitters Nate tends to have every once in a while. Perhaps it would be worth talking to your doctor about?" Mrs. Spencer peered at me through thick glasses lined in dark red. Partnered with her dated short haircut, I couldn't help but think of Sally Jesse Raphael.

"Well, Pete and I will certainly take your suggestions into consideration." I strained to put another smile on my face. I knew Mrs. Spencer was hitting a nerve of truth, and I didn't want to face it head-on. "For now, though, if you'll excuse me, I need to get Nate to the doctor to get his head looked at. You know . . . *just in case*." I rose from the uncomfortable faded pleather chair, and shook Mrs. Spencer's hand.

"Of course. I understand. We hope he didn't hit his head too hard."

I nodded and followed Mrs. Spencer out of her office to greet Nate, who was slumped in his chair, the ice pack thrown aside.

Principal Spencer picked up the discarded ice pack and handed it to me. "Nate, it's probably just a bump, but your mother will take you to get it looked at just to be sure."

Nate blinked at her. He opened his mouth as if he were going to say something, and then shut it before he let go of the words. He blinked again.

"Nate, you gave us quite a scare today. You can't be jumping on desks like that. Do you understand?" Mrs. Spencer pulled her red glasses down onto her nose and stared down at him.

More blinking.

"Nate, tell Mrs. Spencer that you understand," I interjected. Internally, I begged Nate to respond. The awkward situation was growing in its prickly nature into something that felt more like all-out embarrassment.

"I'm waiting, Nate." Mrs. Spencer's voice was firm and unsympathetic. The room filled with silence as she waited, subconsciously picking at a hangnail on her thumb with her pointer finger.

I touched Nate's shoulder and crouched down to his level, talking in a hushed voice. "It's okay, Nate. You're not in trouble. But please tell Mrs. Spencer that you understand that you can't jump on desks."

"No, Mom." Nate violently shook his head from side to side.

I sat next to Nate and placed my hand firmly on his knee. Looking straight into his eyes for as long as he'd let me, I explained quietly but firmly that we were going nowhere until he acknowledged what Mrs. Spencer had said to him.

"I get it, okay? No jumping on desks." Despite his words being laced with rudeness, I settled for his understanding and felt a sense of triumph to have outlasted him. For a moment, I hadn't been sure who would win the battle.

I rose from my chair and explained to Mrs. Spencer that Nate would return to school after he'd been cleared by a doctor. She nodded her head, pursing her lips, and said nothing more as I ushered my son out of the school.

I called Pete from the parking lot to let him know what had happened, and to tell him he needed to take Nate to the doctor.

"How long was he unconscious for? And why didn't they call me as soon as it happened?" Pete asked. I could hear the concern in his voice.

"Apparently he was only out for about a minute. And they didn't call because I walked in soon after it happened. They had just put the ice on his head, and said they were going to call home as soon as they got Nate settled."

"I can't believe this. Seriously, you've got to be kidding."

"Do I sound like I'm kidding? Can you take him? I'll drop him off in my cab. And can you pack a lunch for him? He hasn't eaten yet."

"Yeah . . . sure, I'll take him. I'm assuming you can't do it yourself because you have meetings?"

"Starting at two o'clock, then back to back until six. I can't miss them. I'd take him if I could but —"

"I said that I'll take him," Pete interrupted. His voice was tense, and served as a reminder of the strain that had recently pierced our relationship. For twelve years, we'd had a solid marriage, filled with as much hard work as there was adoration. And the result of our commitment to each other was strength in union — not only for the two of us but for our family as well. But in recent months, an unexplained tension seemed to repeatedly seep into our conversations, showing its unsightly face in what had previously been ordinary moments.

I freed myself of more uncomfortable banter by bringing up the excuse that I needed to call a taxi. When it arrived, I opened the door for Nate and pulled him close to me as the cab pulled away, heading in the direction of our house.

As I watched the storefronts on Bloor Street whizzing by us, I gently kissed the top of Nate's head and inhaled deeply, taking in the unmistakable scent of Johnson & Johnson shampoo. I knew Nate was likely getting too old for it, but I couldn't seem to part ways with the tiny reminders that Nate was my baby for just a little while longer.

Five minutes into the ride home, I noticed twitching in Nate's shoulders. His discomfort was obvious in every movement he made, and maternal instinct told me that it wasn't the blow to his head that was causing it.

"Are you okay, Bean?" I asked gently, calling him by the nickname I'd given him as an infant. He said nothing, and continued to stare out the window. Every few seconds, his shoulders would twitch.

My heart ached for my son, heightened by the fact that I couldn't be the one to take him to the doctor, to be there for him, as all mothers should be for their children.

When we reached our house, I walked Nate up the driveway, anxious about the time it was taking. He was sluggish, but I didn't want to hurry him. When we finally reached the porch, Pete opened the door to greet us, and ushered our son into the house.

"Are you coming?" Pete asked me, cranking his head to look at me as he walked through the front door.

I shook my head, blinking back tears. I was desperate to stay with Nate, but my two o'clock meeting was with Jack, and I couldn't miss it.

Instead, I was forced to wave a final time before returning to the cab. I gave the driver my work address. As he pulled away, I bitterly yanked out my iPhone and returned to the chaos of my workday, firing off answers to the challenges in my inbox.

9
Nate

I'm going to the hospital. Dad said I have to get my head looked at by some doctor.

I don't want to get my head checked. I want to play video games with Noah but Dad said *no way, boss*.

We walk in and see doctors. Lots and lots of doctors. And nurses.

Dad tells me to keep the ice on my head. I sit on the blue chair with lots of other people. Dad talks to a nurse. I wait.

I take off my jacket because I feel hot. Even with the ice on my head. I feel dizzy. I might fall over and hurt my head like I did before. Then Mom will be upset again.

My chest hurts. It goes up and down. Really fast. It won't stop. It's weird. I do not like it. I'm scared.

I can't breathe.

Everything hurts.

"Hey little guy . . . are you okay?" a woman wearing purple asks me. She is sitting too close to me. I tell her to go away.

She stops talking to me. For one minute. Then she comes closer and asks where my mom is. Her breath stinks. Like cat pee and coffee all mixed up. I want her to go away. I yell at her to go away.

"Is everything okay here?" my dad asks. He isn't talking to the nurse anymore. He puts his arm around me. "Are you okay, Nate?"

My arms twitch. Dad hugs harder.

"Is this your son?" the woman asks. "He doesn't seem okay. He was breathing really quickly and he won't stop shaking."

"Nate? Are you okay? You're sweating . . . are you hot?" He sits on the chair next to me.

I can't breathe. I'm scared. I might be choking. My chest hurts.

I hate it here.

I have to go outside.

I run for the door. Fast. Faster. Like my gym teacher tells me to do.

"Nate? Nate!" I hear Dad yelling behind me. He is following me.

I need air. I can't breathe.

I slam into the door. But I'm not fast enough. Dad grabs me. He picks me up. He is holding me too tight. My arms feel all tingly. It's weird.

I'm so scared.

"No, no, no . . ." I scream. I need to get away. I punch Daddy. I don't want to. I love Daddy. But I punch him. I need to go outside. "No Daddy . . . no, no, *nooo!* Leave me *alooone!*"

My dad holds tighter. I kick hard. As hard as I can. Daddy calls for help. He yells so loud it hurts my ears.

Two doctors rush over. "What's going on here?" one asks.

"I don't know," Daddy answers. "I've never seen him like this before."

I'm more scared now that the doctors are asking questions. I need to get out of here. I bite Daddy. Hard. He drops me.

"Code white!" I hear one of the doctors yell loudly as I try to break away from my daddy. I don't know what a code white is.

Two policemen find me. They grab me. They carry me to the back. They put me on a bed and hold me down. I don't know where my daddy is. I'm so scared. I'm going to die.

"Get awaaay from meee! Where's my daaaddy?"

"Right here, Nate. I'm here, buddy." I hear my dad's voice but I can't see him. I feel a squeeze on my shoulder. I think it's him. But maybe it's the policeman.

A new doctor comes in. He shuts the curtain and sits beside me on the bed.

"Nate? Is that your name?" The doctor sits very close to me. "Listen to me, Nate. You are going to be okay."

"I . . . I . . . c-c-c-can't . . . breathe."

"We know you're breathing because you're talking. And that's great. But we're going to work on your breathing to help you feel better. Can you do that for me, Nate?"

I can't do that.

"I will help you. I want you to push your stomach way out. Just like a basketball is in there. Take a big breath and push your stomach way out, okay?" The doctor is holding both of my hands. I try to do what he tells me. My stomach starts to go out.

"Good job, Nate. You're doing great." The doctor smiles at me. "Now, let's count to five. I'm going to count to five, and I want you to breathe in . . . really deeply . . . and turn your stomach into that big basketball. Don't stop until I get to five. Ready? One . . . two . . . three . . . four . . . five . . ."

I try to push my stomach out like a basketball. I try really hard.

"Fantastic! Good job. Now I want you to breathe out slowly for five more seconds. Ready? One . . . two . . . three . . . four . . . five . . ."

The police officers step away from me.

"Ready to do it again?" the doctor asks. "We're going to do it until I get to three this time. Okay? Here we go. One . . . two . . . three . . ."

I keep breathing with the doctor. Over and over. I think it is weird. But then I feel better. I'm suddenly fine. I feel normal again. Except for my headache that is pounding in my brain.

The policemen leave. The doctor asks to speak to Daddy outside.

"Will you be okay if I talk to the doctor for a minute?" Daddy asks me.

I shrug my shoulders. I will be okay if Daddy goes. It doesn't matter. Because I feel like I am alone whether Daddy is with me or not.

10
Ashley

The night of Nate's hospital visit, I made sure that I was home in time for dinner. I had called Pete to let him know that I would pick up Swiss Chalet, Nate's favourite, on my way home.

I doled out the chicken and ribs. Everyone ploughed in except for Nate, who did nothing but push chicken and french fries around on his plate.

"What's wrong, Bean? Don't you feel like eating? It's your favourite."

Nate shrugged, showing no interest in taking his first bite.

"Do you want more sauce?" I asked, forcing a smile and trying to pretend that it was our typical Friday night, which always included takeout and a family movie.

Nate ignored me.

"Is it your head? Does it still hurt? Are you sure there's no concussion?"

"Ash, why don't you stop with the twenty questions and focus on your own dinner?" Pete asked. His voice was flat and slightly irritated. "I told you, the ER doc said Nate will be fine. No concussion. There's nothing to be worried about."

I nodded and took a small sip of my wine. Tears sprung to my eyes and I blinked hard, wishing them away.

"Pete? Can you help me for a minute? In the family room . . . I need to speak to you."

"What? I'm eating. Can't it wait?"

I shook my head, motioning for him to follow me. Thanks to our years of in-sync parenting, Pete instantly knew not to question it again. He followed me so we could talk out of earshot of our kids.

"Are you *sure* Nate's okay?" I asked him in a hushed voice. "I'm so worried. He's not himself at *all*."

"The doctor said he'll be fine. They checked him for a concussion and everything is normal."

"And what about the other thing that happened? How he got all weird and bit you?"

"I told you already. The doctor thinks it was a panic attack brought on by the hospital, which Nate clearly hates. The doc said he sees it occasionally with kids who don't want to be there. So let's not worry about it. Okay?"

"Okay . . . I guess that makes sense." I could hear the uncertainty in my voice.

"Let's go back and finish our dinner with the family. I think the best thing to do is make things as normal as possible for Nate."

I nodded and followed Pete back to the table, forcing a smile as I sat down with our kids. I turned my attention to Grace. "How about you, hon? How was your day?" I stabbed a piece of chicken with my fork. I hate Swiss Chalet.

"Amazing! I just *love* Fridays. Especially *this* Friday because Luke passed the ball to me in gym class. Well, really he threw it at me. We were playing dodgeball, you know? But then he told me afterwards he felt absolutely *awful* because he hit me so hard. Right here, on my arm. See? Look at my bruise . . . don't you *love* it?" I nodded at Grace, half listening to her drone on about her twelve-year-old crush of the week. I was grateful for the distraction and happy when my chatterbox daughter filled the rest of our dinner with constant babble. She was the perfect fix to our uncomfortable family silence.

After dinner, of which Nate ate almost none, we let him pick our Friday night movie. As he always did, Nate asked for *Spider-Man*. But twenty minutes into the movie he stood up, said nothing, and walked out of the room as though he couldn't get out of there quickly enough.

"What's with him?" Grace asked, nodding towards the door. I glanced at Pete, who shrugged.

"I cannot *stand* this movie. And Nate *always* picks it," Grace continued, rolling her eyes. "So, like, if we're not watching *Spider-Man*, can I go too? I want to text Emma and Keira to tell them my bruise is getting *bigger*."

I closed my eyes, digging deep for patience with my overly dramatic daughter, and let her go so she could text her best friends. Against my better judgement, Pete and I had recently given in and bought her an iPhone. Although it was for emergencies only during the week, we became a bit more lax with it on the weekend.

"And then there were two . . ." I said. With our children gone from the room, Pete and I sat across from each other on facing couches. We were both still drinking from the bottle of wine we had opened at dinner.

Pete nodded, knocking back his wine. He turned his attention back to the movie, clearly ignoring me.

"Are you . . . are you mad at me?" I asked sheepishly. I felt too exhausted to get into the conversation, but couldn't stop myself from asking.

Pete shrugged, reminding me of Nate in the cab ride home earlier that afternoon.

"Well?" I pressed him. If we were going to have it out, I wanted to get it over with so we could enjoy the rest of our weekend.

Pete refilled his glass and took another gulp of wine before looking at me with icy eyes. "You say you put this family first, Ash. Is that right? No matter how crazy your schedule is . . . or how high on the ladder you climb? Well, our son had to go to the *hospital* today and you couldn't even take him to get checked out. And why? Because you had some *very important* meeting at work." Pete snorted. "I think you should take another good look at those priorities you claim to have established."

I swallowed hard, listening to my husband dump more weight onto the feelings of self-reproached guilt I'd been carrying on my shoulders all afternoon. My pulse quickened as his words danced on my insecurities as a working mother.

But soon into the silence that followed, I switched gears and started to feel defensive. Pete was being unfair. When we had decided Pete would stay home with the kids, we had agreed that the bulk of the appointments, games, illnesses, and anything else that popped up would fall onto his plate. Pete knew what the corporate world was like. He lived in it for *years* before staying home to freelance and take care of our children during the day. There was no reason he couldn't — or shouldn't — have been the one to take Nate to the hospital that afternoon.

"Come on, Pete . . . please don't do this again. We both agreed that you would be the primary caregiver during the week.

I had a video conference call with Jack and New York. There was no way I could miss it."

"Not even for your son? The one who had to go to the hospital?"

"Look, if you would like to discuss changing our agreement . . . if you would like to consider going back to work so we can more evenly divide the responsibility for these types of things when they come up, then let's do that. But you goading me? Pestering me with something you know I'm sensitive about? Well, it isn't healthy for any of us."

Pete didn't respond. The room filled with sounds of the movie, with Uncle Ben saying to Peter Parker, "I don't mean to lecture and I don't mean to preach. And I know I'm not your father . . ."

The irony of Uncle Ben's words didn't go unnoticed.

"Pete?"

He continued to ignore me.

"Well, if you won't talk to me, and we're clearly done here, I'm going to check on Nate and then go to bed. I'm exhausted."

"Whatever . . . suit yourself."

I left quickly, climbing the stairs to Nate's room, only to find him lying on his bed, staring at the ceiling with wide, haunted eyes. He looked very sad.

"You okay, Bean?" I asked. I motioned for him to move over, and climbed into bed with him. He immediately curled up into me, and shook his head.

"Anything I can help with?" I asked him gently. "You can talk to me about anything. You know that, right?"

Nate shrugged.

"Well, I'm here for you when you're ready to talk. *If* you want to talk. Or I can just lie here with you . . . if that's what you prefer?"

He shrugged again. But he didn't kick me out as he sometimes did.

I snuggled into his single bed, rubbing his arm with the tickle strokes I knew he loved. Just when his breathing slightly changed and I thought he was about to fall asleep, he popped up. I immediately sensed his urgency.

"Where's Noah? I need to find Noah! I want my best friend."

"Shhh . . . shhh. It's okay, Nate. I'm here with you. Noah isn't here, but I am. Come back and cuddle with me. I'll tickle your arm until you fall asleep."

Nate looked uncertain. Unwilling. Hesitantly, he crawled back into my arms, and I noticed his breathing was quick and rapid. My own pulse matched his as my worry escalated.

"It's okay, sweetie. Close your eyes and think happy thoughts. Like . . . hot chocolate on a snowy day. With marsh-mallows. You love that, right? Or a puppy's wet little nose? One who likes to kiss you hello. Let's think of the happy thoughts and I'll stay here until you fall asleep, okay? Close your eyes . . ."

Nate didn't answer, but I kept my promise anyway. I lay beside my son in silence, tickling his arm and trying to make the pounding in my heart stop. I knew in my soul that something was very wrong with him.

Somewhere in the night, I fell asleep, hugging Nate as I lay beside him in his single bed. I stayed there, just like a mother of a sleeping newborn who is nestled into her. Except my baby was nine and broken, like a wounded little bird.

The sleep I desperately needed kept me glued to Nate's bed all night, uninterrupted. And by the time I woke up early the next morning, my baby was gone.

11
Nate

I lift Mom's hand off my arm. Why is she still with me? It's morning. It's weird that she slept with me.

I sneak out of bed and walk towards my window. I am very quiet so that Mom won't wake up. I wait.

Outside, the sun has started to come up. It is light, but no one is on the street. Birds are chirping. One flies out from the tree it is sitting in and lands on my windowsill. I look him right in the eyes. He looks back at me. We stay that way, quiet and staring, for a long time. I think the bird looks sad as well. Like me.

The bird flies away and I am alone again. I continue waiting. Waiting for my sign. Waiting to see Noah.

After what feels like forever, I see Noah ride his bike down the street. He stops at my driveway. He shields his eyes from the sun and waves when he sees me standing in the window.

I glance at my mom, who is still sleeping. I can make a run for it and she won't wake up. She won't know that Noah and I decided to meet each other super early in the morning to ride our bikes.

I run to meet Noah. When I get outside, he is still waiting on our driveway.

"Let's hit the good park, guy. No one will be there at this time." Noah fist-bumps me because it's our standard greeting. We do it every time we see each other, just like the other kids at school. That's where I learned it. But the kids at school never do it with me. Only Noah.

I jump up and down. I am excited. I love the park when no one is there. Especially the good park.

I keep jumping. Up. Down. Up. Down. I jump in one spot until my lungs burn from the cold air. My teeth rattle and I bite my lip when my feet hit the ground. I taste blood.

"Look!" I show Noah the blood.

"You're fine. Don't be a baby," Noah answers. He jumps on his bike. I think he is going to go to the parkette a few streets over. But he starts heading towards the *really* good park. The one with the zoo.

I grab my bike from beside the house and begin to follow him. I try to ignore the blood. My lip stops stinging.

Noah is ahead of me. I ride fast to catch up. The cold air keeps burning my lungs. I ride faster. I laugh out loud because my insides feel cold but my skin feels like it's burning.

We get to the park. We sit on the swings. I pump my feet as hard as I can. I want to go high. As high as Noah.

Higher.

Higher.

Higher.

I feel excited.

Then I get scared. But I kind of like it. I like feeling scared. So I jump off the swing. I hit the ground. I hit it hard.

Really, *really* hard.

12
Ashley

The minute I realized Nate was gone, I jumped out of bed and ran down the stairs. I tried to convince myself he was likely eating Cheerios and watching cartoons, or perhaps he had sneaked outside to play in the backyard. But a stronger sense in the pit of my gut told me it was something else. Something bad.

"Nate?" I called out. The house was silent. Upstairs, Pete and Grace still slept.

I raced around the house, looking in every spot Grace and Nate had ever used while playing Hide and Seek.

No Nate.

I poked my head out our back door and called his name, hearing nothing in return but creaks from the empty swings that were dancing in the wind. Nate wasn't in the front yard. Or the garage.

When I was convinced he wasn't on our property, I ran upstairs to wake Pete. He rose instantly, jumping into the warm-up pants he had thrown on the floor beside our bed when he went to sleep the night before.

I followed Pete downstairs. He grabbed his keys from the foyer table. "Do you want me to come?" I asked him.

"Probably not the best idea since the last time I checked it was illegal to leave sleeping children alone in the house." Pete's voice had a mean bite to it. When he saw the tears spring to my eyes, he continued in a softer voice. "Ash, you need to stay here. I'll go. Just try not to alarm Gracie when she wakes up. You know how she can get sometimes when she's scared. Maybe just say I've gone out for a drive or something. Okay?"

I nodded, hoping I wouldn't have to have that conversation any time soon. I wasn't in the frame of mind to pretend like everything was okay. I was worried sick about my son.

Feeling woozy, I tottered into the kitchen and tried to think of what to do next. Should I call the police? No, it had only been about twenty minutes since I'd realized he was gone. Should I call a neighbour so I could look for Nate too? I couldn't, because that would definitely create suspicion when Grace woke up.

Instead, I put on a pot of coffee, hoping it would calm my jitters. When it finished percolating, I slugged back the piping hot brew and immediately burned the inside of my mouth.

"Shit!" I said, grabbing some ice from the freezer door. I popped it in my mouth and took relief in the icy chill that numbed the pain.

Three minutes later, after what felt like an eternity, I couldn't wait any longer. I texted Pete.

Did you find him?

His response came almost instantly.

No, not yet.

I took my coffee out to the front porch and sank into the thick cushion on one of our portico chairs. The icy October chill immediately found my bones, and I shivered as I waited impatiently for Pete to find Nate. I thought about going inside to get a coat, but didn't want to remove my eyes from the street.

Neighbours were starting to poke their heads outside to greet the morning. Many of them quickly picked up their papers and retreated back indoors, ready to absorb the Saturday news alongside their own coffees. A few ventured farther outside to take their dog for a morning walk or rake leaves on their lawn.

"Morning, Ashley!" a voice called out. I looked up, dazed, to see Bernie, our neighbour from across the street, waving at me. He pointed at the Sold sign hanging on his front yard. "Did you see? We sold our house yesterday. Won't be long before we're off to Oakville. We need to get to the suburbs. Having nowhere to park our car is driving my wife nuts."

"Congratulations," I managed to call back. I could barely focus on what Bernie was telling me. I hadn't noticed they'd sold their house. Bernie gave me the thumbs-up before picking up his copy of the *Globe and Mail* on the front porch. He examined the front cover, then waved a final time before disappearing back into his house.

I wrapped my sweater tighter around me. Since I hadn't made it out of Nate's bed the previous night, I was in the same outfit that I'd worn to work the day before.

I sipped at my coffee, now at a tolerable temperature, and hugged the mug for warmth. With each passing minute, I became more desperate to see our car pull into the driveway, complete with Nate's lopsided grin shining from the back seat.

"Mom . . . ? What are you doing out here?" I jumped at Grace's voice and spilled coffee on my pants.

"Pardon? Oh, I just thought I'd get some air. Enjoy the morning, you know?" I forced a smile. "Want to join me?"

"No, thanks. I've got to go text Emma. Plus, it's *freezing* out here." Grace flipped her long blonde hair behind her shoulder and retreated back in the house.

Shaking my head, I sensed that Grace didn't even realize Nate was gone. Depending on her mood, she so often modelled the classic twelve-year-old whose world seemed to start and stop with her ever-evolving group of tween friends, and she became oblivious to everything else.

I turned my eyes back to the road, straining my ears to hear the sound of our car. Each time I thought I heard one I jumped up, frenetically gawping down the road. I was clinging to hope.

I needed someone to talk to. I thought about calling my best friend, Tay, but I knew she'd be in the middle of her chaotic Saturday madness, trying to get her four children ready for their various morning activities. Plus, I didn't want to worry her.

Tears threatened to fall, then coursed down my cheeks. The longer Nate was gone, the less successful I was at fighting my anxiety over his absence. I could only keep calm for so long. I was losing control of my ability to smack logical sense into the powerful dose of pre-grief agony that takes over a mother's soul when she is waiting to hear if her child is all right.

13
Nate

My ankle is burning. It hurts so, so much. I want my mommy. Where is my mommy?

I'm lying on my back. The big sky is grey. I wanted Noah to stay with me but he got scared when I fell. So he left. He said his mom would kill him for sneaking out of his house so early.

I know Noah is sorry for leaving me by myself when I am hurt. He was just scared. Like I am now. Because now there is no one to help me. And I am all alone. And I am lonely.

I'm cold. And my ankle is killing me. Where is my *mommy*?

The swing keeps swinging over my head. It creaks every time it goes back and forth. Back, *creak*. Forth, *creeak*. Back, *creeeak*. Forth, *creeeeak*.

I can't breathe. *Where is my mommy?*

There is no one at the park. I need help. *Where is MY MOMMY?*

I'm scared. Freaking out. And my ankle hurts so bad. It really, really hurts.

I need help. I want my mommy.

14
Ashley

After forty minutes, I couldn't take it any longer. I called Tay, desperate for someone to calm me down.

"Ashley? Slow down. What's wrong?" Behind Tay's voice were the shrieks of four children, likely eating breakfast.

"It's Nate. He's gone."

"Gone? What do you mean *gone*?"

"I . . . I woke up and he wasn't there. Not in his bed. Not in our house. Not anywhere!"

"Okay, Ash, listen to me. We'll figure this out. But just hang on one sec." I could hear the muffled sound of Tay covering the phone, instructing her eldest daughter, Julia, to take over and watch her younger siblings.

"Okay, I'm back. Now tell me. And start from the beginning," Tay demanded, her typical bossy demeanour emerging. Although she had stopped practising as a physical therapist so she could stay at home with her children, her ability to use words to control a situation and get someone to do something had always stayed with her. In better times, I had often joked it was because she needed to retain the skill in order to keep her house running smoothly.

"Well . . . Nate . . . he, uh, he isn't doing too well these days. He isn't himself. I don't know . . . he's just different. Yesterday he acted really weird in school and ended up whacking his head."

"He did? Is he okay?" Tay asked.

"Yeah, he's fine. Just a bump. No concussion. But his behaviour is still so odd." I took a big breath and dove into the story.

"So, you slept in his bed, and he just wasn't there when you woke up? When's the last time you saw him there? Did you wake up through the night?"

"No, I was exhausted. I must have fallen asleep right after he did, and the next thing I knew it was morning and he was gone."

"*Mom?* It's eight-thirty. I have gymnastics in half an hour. Aren't we going?" Grace's voice startled me and I wiped away my tears before turning around to face her. I was still on the porch, shivering and talking into my iPhone.

I put my phone down and looked at my daughter. "Oh, right. Yeah, we're going. Just give me one minute to finish up my call with Aunty Tay, okay?" I returned my attention to the phone.

"Ash? You can't take Grace to gymnastics now. You have to stay there. I'll get Braeden to run my crew around to their activities, and I'll come pick up Grace and take her myself. You just stay there and wait for Pete to come home with Nate."

"Are you sure?" I hated to take advantage of Tay and her husband, but I needed her help.

"Yes, of course I'm sure. I'll be there in ten minutes. Tell Grace to be ready because I won't have time to come inside to get her."

"Okay. And Tay? Thank you."

"I'm here to help you, my friend. And it's going to be okay. You know that, right?"

I nodded my head at the phone. I clicked off and told Grace that Tay would be taking her to gymnastics because I wasn't feeling well.

"But *why*? I want *Daddy* to take me," Grace whined. For a twelve-year-old, she could sometimes mirror a toddler. A split second later, she realized her father wasn't there. "Where is Dad, anyway? Why isn't he here?"

"Dad had to go out for a bit. He'll be home soon," I replied quickly, anxious to think of something that would distract her from asking questions. We knew from experience she didn't do well with separation, and I didn't want her to know Nate was missing. "Why don't you run and grab a few mini chocolate bars from the Halloween stash in the cellar downstairs? Tuck them in your bag and you can have them after gymnastics as a treat."

Grace looked at me with a funny glance. She paused for an instant, suddenly looking like she was going to ask more questions. I peered back at her, and our eyes locked in a staring contest. She blinked. Lucky for me, the urge for chocolate won and she pranced back into the house, excited to be given free rein on the kids' most coveted stash.

True to her word, Tay pulled up ten minutes later. When I poked my head inside to call Grace, she bounced from the house and climbed into Tay's back seat. I followed her and kissed her goodbye. She had chocolate on the side of her mouth, and I wondered how many bars she'd eaten before coming outside.

I stepped away from the car and waved to Tay as she backed out of the driveway. When she reached the street, she used the hand signal for "call me." I nodded, assuring her that I would.

Returning to the porch, I texted Pete again. Twenty minutes later, I was still waiting. I tried to convince myself that hearing nothing could be a good thing. Maybe Pete had found him and was so busy yelling at him that he couldn't hear his phone. Or perhaps Pete had gotten so distracted in his happiness that he'd taken Nate for breakfast and left his phone in the car.

I'd just about convinced myself that Pete and Nate were gorging on waffles when my phone rang and scared me half to death.

"I found him. He was at High Park. Can you believe that? He rode his bike. I have no idea how he was even able to ride there, though. It's so far. Honestly, it's got to be —"

"Oh, thank God!" I interrupted, my open palm flying to my forehead. I finally exhaled, feeling as though I'd been holding my breath for over an hour. "I've been freaking out here, with way too many horrible thoughts running through my mind . . ."

"Ashley? You should know that he has a pretty banged-up leg. He jumped off the swings to keep up with Noah. And I think . . . well, I actually think his leg might be broken. I'm going to take him to the ER, just in case."

"Keeping up with Noah? We're back to this? *Again?*" A blend of emotions took over, replacing the utter panic I'd been feeling since I woke up. Fury fused with concern. Frustration mixed with uncertainty. But above all else, exhaustion reigned supreme.

I bowed my head, placing my forehead in the palm of my hand. The day had barely started and I felt defeated already. "Okay, well I'll meet you guys there, then. Give me twenty minutes." I hung up the phone and messaged Tay to let her know Nate was safe and somewhat sound.

When I flew through the emergency doors, I found Pete and Nate sitting side by side on the blue chairs in the emergency room. For the whole ride to the hospital, I'd been dreading that Nate would be having another panic attack, but when I got there he wasn't freaking out at all. Instead, he was staring straight ahead, seemingly oblivious to his rapidly swelling leg that was poking outside of the pajama shorts he was still wearing. It was unnerving to see him so still, given how puffy his leg had become — and equally unsettling to see that he hadn't changed out of his summer pyjamas before he took to the streets at some point in the night.

"*Nate?* Oh, my baby, Nate! I was *so* worried about you!" I flew to his side and buried his head in my neck. "Where were you? *Why* would you leave the house like that?"

I waited for Nate to respond. Seconds passed, but I got nothing except his continued stare at the empty row of chairs in front of him.

Pete looked at me and shrugged, exhaustion showing on his face.

"Nate? Nate . . . listen, sweetie . . . you aren't in trouble. But we need to know why you left the house. Why would you go in the middle of the night? You scared us, baby. I was really worried. Why would you go?"

Nate turned his head and said faintly, "It wasn't the middle of the night. It was morning. And I wanted to do what Noah was doing. I didn't want him to think that I was a baby."

"Oh, Nate." I brought my son in for a hug, unsure of what to say to make him feel better. It was all I could muster before we were called from our seats.

"Nate Carter?" A nurse holding a chart emerged from behind the desk and looked around the waiting room inquisitively. When Pete waved to show we were who she was looking for, the nurse nodded. "This way, please."

Pete gingerly lifted Nate from his chair and carried our forlorn boy through the emergency room doors towards the examining rooms.

"Are you his mother?" the nurse asked as we passed.

I nodded my head. I knew there was worry in my eyes as they met hers.

"When your husband checked Nate in, he mentioned what happened yesterday. We got Nate in as quickly as possible. Looks like it doesn't seem to be a problem this time, though, which is good." The nurse smiled at me. Her eyes were warm. Compassionate. "We'll take good care of your son, Mrs. Carter. I think the doctor will want to X-ray his ankle to see if it's broken, but we'll be as gentle as possible and try not to add to his stress. He'll be okay."

"Thank you. I appreciate that," I responded. In my moment of vulnerability, her kindness went a long way.

Through it all, Nate said nothing. He refused to answer any of the doctor's questions, and seemed to look through anyone who tried to speak to him. Pete explained to the doctor that Nate had fallen off the swings. I was relieved when the doctor didn't probe us on why Nate was wearing his summer pyjamas; we'd kept silent on the fact that he'd left at some point in the night, for fear of raising any social services flags.

While we were waiting for the X-ray results, a young nurse came in with stickers and lollipops, and tried her best to raise Nate's spirits. He shook his head and refused what she offered.

I tried to shake the embarrassment that flooded through me. I felt awful about being embarrassed about my son, yet I desperately wanted him to act normal. To stop staring at nothing as though he were absent from every moment in his life. I wanted him to cry. Or scream. Wail, even. He needed to *wail* the way most children would if they'd broken their ankle. Not be silent, staring into nothingness.

Half an hour later, a nurse came to put Nate's ankle into an air splint. He'd suffered a bad sprain. The doctors warned Nate to be careful, telling him that he had gotten off easy with only a sprain. They felt it was good news that it would be only a few weeks before it healed.

I couldn't help but think that a few weeks would seem like forever to a nine-year-old who also wasn't speaking, and fear flooded through me as I wondered what it would do to his already saddened spirit.

15

"Mrs. Carter?" The doctor who had examined Nate's ankle ran to catch up with me as we left the hospital. Pete was pushing Nate in a wheelchair. He turned around when he heard the doctor call my name.

"May I have a word with you?" she asked. Something in her tone indicated that she wanted to talk privately. Without Nate around us. Pete picked up on her request for discretion and he suggested they keep going.

"Thanks, Pete. I'll catch up with you in a minute."

"Your son, Nate. I'm wondering if he's always so . . . silent. Does he always act so distant?"

I shook my head. I needed to be honest with her. "No. He's

been acting this way now for several weeks and I . . . I'm not really sure that I understand why."

The doctor nodded in sympathy. When she saw the tears spring to my eyes, she placed her hand on my back and guided me to a private corner. "So, recently he's become quiet like this for an extended period of time? How often do you see this happen with him?"

"Frequently. It does come and go. And I never know when to expect it."

"Is it brought on by anything in particular?"

I shook my head.

"How long does it usually last for?"

"It varies. Sometimes a day or two, I guess. Other times, longer."

The doctor nodded her head, taking in what I was saying. "And how is Nate doing in school? Does he like it?"

"He used to, although he's had some tough times with bullying. Lately he sometimes complains about going to school, but we're keeping a close eye on things, and I don't think he's being bullied by anyone."

"And what are his teachers saying?"

I shrugged my shoulders as Nate's principal's words came skipping through my brain. "I was actually planning on booking a meeting with his teacher this week. He fell yesterday in his class. Hit his head. I spoke with his principal about it when I picked him up, but not his teacher."

"Yes, I saw that in his file. You brought him in because of the concussion scare, but everything was okay, correct? That's good. I'm glad. I also saw that Nate had what the doctor on call thought was a panic attack while waiting to be admitted. Has Nate ever had that before?"

"No, that was definitely new."

"It's something you should definitely watch, Mrs. Carter." The doctor scratched something down on the pad of paper she was holding. She tucked a brown curl behind her ear. "And what activities does Nate do? What does he enjoy?"

"Why all of the questions, doctor? Is there something you're worried about?" Doctors seeking out a patient's parents to ask questions in the hallway couldn't be a good thing.

The doctor nodded her head, and closed the pad of paper she was holding. "I'll cut to the chase, Mrs. Carter. I'm worried that Nate could be suffering from childhood depression. His behaviour, and the look in his eyes, not to mention his silence, well . . . I see some red flags that we need to watch out for."

I looked down, taking in what the doctor was saying but not wanting to greet her eyes.

"And we know that depression is often linked to anxiety. Anxiety that presents itself in ways such as the behaviour we saw yesterday."

"I see. And what do you think we should we do about it?"

"Keep a very close eye on him. Monitor his moods. Write them down, even. If he keeps acting the way he did today . . . if his bad or quiet moods last for a long time, I advise you to take him in and speak to your family doctor. She or he will be able to advise you from there, and they might want you to book an appointment with a child psychologist. Just in case."

There were those words again. They seemed to be finding me a lot.

"Obviously it's early, so I don't want to scare you, but the more quickly you can understand what's going on — *if* something's going on — the better."

"Well, thank you for taking time out of your busy schedule to grab me on the way out."

"You're welcome, Mrs. Carter. And I hope Nate's leg doesn't cause him too much pain or discomfort. Don't forget to ice!"

I walked towards the parking garage with the doctor's words ringing in my ears.

"Everything okay?" Pete asked when I got to our SUV. He was waiting outside by himself, leaning against the driver's door.

"We'll chat later," I responded. I had no idea how Pete was going to respond to all of this. I stuck my head in the Enclave to see Nate, who was sitting lengthwise in the back row. His leg was propped up with a pillow the hospital had given us, and Nate was leaning the side of his head onto the back of the seat, almost like he was trying to burrow and escape.

"You okay, Bean?" I asked, calling over the middle row of our SUV to the backseat. "Ready to go home now? I was thinking we could pick up pancakes on the way home."

I waited for him to say yes to his favourite breakfast, or at least manage a semi-smile at the suggestion. But his only response was to turn his face away from me, trying to burrow further as he smashed his nose into the fabric.

16

When we returned home, we got Nate settled into his room. It took five big pillows — two behind his back, one under his hips, and two under his ankle — before he finally seemed to be comfortable. We had offered to put him in the family room, in front of the big TV, but Nate had refused.

"Don't you want to watch some cartoons?" I asked him, anxious to see a flicker of light appear in his eyes. "One of the good parts of having a sprained ankle is that you get to watch them all day."

But Nate only shook his head, repeating, again, that he wanted to be by himself in his room. He refused to eat. He didn't want to play video games. And he asked me to leave when I offered to stay.

Pete wanted to talk to him about why he left the house, but I convinced him to let it wait. I was worried about the slump Nate was in, and didn't want to push him.

On Monday, Nate begged us to let him stay home from school. We gave in to his request, worried that he might not yet be ready, and concerned about how the other kids might treat a kid on crutches. On Tuesday morning, we echoed the decision and Nate stayed home once again, isolated in his room.

I forced myself to return to work for a mid-morning meeting that I couldn't miss. I'd managed to work from home the day before, calling into my meetings and using the time when Nate napped to plough through my quickly building email pile.

But I couldn't stay away from work any longer. The pressure was mounting with three of our most important accounts, and Jack had clearly expressed that he needed me to be directly involved with every aspect of managing our new client.

By Wednesday, Pete convinced me to make Nate go to school. It was obvious his ankle was already healing by the amount of pressure he was able to put on it when we forced him out of bed to brush his teeth and take a bath. And it wasn't healthy for him to continue to hibernate in his bedroom.

After forcing myself to bury my swelling stress levels, which had heightened after one of my top team members had resigned the day before, I cleared my morning meetings to take Nate to school. It was the only real request he'd made when we'd given him no choice. I helped him get dressed, then walked at a snail's pace beside him as he made his way to the car on crutches.

When we got to school, I brought Nate straight to his classroom. A group of kids from his class snickered and began whispering. One boy I didn't know pointed right at us.

I inhaled sharply. "Hey guys," I said. "Nate hurt his ankle

and could use some friends to help him out until he's better. Can you do that?"

"Yeah right," one boy snorted. The others snickered outwardly. Then, more quietly, the instigator said to his gang of friends, "Like we'd *ever* help a hyena!" The entire group burst out laughing.

"*What* did you say?" I stopped in my tracks to look straight into the eyes of the obnoxious ringleader.

"Your kid's a hyena — and *we* don't *like* hyenas." The boy returned my stare as the rest of the group barked hysterical laughter. I ignored them, refusing to back down.

The boy crossed his arms. He took two steps in front of his gang and gave Nate a menacing stare. Beside me, I felt Nate start to tremble and, in that moment, my heart broke for my son. There were no friends at this school for Nate.

"Come on, buddy. Let's get you to see Mrs. Brock."

When Nate crutched forward, I turned to look back at the brat behind me. "By the way . . . what's your name? I'll be sure to tell Mrs. Brock that we had a chat."

The boy answered my question by running in the opposite direction, his crew of unruly urchins following closely behind him. One even gave me the finger as they loped away to the playground.

I was astounded by how outwardly obnoxious they were. I'd recently read an article that encouraged parents to pay attention for signs of bullying from even the most amiable kids, some of whom had a knack for laying on the charm in front of adults, only to turn on their prey the minute it was kids only. The manipulation of the whole act would make it even harder for parents to separate truth from fiction, as many would find it hard to believe the charming kid at school would actually bully their child. If the boys in Nate's class were so openly vulgar in front of his mother, I shuddered to think of what they might be doing when I wasn't around to protect him.

When we reached Nate's hallway, I helped him leave his things in his locker and get settled in his class. There were ten more minutes before the bell rang, and I hoped Mrs. Brock would make an early appearance so I could talk to her about Nate. I needed to let her know what had happened on our way into the school.

Nate and I waited for Mrs. Brock in silence; I tried to ask him questions but he wouldn't respond. Seven minutes before the bell, Mrs. Brock walked into the room, carrying a mountain of papers with her.

"Nate! You're back. We're so happy to have you. How is your ankle?" Mrs. Brock dropped the papers at her desk, and walked directly over to Nate. She crouched down beside him so they were at eye level, and smiled broadly. "Are you comfortable? Do you need to put your foot up at all?"

Nate shook his head. It was the first day his ankle hadn't been propped up, but I sensed he didn't want to do anything to call more attention to himself. Given the combat we'd just had in the playground, I decided that he might be right.

"Mrs. Brock? May I have a word with you in the hall?" Nate stared at the top of his desk while I waited for Mrs. Brock to answer. She looked concerned about leaving Nate, but ultimately agreed to join me in the hall.

"I know we don't have long before the bell, so I'll cut right to the chase. I'm concerned about Nate. Both because he hasn't been himself lately, and because there were a group of kids just now who were downright cruel. They made fun of him, calling him a hyena and other nasty words. One even gave us the finger!"

Mrs. Brock raised an eyebrow at my last comment, but I sensed from her reaction that what I was saying wasn't a surprise to her.

"The kid who was teasing him . . . I assume it was Tyson and his group?" Mrs. Brock asked. I told her that I didn't know the kid's name as he had run off when I'd asked him.

"Tyson is a bit of a class ruler, with a group of kids following his lead. And he isn't always nice to Nate, I'm afraid."

My protective warning bells that had started to ring when we'd confronted the group on our way into school now went off like there was a bomb scare. I took a deep breath before asking, "How often is it happening?"

"It goes in fits and spurts, but I'd say twice a week. Sometimes more."

"Twice a week?!" I spurted. "Why hasn't anyone contacted me before now to let me know? I was just with Mrs. Spencer last week and she said nothing had happened at this school!"

"Nothing severe enough to involve the principal. So Mrs. Spencer hasn't been involved at all." Mrs. Brock looked at me inquisitively as she continued. "Mrs. Carter, hasn't Mr. Carter told you about this? I've had several conversations with him about it. Knowing what has happened to Nate at other schools, I've been very proactive about informing your husband about everything that goes on here."

"No. He hasn't . . ." I was livid, and ready to hurl words at my husband when I saw him next. I felt my face turn a hot shade of red.

"As far as I know, they haven't physically hurt him at all. But they do like to tease him quite a bit, unfortunately." Mrs. Brock paused. She shifted her weight from one foot to the other, looking mildly uncomfortable. "I think Tyson and the others who go along with him see Nate as an easy target."

"But why Nate? Are there others that get picked on too?"

"Occasionally. But, Nate . . . well, he sometimes does things that the other kids aren't used to. He acts a bit different from the other kids." Mrs. Brock paused again. I met her glance and found compassion in her eyes. I knew she was a wonderful teacher who cared about Nate's best interest.

"Such as jumping on the desk and acting like a hyena?"

Mrs. Brock nodded. Of course the other kids would have

73

thought that was odd. His own mother thought it was strange behaviour.

"How about other things? Do you have any other examples of things?" I asked, beginning to absorb what Nate was facing on an everyday basis at school.

"He does sometimes act out of character and gets fairly wild. I have a hard time containing him, on occasion. But other times he goes into a shell and won't say a word to anyone around him, including me. I don't push him too hard when he gets like that because his teacher from last year said it didn't work very well." Mrs. Brock looked directly at me. "I have to tell you, Mrs. Carter, that I *am* concerned about Nate. He flips back and forth between extremely frenzied and then, out of the blue, almost nonexistent. I've never seen such an extreme spin of emotions."

"I see. And have you talked about this with Pete, too?"

"A little bit, but our conversations have been more centred on the teasing from the other kids." Mrs. Brock glanced at her watch. "We're almost at the bell, but I don't want to brush this off. I'm always available to talk about Nate. Perhaps we could book an appointment with both you and your husband to discuss this further, if you'd like to chat more?"

"I appreciate that, thank you. You've given me a lot to think about."

"You're very welcome. And I will take very good care of Nate and his ankle today. Will it be you or your husband picking him up at lunch?" Mrs. Brock now rushed her words, anxious to finish our conversation before the bell rang.

"Pete will be here. I need to get to work."

"Of course. Well, I'll be sure to relay anything to Mr. Carter that you both need to know."

I thanked Mrs. Brock again and rushed into the classroom to say a final goodbye to Nate, who hadn't moved an inch and was still staring at his desk. As I kissed his cheek and brought him in for a hug, I saw the haunted, hollow look in his eyes, and knew without a shadow of a doubt that my son was, indeed, somehow broken inside.

17
Nate

I am back in my bedroom. By myself. But that is okay, because I want to be alone. I do not want anyone in my room with me.

Talking makes my heart hurt even more. I have never had it hurt like this. It's like someone is kicking it. Or squeezing it too hard. And it hurts, but it also feels numb. It is weird. And it hurts even more than my ankle did. And it feels way different.

I am glad everyone is staying away. I do not want to be near anyone because no one wants to be near me. Everyone hates me. Even my mom and dad and Mrs. Brock. And especially stupid Tyson.

I know my mom and dad hate me because they are fighting.

They are fighting about me. They are yelling at each other. Over and over and over. It is all my fault.

I am the only one at home and they think I am sleeping. So they are yelling at each other. They think I cannot hear them. But I can hear every word.

Mommy is mad at Dad. She says that he does not tell her anything about me. I know it is my fault they are fighting. It is always my fault. If I just went away they would not fight anymore.

Mommy keeps yelling. She is telling Dad that she has a right to know things about me. That everything is *not* typical kid stuff.

I wonder what she wants to know about me. There is nothing to tell. I am boring. No one likes me. I am nothing.

I feel sad. Very, very sad. I do not like feeling sad. I do not want to do anything but sleep. But I am not tired. I cannot sleep.

I want this feeling to go away. But it won't.

I just want to die.

18
Ashley

After Nate's first day back to school, we had a tense family dinner and I decided to go to bed right after Grace and Nate had said their good nights. I was mentally and emotionally exhausted, and couldn't entertain the thought of anything but sleep. I'd had another gruelling day at the office, and a second resignation had forced me to examine where we were going to get the brainpower to execute against everything we needed to deliver. Combined with what was going on with my son, it was all too much, and I felt as though I was teetering on a ledge that could send me straight into a world of complete instability.

As I lay in bed, I thought about what had happened earlier that day. Despite the chaos that had been going on around me at the office, I hadn't been able to concentrate on anything at work, so I left early to meet Pete. I wanted to pick up Nate together. I worried about how his day had gone, what his mood would be like. If he'd had any more outbursts. And if Tyson or his bully friends had picked on him.

If Mrs. Brock had any updates she should tell Pete and me together. With my own husband not relaying any messages or concerns to me, I felt as if I didn't know anything about what was really going on with our son.

Mrs. Brock waved when she saw us, and relayed that Nate's day had been fairly uneventful, but very quiet.

"And how were the other . . . kids? Did they pick on him today?" I asked quietly.

Mrs. Brock shook her head. "Not that I saw, which is good. I took Tyson out in the hall right before I started the first period lesson to let him know that you and I had talked. I told him that if there was one mean word to Nate, he'd be going to the principal's office. Threats don't always work with him, but it seemed to work today."

I nodded, grateful for Mrs. Brock's full support, and we said our goodbyes.

Given that Nate had no after-school activities, we took him home. When he finally hobbled his way into the house, he told us he just wanted to rest and go to bed.

"Do you want to talk about today first? How was school? Was it tough being back with a sprained ankle?" I pried. Nate slowly made his way up the stairs to his room. I knew I was pushing too hard. I had asked him the same questions repeatedly in the car, but he'd ignored them.

I tried to tell myself to relax. That Nate would open up when he was ready. But I was anxious about his well-being and nervous that my little boy was being picked on by bullies.

I regretted what came next. When Nate was in his room with the door closed, I couldn't wait for one more minute to ask Pete why he hadn't told me about the kids at school picking on Nate. Or why he hadn't mentioned that Mrs. Brock was concerned about Nate's mood swings.

"Ashley . . . you're being dramatic again. I know what happened at the other school was brutal. But he's at a new school now, in a new year with a new class. And you have to remember that Nate is a *kid*. With kid friends. And guess what? Kids sometimes tease one another. It happens. It's happened since we were little kids ourselves. Didn't you get picked on? I still remember Tommy Shields and how mean he was to me. But it gave me tough skin. It was character building, and it will be for Nate too. He'll be fine. So stop worrying so much."

"It's not character building; it's just plain *mean*. And I won't stand for bullies picking on my son!" I retorted. "And . . . you! *You* didn't even have the consideration to let me know. To tell me about our son being picked on by those stupid little shits at school . . . especially after everything Nate has been through. I'm his *mother*, Pete. I have a right to know these things."

"Sometimes I need to make a judgement call, Ash. You're at work all day . . . I can't tell you about every little thing that goes on around here. I always tell you the things that I think are important. You're completely overreacting to me not telling you that some of the kids are teasing our son."

"Overreacting? Is that what you think this is? And do you think Nate's principal and teacher and the doctor at the ER are overreacting too? That they don't know what they're talking about when they express concern over Nate's strange behaviour or the funky moods he gets in? I've told you several times that the ER doctor indicated Nate might suffer from childhood depression. And you always just shrug it off, like that's no big deal."

"Childhood depression? Come *on*." Pete snorted. His face was quickly turning into a shade of purply red. "What a load of medical psychobabble bullshit. And, yes, I do think they are overreacting. Nate is a nine-year-old boy. They get hyper. Then they get sad. They're little emotional balls of energy. They're *kids*, for fuck's sake. And *you* need to stop overreacting."

Pete and I had never talked to each other this way before. It felt awful. I barely recognized the person I knew my husband to be; the person standing in front of me was a fuming mess of a man in complete denial of a situation that I was desperate to resolve.

As our fight grew in strength, I thought about Nate upstairs. The only thing that provided me comfort was the fact that he was the only one at home, and I suspected he was sleeping.

Pete and I managed to park our anger during dinner and the kids' routine homework sessions that always followed, speaking tersely to each other when we were forced to converse. And then I crawled directly into bed without bothering to wash off my makeup. But despite how tired I was, I couldn't sleep. I felt awful about my fight with Pete and desperately wanted to be a team again.

Pete finally came to bed about an hour later. I stiffened as he entered the bed, and pretended to sleep. I didn't want to start fighting again.

After a few minutes, Pete slowly inched towards me underneath the covers, nudging me with his toe. Inch by inch, he came closer, eventually spooning my back and nuzzling his nose into my neck. "I'm sorry, Ash. The last thing I want is to be fighting with you."

Tears sprang to my eyes, and I didn't answer. But I also didn't move out of Pete's embrace.

"I really think you're taking this a little too seriously, sweetie. And I don't want you to worry. Nate will be fine. He's just a little kid. And you know kids are like this. They tease each other," Pete whispered. I could feel the warmth of his breath directly on my ear. "I'll make sure to keep closer tabs on Nate at school, okay? And I'll make sure to relay anything I find out to you as soon as it happens. I feel bad that Nate is being picked on at school, too, but it's part of growing up. And it's completely different from what happened last time. We can't overreact to cruel words and think it's the same thing as black eyes."

I sat up. "And what about the other things? The fact that we've now had three people, including a teacher and a doctor, tell us that Nate is behaving strangely. That his 'typical kid mood swings' might be something more? Something bad?"

"Then we keep a closer eye on him. Like I said I was going to. But you've also got to consider that we've just got an extreme kid. One whose emotions swing a bit further than most."

"I don't know, Pete . . . something feels off. I can feel it in my gut. Call it mother's instinct, but I can't shake the fact that something might be really wrong with Nate. And it's scaring me."

Pete drew me in for a hug. "Don't be scared. We're in this together. You need to know that everything will be fine."

Pete could see I wasn't convinced. "Honestly, Ash, I think we should stop talking about it. It's making you panic and that's not good for anyone. I already said I'd keep a closer eye on him at school, and if anything else happens, I promise I'll let you know."

Pete's response made me ache all over. He was sweeping everything Nate was going through under the carpet and making it seem like it was normal. And I knew it wasn't.

"Think of it this way . . . wouldn't you be bummed out if you sprained your ankle and couldn't do any of the activities you loved most?"

"But that's just it, Pete. I don't think it's the ankle that's bumming him out. And I don't think that it's why he doesn't want to play hockey or any of the other things he used to love. He's just so disengaged. From *everything*."

"Well, maybe he doesn't like those things anymore. Kids change . . ."

I shook my head. "Not this drastically, they don't. And what about him running away in the middle of the night? Or taking off in the middle of the day to go buy gum in his underwear? That stuff is not normal. Maybe he's so depressed he's crying out for help or something—"

"You just don't know what it's like to be a nine-year-old boy. They're different than girls," Pete interrupted. "It's like their brains are sometimes without logic. He's just a kid, Ash. And I'm sure this won't be the last of the unusual behaviour. He's a *boy*."

"I don't know . . ." I knew in my heart of hearts Pete wasn't right. And no matter what he said, he would not convince me.

"Well, for tonight, we know that Nate is safe and sound. Tucked in his bed. So let's get some sleep and take each day as it comes," Pete suggested. "We don't really have any other choice right now, do we?"

I shrugged, knowing Pete was right. About the last part, at least.

I lay awake in bed for hours that night, listening to Pete snore softly beside me. It didn't seem that what was going on with Nate was affecting him in the same way it was haunting me.

At one point, I tried waking Pete up. I was frantic to keep talking about what was going on with Nate, and I felt that if we kept the discussion going we might just come across the answer of what we should be doing.

But Pete rolled over, turning his back to me when I tried to gently nudge him awake. I had no idea if he was still sleeping or if he was faking it and using it as an excuse to end the conversation he didn't want to be having. I suspected the latter.

With nothing around me but the quiet sounds of a house in the middle of the night, I felt sad. It was as if there was no one to turn to, to talk to, even though my closest family members were under the same roof. They were all sleeping in close proximity, yet it felt like they weren't really there at all.

As the minutes ticked by, the fist of despair clenched my heart even more tightly. I was aching from loneliness. I had no one to turn to.

And the worst part was the recurring thought that wouldn't escape me. The unshakeable, persistent fear that the wee boy sleeping in the room down the hall felt the exact same way as I did — except much, much worse.

19

The next morning, I got up thirty minutes before my alarm. I sent an email to Emily to cancel my early morning meetings again so that I could take Nate to school. I tried to ignore the guilt of missing yet another meeting I knew I should be at; Jack would lay into me about it when I got to work, so there was plenty of time to feel bad about it.

At breakfast, Pete raised his eyebrows at me when I told him I would be taking the kids to school that morning.

"But I keep telling you that I want to *walk*. By *myself*," Grace whined, her mouth full of cereal. "Come on, please can you let me? My school isn't that far, and I promise to be careful."

"Grace, don't speak with your mouth full." I clenched my

teeth, trying to find patience. Even the tiniest things were dancing on my nerves. "You know what? You can walk, since you're able to do so — and since you *want* to so badly. I'll just take Nate. Okay, buddy?" I looked at my son as I took a gulp of coffee and watched for his response. But there wasn't one. His untouched toast lay in front of him.

"Are you going to eat any of your toast, Nate?"

He ignored me.

"You need to eat something, buddy. I'm prepared to wait." I took a seat at the table and braced myself for battle. I nudged his plate towards him. I wasn't leaving until he ate something.

Slowly, Nate took his first nibble of toast. When he finished half of it, I declared myself the victor. I helped him out of the chair and we began the slow crutch-walk to the car. Nate was silent the whole way.

I once again took him directly to class. Nervously, I scanned the playground, keeping watch for Tyson and his crew. When I couldn't find them, it dawned on me that I should be embarrassed to be uneasy about running into a kid. I was almost thirty years older than him.

Once Nate and I were safe in the classroom, Mrs. Brock greeted us energetically. "Good morning! How are you today, Nate?"

"Okay," Nate responded quietly. They were the first words I'd heard him utter since he got up that morning.

"Well, I've been excited to tell you that I have a very special surprise for you. I remember you telling me that you love zoo animals, so I've decided that we're going to learn all about elephants and rhinoceroses today. Does that sound good to you?"

I noticed a slight flicker enter Nate's eyes. Then, the tiniest smile crept upwards into his cheeks.

"Look, I brought in animal books from the library that we can read today." Mrs. Brock crossed the room and pointed to a display of books she had set up. "And I thought we could also paint some ostrich eggs . . . and play a game called Mammalian Madness. What do you think, Nate?"

As his smile increased, so did my relief. For the first time all week, I felt happy as I left my son, and I hoped he felt the same way.

At work, I had barely hung up my coat when Jack walked into my office. He shut the door swiftly behind him and sat in one of the wingback chairs on the other side of my desk. "Where were you this morning?" he asked curtly. "You missed the senior management meeting. Again."

"I know, Jack. And I'm sorry. Did you get my email?"

"I did."

"Well, you know I wouldn't miss it if I could help it. I'm . . . I'm a bit worried about my son, Nate, and it's requiring a bit more flexibility these days."

"Ashley, you know I've always given you complete flexibility with your career and your family. And you've never disappointed me within that very loose rein. Part of the reason I've never questioned you is that you have a razor-sharp ability to prioritize and know what meetings you absolutely need to be at."

I nodded, feeling the heat rise to my cheeks. As an obvious favourite at the company, I wasn't used to being in Jack's hot seat.

"I was surprised by your decision to miss the meeting this morning. It was an important one. One you shouldn't have missed."

"Yes, I'm aware . . ."

"Well, then perhaps you should have made a different decision."

"I'll connect with Cruz and find out everything I need to know. I'll catch up. This morning."

"That isn't the point, Ashley. You should have been there for the group discussion. To contribute to the meeting."

"I know, Jack. You're right. It won't happen again."

"That's good. Because we need you around here. Our client list is growing, as you're obviously aware, and we need to be upping our creative game." I tuned Jack out as soon as I heard his remarks on needing sharp creative. Jack liked to think he was motivating me, but the truth was he knew nothing about running a creative shop. While Jack was a businessman who had the right knack for ensuring profitability every fiscal year, he didn't have the foggiest idea of what constituted strong creative.

I continued smiling and nodding, pretending to listen to Jack ramble on about how important I was to the business and why he needed all of my focus. When I couldn't take any more, I gently interrupted him. "I hear you, Jack. I really do. But right now I'm late for another meeting that I need to attend. The 110 percent focus that you just talked about needs to be on our next campaign. We're working on a deadline for Campbell's. We present tomorrow morning at eight-thirty. The team needs me to provide final feedback and approval, and I don't want to keep them waiting. Okay, Jack?"

"Yeah, sure. Makes sense. Go get 'em. And good talk. I'm glad we see eye to eye on this now." Jack scratched his head as he rose to his full height. It took every bit of my strength not to roll my eyes at him. While the two of us usually got along well enough, his overbearing side was tough to take in anything more than small doses.

When Jack was gone, I grabbed my Campbell's file folders and made my way to the creative boardroom, where I knew the team was working on the digital campaign. They were heads down when I walked in the room.

"How's it going, guys?" I asked, peeking over their shoulders to look at the comps that had been put together.

"It's going . . ." James, my associate creative director, piped up without glancing from the comp that consumed him.

"Do you like where we've landed?" I asked him. He finally looked up, and pushed the comp in my direction for me to take a look at. My heart sank when I saw it. The idea was flat and dull. And it wasn't on strategy. I knew the client would be disappointed.

"James . . . are there other options?" I asked hopefully. I decided to give him the benefit of the doubt and assumed that there were alternatives.

"Nope. Unfortunately not. This is the best we've got," he responded, looking disappointed. "I can tell by the look on your face that you feel the same way I do, which isn't great. But we're going to fix this, Ash. We'll work all night if we have to."

I glanced around the room and saw something close to defeat on the faces of my creative team. I knew they'd been working long hours on the campaign, but hard work without on-strategy, effective creative wasn't going to cut it for our client meeting the next day.

"Okay, well let's take a look at what you've got. Maybe there's a thought starter in one of the other ideas." I set my file folders on the table and sat down, reaching for the other comps. Each one was worse than the previous.

Awkward silence filled the room as I took one more look at each comp. There was nothing there we could work from.

"Uh . . . we could really use your help, Ashley," James stammered. He was a strong mind that had been responsible for a tremendous amount of award-winning campaigns, but he was clearly struggling with what had been asked of him this time around. "We've been at this for a few weeks now and, to be honest, I think we're starting to suffer from brain burnout."

"Not yet you're not," I responded with a smile and a wink. "We can do this. We'll do it together."

James shifted awkwardly in his seat.

"Here's what we're going to do," I continued. "I'll send Emily on a Starbucks run, and get her to bring back a whack of brain food . . . cookies, muffins, yogurt, candy . . . whatever you guys want, we'll get. Then, we'll start at the beginning. Together.

We'll throw out all of these ideas and start fresh. Who knows . . . we might circle back to one of them eventually, or borrow a general theme, but for now I don't want to be limited to them. I want us to think bigger. To be more on brand. And definitely more on brief. We *really* need this campaign to be an evolution of last year's creative, and to fit like a glove within Campbell's three-year strategic plan. Does that sound good to everyone?" I paused to look around the room. The previously sluggish faces began to perk up. The team sat taller. Energy began to fill the room.

"Sounds great. Thanks Ash," James responded. Around him, the team nodded their heads in unison.

"Let me just see if Ben can lend us a few members of his team so we have some new thinkers in the room." I picked up my phone and sent Ben a message marked urgent. "You guys definitely know the brand and the brief, but having fresh minds sometimes helps to spark ideas."

Twenty-five minutes later, we all sat around a food- and drink-filled table with a few new faces eagerly waiting to get started. I took my position at the white board and said, casually, "Let's start with the easy stuff. Don't think too literally. Or specifically. Let's let our minds open to *all* ideas and *all* concepts that revolve around coziness during the holidays. We'll throw them up on the whiteboard and go from there. And remember, no idea is a bad idea. No matter what. It might not be what we'll go with, but you never know what will spark the next idea, which could be the winner." I smiled again at the group. I didn't want them to be frustrated. I needed them to be filled with energy. We had about a week's worth of work in front of us with less than twenty-four hours in which to do it. We were going to need to dig deep to pull it off. "So. Who wants to start?"

"How about flannel pyjamas?" A twenty-something guy named Hunter suggested. He was one of the new additions from Ben's team, and I was thankful Ben had sent him, given what I'd heard about his brainstorming contributions. I nodded my head and wrote it down. "Anything else?"

"Roaring fires," Nicholas threw out. On the whiteboard it went.

"White twinkly lights."

"Snow falling in the woods."

"The smell of apple pie baking in the oven."

"A new pair of mittens. You know . . . the really soft kind. Like cashmere." I wrote quickly. The ideas were beginning to tumble out of the team's mouths and, within thirty minutes, we had two oversized whiteboards filled with marker.

I glanced at the clock on my phone. I was ten minutes late for my next meeting, but I knew I couldn't leave. It was internal, so I wasn't as concerned about bailing as I would be if it included clients, and there was no way I could risk our momentum falling to pieces if I moved on.

Inwardly sighing, I sent Emily a note asking her to reschedule my next meeting. I knew it was likely going to be at seven a.m. the following day, given that it was time-critical and I was already stacked with meetings for the entire day. There was zero wiggle room in my schedule.

"Okay," I said, turning back to the team. "Let's keep going. There are some obvious idea keepers that we've put on the left side of the whiteboard, but there could be some others over here as well. Before we abandon them, let's go through the list to prioritize the better ones and see if anyone has ideas for how we could build on them to support the brief we've been given by the client."

Together, we worked for three hours, prioritizing the list and fleshing out the ideas we knew could work.

In the middle of the afternoon, I left the group to go to a client meeting that I couldn't miss, and returned a few hours later to check in on their progress. While I knew my chances were hovering somewhere just above zero, I was keeping my fingers crossed that the team would be far enough along that I could let them officially take over.

"How's it going?" I asked, forcing a smile.

"We've made some progress, for sure. But we're glad you're back, as we need your opinion on a few things . . ." James replied.

I glanced at the sketches on the table, and felt my shoulders drop as I realized how much work there still was to do. We were on our way but definitely nowhere near done.

At six o'clock, I excused myself to call Pete. I was dreading the phone call, but knew I had to let him know I wouldn't make it home for dinner.

"How's Nate? Did he have a good day?" I asked, once I'd given Pete my disappointing news.

"Unfortunately not, I'm afraid. Mrs. Brock said that, at first, she thought he was going to love the zoo animals. But when the rest of the class came in he barely said a word. Apparently she tried her best, and coaxed him all day to participate —"

"But he didn't?" I interrupted. Pete wasn't getting there fast enough.

"No, he didn't. And she thinks he was using his ankle as a crutch, so to speak. The only thing he *did* say was that his ankle was hurting and that he wanted to sit by himself in the back of the classroom."

My heart ached. I had no words to reply.

"And those little bullying shits in his class seemed to take advantage of him being that way, too. Mrs. Brock overheard them laying into him pretty good at the back of the class, calling him a baby and a wimp. She kept him inside at recess and tried to talk to him, but she said he just stared out the window."

"I'm going to come home. I don't care about this creative presentation anymore. I need to see Nate."

"No, no . . . you stay there. We're just about to sit down to dinner and then he'll be in bed soon after that. I get it . . . you need to be at work right now. I've got things covered here."

I didn't respond right away, trying to decide if I should listen to my husband or my gut. I knew I should go home to Nate. He needed me.

"Seriously, Ash. Nate will get it too. We all do. Just do what you have to do, and come home when you can."

I began to feel Pete push me towards my acceptance of fate. Before I could respond, I felt a sharp pain on my thumb, and looked down to realize I'd subconsciously peeled away a hangnail using my pointer finger, causing my thumb to bleed. I was more stressed than I realized.

"Ashley? Are you still there?"

"Yeah, I'm here. Look, I'm going to try my best to make it home by bedtime. But I'm not convinced it will happen, unfortunately. We've got a long road in front of us."

"Sounds like it. Don't worry about it, hon. We'll see you when we see you."

I was appreciative of Pete's change in attitude and of his support of my working hours. It was a long cry from the guilt he'd recently shoved at me and I wondered what had changed.

At two o'clock in the morning, I unlocked our front door and fell onto the hall bench to take off my boots. My whole body ached, and I longed for sleep. All around me, our house was dark and silent.

Pausing in the kitchen for a glass of water, I noticed a new drawing that had been stuck to the fridge door with Nate's favourite magnet, a bright red replica of the Golden Gate Bridge. It had been a gift from my father after he'd returned from one of his trips to San Francisco. Nate was obsessed with it, and used the magnet whenever he was particularly proud of something he'd created and wanted to display proudly.

I peeled the artwork from the fridge, and took in the picture of an angry-looking elephant. It had sharp, pointed tusks and deep red eyes. Almost bloodshot, but more intense. The elephant had been coloured a shade of grey that was so dark it was almost black, and was snarling to show its mean-looking teeth. All around it, black clouds closed in on the scary looking creature, and a bolt of yellow lightning shot across the page. The picture was both aggressive and frightening.

I shuddered, wondering why Nate would draw such a disturbing picture. I hesitated before putting it back up on the fridge; I didn't want such an angry-looking elephant up on display in my house, but I knew Nate would be crushed if I took it down, given that he'd used his favourite magnet; it was an obvious signal that he was very proud of his drawing.

After filling my glass with water from the fridge, I crept up the stairs, pausing first to kiss Grace's sleeping cheek, and then to peek in on Nate. I was more than five hours too late, but still wanted to say good night, even if it was to already sleeping bodies. I paused a long time to watch Nate sleep. His breathing was rapid and shallow.

I took his little hand in mine, but he didn't react. He didn't even flinch. Taking it as a sign that he wouldn't wake up, I buried my head in his little chest, happy to be near him again. When he still didn't stir, I crawled in next to him, careful not to wake him or hurt his ankle. I listened to his heartbeat. Felt my head rise with the rhythm of his breath. He was so peaceful, and perfectly at ease.

With his eyes shut, I couldn't see the lurking demons that haunted the baby blues I had loved for a lifetime. I couldn't see any of the tell-tale signs of whatever it was that was suffocating my baby's soul. Everything was hidden by sleep. Guarded by closed lids.

Lying with my sleeping son, I felt I was also temporarily at peace. I liked that it was hidden, that I couldn't see what was truly going on. I *liked* that I couldn't see the foggy gaze that now trumped Nate's former bright, shining eyes.

And when my tears came moments later, I also liked that my son couldn't see his mother cry.

20
Nate

It's still dark. I lie in bed. I slowly turn my ankle in a circle. It feels way better but I still cannot walk on it by myself. I need crutches. Or someone to carry me. Mostly that is Dad. But sometimes Mom carries me too.

I miss my mommy. She did not come home last night. Dad said she was working. She always has a lot of work to do. Dad told me Mom would be home in the morning.

I wanted to know more about what Mom was doing last night at work. But I couldn't seem to find the words. Or make myself talk. I want to talk. But I can't. I don't know why.

Dad says Mom has a lot of work to do. I wonder if she misses me too. I want to ask her. I want to find her.

I sit up in bed. I feel all fuzzy in my head. Mom says that is called *groggy*. I wait a minute. It goes away.

Outside, I can hear rain. It's hitting hard against my window. I wonder if the bird I saw staring at me is getting wet. I wonder if he is still as sad as I am.

I edge my way to the side of my bed. I put both feet on the ground and test my ankle. That is how Dad told me to do it. It hurts a little bit. I think I can step on it. I think I can get to Mom's room without my crutches. I hate my crutches.

I walk slowly in the dark. I feel my way. I touch all of the walls. It helps me to get to Mom's room. It helps me walk with my sore ankle.

The door is shut. I open it.

The room is quiet. And dark. It makes me feel sad.

I walk in. I go to her side of the bed. I want her to hug me.

I can't see her. I need to see her.

I turn on the lamp beside her bed.

Mom is not there. But Dad sits straight up.

"Huh? What? What's going on? *Nate?* Hey . . . what's up, buddy? Why are you up so early? It's only a quarter after six." Dad is squinting into the light. He is holding his hand up to his forehead. I think he is protecting his eyes. I wonder if his eyes hurt. Like mine do. The light is hurting my eyes.

I want to ask where Mommy is. She is not in the bed. She is gone.

I still can't find the words. I still cannot make myself talk. I do not know why. I feel like I can't breathe. Can't find the words. I think it is called suffocating. Whatever it is, it hurts.

Dad must be used to the light now. He takes his hand down from his forehead and reaches for me.

"Are you okay, buddy?"

I feel myself blink. No words come out.

"Do you want to come into bed with me?"

I do not. I want my mommy.

"Come here, bud. Mom had to go into work early. She had a seven o'clock meeting. But she'll be home tonight."

I do not believe him. Because Mommy is always gone.

21
Ashley

I sank further into the soft leather of the town car back seat, and sipped at the complimentary water, wishing it was some sort of caffeine. My body was so tired that it ached all over, and I longed for sleep. I wished I could tell the driver to turn around and take me back to my bed.

I squinted to see through the windshield. We were speeding, and the rain was so heavy that the wipers couldn't keep up. Blurred lights streaked by at lightning speed.

It was far too dark to be en route to work.

My pulse quickened and I thought about asking the driver to slow down. I likely would have, except I was afraid I would be late for the seven o'clock meeting I couldn't miss.

I longed for a double espresso latte, but knew we didn't have time to stop. The impact of the late hour from my night before was making my brain feel completely foggy, and I needed to find caffeine quickly in order to have half a chance at making it through my meetings.

With five minutes to spare, I got to work and was walking to my office when I noticed Emily sitting at her desk.

"Emily? What are you *doing* here so early?" I asked her, searching for my keys in my oversized bag.

"I knew you had the numbers meeting this morning, and I suspected you were here far too late on the Campbell's creative. So I thought I'd join you in case there was anything you needed. . ."

"You're such a gem. Thank you, Em." I managed to find my keys and let myself into my office. It was pitch dark and felt far too chilly.

Emily followed me into my office. She handed me a venti latte, perfectly made-to-order, with non-fat milk and one raw sugar.

"Oh Em! You're a lifesaver. How did you know this is exactly what I needed?"

"Because you never have time to stop and you always need a morning latte."

I flashed Emily my biggest grin. She made every difficult part of my work life easier, and I'd walk over coal to keep her as my assistant.

"Andrew is waiting for you in the boardroom," Emily informed me, referring to our chief financial officer. "He got here about ten minutes ago."

I smiled at her again as I grabbed my files for the meeting.

"Here!" Emily said as I flew out the door. She raced towards me and handed me my favourite sketch pen, which I had at every meeting. She walked with me the rest of the way to the boardroom to fill me in on some changes to my meetings later that day.

Andrew was already seated at the table, nose deep in his BlackBerry.

"Andrew, thanks so much for rescheduling. And for coming in at this crazy hour." I took a seat opposite to him and braced myself for an uncomfortable conversation. Andrew needed to speak to me about the creative hours that had been creeping upwards in recent weeks.

"Not a problem. I know how crazy busy this place can be." Andrew grinned at me. As far as finance and creative people went, Andrew and I were at the top of the list in terms of getting along. "And I just got a BBM from Charlee. She'll be here any second."

Just as Andrew finished his sentence, Charlee Browers, our head of accounts, flew through the door. She looked soggy from the rain.

"Sorry, guys!" she said, breathless. She wiped the drizzle from the shoulders of her fall coat. "I had a tough time getting a cab and, of course, forgot my umbrella."

"Let's get started," Andrew said, his stern side emerging. "I know you're under significant pressure to deliver creative, Ash. But the hours the creative team has been billing lately are crazy. And as Charlee can attest to, we're getting significant push-back from almost all of our clients."

"It's true, I'm afraid," Charlee jumped in. Her pretty face wore a sheepish grin. "My team has been fielding calls left, right, and centre from clients who are questioning the hours spent on creative development. We need to fix this, Ash. And soon."

"You weren't at the senior management meeting yesterday. But this was a big part of our discussion, and Jack's worried we're pissing off clients." Andrew explained. "With the economy the way it is right now, budgets are tight, and we have to be account-able for every hour billed."

Hearing Andrew mention the agenda at the meeting I'd missed the day before caused guilt to creep up my neck. With the discussion revolving around creative hours, I should have been part of it.

"In my opinion, as you know, we need to revisit the whole billing model for creative," I responded. "It's not effective. You can't always forecast how long it will take to come up with the creative that a client needs. You can't just say, 'Be creative *now*' to a team and then start a stopwatch. It doesn't work that way."

Andrew and Charlee nodded. They'd heard the argument before, and I knew they didn't disagree.

"Plus, the creative team is on the junior side right now. It takes longer. That's just the way it is. I want to hire more senior creatives but Jack hasn't approved the positions. If we had more experienced creative minds working on our clients' business, it wouldn't take as long."

"Yes, but those experienced minds come with more expensive salaries . . ." Andrew responded, and we were caught once again in the same vicious circular argument we always were.

Further into the meeting, it became more obvious that I'd missed an extremely important discussion the day before. We needed to bring in Jack and figure out a way to change how our creative team billed for their hours.

"For now, let's just agree to bill clients for what they've signed off on, and we will eat the rest until we figure out the new estimation model. Does that work for you guys?" I asked. We all knew we couldn't risk pissing off our clients by billing them for hours that were out of scope.

Our meeting broke just before eight o'clock, and I left the boardroom to head to the meeting at Campbell's. Emily waited outside the boardroom with my coat, an umbrella, and a cab chit. I had just over thirty minutes to make it across town.

"James and the others are already in the lobby. I told them you'd meet them there," Emily explained as I shrugged my arms into my coat. She walked with me to the elevator and punched the button for me.

When I reached the lobby, I was greeted by sleepy smiles that matched my own. I knew the team was suffering from lack of sleep as much as I was but, despite our tired brains, we managed to breeze through the creative presentation and get instant approval from the Campbell's marketing team. We were back at the office just before noon, and I headed to my working lunch brainstorm. Famished, I filled my plate with catered sandwiches and salads, hoping it would give me enough energy to keep my steam for the rest of my afternoon meetings.

By the time I got home, I practically fell through the door. I was exhausted from head to toe, and didn't know how I'd make it through dinner.

"Smells like pizza!" I said as I walked into the kitchen. It had arrived just before I did.

"Pepperoni and bacon," Nate said, hobbling up to me and giving me a squeeze. Shocked, I returned his hug and looked questioningly at Pete over Nate's head. Pete shrugged his shoulders, and motioned he would explain later. "What *happened*?" I whispered to Pete as we got out plates and napkins. "I haven't seen that smile on Nate in forever and a day. It's amazing!"

"Yes, it is. And I have no idea what happened," Pete whispered back. "I picked him up from school today and he was like that. It's like he went back to being his old self. Mrs. Brock said he was quiet in the morning, but seemed to be in great spirits when I took him back to school after lunch."

"Oh, thank God. I've been so worried!" Relief spread its wings, giving my exhausted body the bout of energy it needed. The tension I'd been carrying in my neck began to dissolve.

"How was he at lunch?"

Pete shrugged. "Kind of normal, I guess. He talked a bit more than he has in the past few days, but nothing like this."

"Well, I'll take what we've got now!" I responded. Pete nodded in agreement as he finished setting the table, and we all sat down to dive into the hot pizza. Pete opened a bottle of wine, and I sipped it freely, taking in the sight of my happy family.

When we were all full of pizza, we watched *Spider-Man* at Nate's insistent request, and even Grace agreed to watch the movie again. I could tell she also noticed a difference in Nate, and was happy to have her brother back.

Together, we ploughed through a bucket of popcorn and a bag of Sour Patch Kids. Somehow, I didn't even fall asleep.

When the movie ended and the kids bounced upstairs to put themselves to bed, I sat back on the couch and enjoyed the peace. I took in the moment. Relished in the joy. And felt blessed by bliss. My day at work had been both challenging and rewarding. Nate was clearly back. And my family was happy.

Life was good.

22

The next few weeks flew by at lightning speed. Work escalated and became frenzied, and my family bounced back into the normalcy of routine. With Nate's ankle growing stronger every day, much like his demeanour and behaviour, I was able to return my focus to my career and give Jack the drive he was looking for.

"Mom?" Nate asked. He walked into the kitchen early one Sunday morning without even the slightest trace of a limp. "Can we have pancakes?"

"Can we have pancakes . . .?" My voice trailed off as I waited for him to finish the sentence.

"Can we have pancakes, *please*?"

"We sure can, Bean. How about chocolate chip?"

"Yeah!" Nate pumped his fist into the air. I took that as a good sign.

While I pulled out all of the ingredients to make my family-famous homemade chocolate chip pancakes, Pete walked lazily into the room. He looked tired, as if his full night of sleep hadn't fixed his exhaustion.

"Coffee?" I asked him. He nodded sleepily in response, before coming up behind me to give me a hug and kiss my cheek.

"So gross!" Nate jumped in. "Take it somewhere else, would you?"

"Go wake up your sister and tell her to get out of bed. And if she threatens to throw you out, tell her there will be no bacon for her unless she's down here in ten minutes to help."

Nate bounced from the room.

"It's nice, right?" I asked Pete, turning to face him.

"What's nice?"

"This. Us. Our family. It's wonderful for everything to feel *nice* again."

He nodded, handing me the eggs for the pancake batter. He had already put the bacon into the oven, and the intoxicating smell of Sunday morning started to fill the house.

A few moments later, Grace came into the kitchen and asked if she could go over to Emma's house that afternoon.

"Nope. Not today, hon. It's Nate's first hockey game since he sprained his ankle, and we're all going as a family to watch him play."

"Come *on* . . . really?!" Grace retorted. Clearly she'd had other ideas about how she was going to spend her afternoon.

"Yes, really." I ignored the dirty look she shot my way. I didn't want to ruin my feeling of nice. "Now, why don't you help me by setting the table?"

"Well . . . can I go over to Emma's *after* the hockey game?"

"If you help me set the table, we'll see." I'd learned a long time ago to accept the fact that bribery wasn't beyond the scope of my parenting tactics.

"You ready for the big game today, bud?" Pete asked, taking the plates from the cupboard to help Grace set the table. She was the proverbial daddy's girl in every sense of the phrase, and Pete was constantly helping her when I asked her to do something around the house.

"I guess. I just hope my ankle doesn't hurt too much."

"It looks good as new to me, bud. I think you'll be okay." Pete winked at Nate. "Now, who's hungry? These pancakes look fantastic!"

I poured the kids some orange juice, and within minutes, they'd scarfed down six pancakes each.

After everyone helped to clean up, Nate and Grace bounded upstairs to get ready for the day. We planned to run errands before lunch, yet another thing Grace had to complain about.

We took the kids to our favourite place for lunch, an old-school pizzeria with black and white tiled floors. They served their steaming pies on high stands.

Once we'd ordered, Grace catapulted into her never-ending narrative, chattering on about who she might see at Nate's hockey game, and asking if her hair looked okay in case it was Devin, the cute boy she had met there the last time we went to Nate's hockey game. I assured her it did. The half-pepperoni, half-Hawaiian pizza that arrived was the only thing that seemed to halt our talkative daughter in her long-winded tracks.

"Are you excited about your game today, Bean?" I asked Nate. He shrugged, pushing at the pizza on his plate.

"Aren't you hungry?"

He shrugged again, before answering, "No. Not really."

"Well eat up, little man," Pete interjected. "You've got a big game in front of you!"

Nate begrudgingly ate the half a piece we forced him to have before we paid the bill and returned to our car. By the time we made it to the parking lot at the arena, I couldn't help but notice that Nate seemed quieter. Eerily silent, in fact, and even more so than he had been at lunch. I wondered if he was nervous about getting back on the ice. But when I asked him, he simply shook his head and said that he felt tired.

"You sure, Bean? You're sure everything's okay?" Panic tainted my voice, but I couldn't help acting paranoid. Even the slightest twist of energy in Nate was enough to start the crackle of my nerves.

Nate shrugged. "I don't know. I told you before that no one likes me on my hockey team. I'm not sure that I want to play anymore."

"But you've always loved hockey! And of *course* the guys on your team all like you. I'm sure they've missed you while you've been gone." It was a white lie. The boys on his team didn't have the same bond with Nate as they did with each other. But the strict no-bullying rules of the league ensured that no one would say one mean word to any other player, and I'd always hoped that, over time, the kids on Nate's team might think of my son as their friend.

Pete slammed the car door shut and threw Nate's hockey bag over his shoulder. He whisked our son up in the air, and called out that he thought Nate would be late unless they moved quickly. Within seconds they were gone, and Grace and I went to buy hot chocolates before taking our seats across from Nate's team's bench.

"Let's gooo, Naaate!" Grace called out as Nate stepped onto the ice. Her indifferent attitude from breakfast had taken a back seat to the sisterly pride I knew she always felt when she watched her brother play hockey. Despite his lack of kinship with the team, Nate was good at the sport, particularly for his age, and typically scored the majority of the goals.

About halfway through the game, Nate skated off the ice and benched himself for no reason. The whistle hadn't even been blown. I strained to see what had happened, but couldn't make out what Nate was doing or saying on the bench.

"I'm going to see what's up," I murmured aloud to no one in particular. Pete shook his head in disagreement, but he knew not to try to hold me back.

When I made it across the arena, I called Nate's name, and motioned for him to come and see me. He ignored my plea, and turned his attention back to the game.

"Nate!" I called out, this time louder. He turned, finally, and looked blankly through me. His eyes seemed hollow again. Empty. He refused to come talk to me, no matter how many times I called his name or waved him over.

When I started to feel like I was making a fool of myself, I gave up and went back to sit in my seat. Nate didn't play again that day, and when I was finally able to ask him why he'd left the game, he said simply that his ankle was hurting and he hadn't felt like playing.

Our drive home was quiet, and I stared out of the window, lost in thought about what had happened in the middle of the game. The more I thought about Nate's behaviour, the more I was convinced that something had snapped in him to make him slip back into the odd behaviour of recent weeks. He had regressed.

With every block we drove, my fearful thoughts became so rampant they almost took on a hyper state, and I made a mental note to book a doctor's appointment for Nate the minute the office opened the following day.

—

"Ashley! You're crazy. There is nothing wrong with Nate. Why are you saying this *again*?" Pete practically snarled at me while brushing his teeth. We were getting ready for bed, and I had brought up what had happened at Nate's hockey game earlier that day. Pete spit into the sink and put his toothbrush back into the holder before walking around me to retreat to our bedroom.

"Pete . . . you're not *listening* to me. There's something wrong with Nate. I know it sounds extreme because he's been so good the past few weeks, but I know what I know. I can't explain it. Every motherly instinct is telling me there's something up with him. Something's not right." I followed Pete into our room and sat beside him on the bed. He clicked on the TV and switched it to sports highlights.

"Don't be rude, Pete. I'm trying to talk to you about our son."

"Yeah . . . I heard what you have to say. And I responded. So we're done talking about it. Got it?" Pete turned the volume up on the TV, which increased at about the same speed as my rage.

"No. You're not ignoring me this time. I'm seriously worried. What if Nate leaves in the middle of the night again?"

"That's why we got the alarm," Pete responded. We'd installed it shortly after Nate had broken his ankle. I couldn't deal with another episode of Nate deciding to go on a joyride in the middle of the night.

"That's not the point, and you know it," I retorted. But I was getting nowhere. I paused, searching my husband's blank face. "Pete, I think we should take him to see a doctor."

"He doesn't need a doctor, Ash. He's a *boy* who's acting perfectly normal. So he has a few mood swings . . . so what? It's not a big deal. Nate said his ankle was bugging him today, which is perfectly understandable, so why don't you just drop it already?"

"But —"

"Look, I don't want to talk about it anymore. He's fine. Now drop it." Pete turned the volume on the TV even higher, as if to make a point, and I gave up trying to pursue the conversation. Instead, I walked into our bathroom and purposely locked Pete out, just as he was doing to me, before drawing myself a bubble bath.

Frustrated by my husband and feeling very much alone, I

sank deep into the searing fizzy water, which bit at my skin and caused it to turn a deep shade of red. The sting of the heat was prickly and somewhat painful, but it was enough to finally disrupt the raw, maternal panic that I otherwise couldn't seem to shake.

23

I kicked off my Cole Haan flats and tucked my feet up underneath me. I was flying to New York for the Amex meetings, and was taking the nine p.m. Sunday flight out of Toronto. Sitting on a black leather chair in the Maple Leaf lounge, my heart was heavy. The deep navy sky provided a backdrop to the polka dot lights that lined the runway, and an oversized plane lazily taxied into its spot before being connected to a gangway.

Pete and I had lived through another tense day, snapping at each other far too quickly about things we both recognized as being unimportant. I knew our bickering was the symptom and not the cause, but it didn't make it any easier.

Nate had continued to walk about the house in a fog all week.

We had taken him to another hockey game earlier that day, and he had begged to be benched. When the coach said no, he actually sat down on the ice and refused to move until the coach let him sit out.

I was grateful when the other mothers tried to make light of the situation by saying he was probably just not feeling well or his ankle was probably sore. I appreciated the gesture, but couldn't help but feel judged as they sipped at their fat-free lattes and occasionally cheered for their own sons.

When we got home from the game, Nate asked if he could take a nap.

"A *nap*?" Grace had chided Nate. "What are you? Like *three* or something? What a wittle baby you are."

And Grace wasn't far off in her assessment. Nate had bawled like a newborn when the town car had pulled up to our house to take me to the airport that night. When he realized I wouldn't give in and stay, he threw an unreasonable temper tantrum, kicking his feet and smashing his folded fists into the ground. Pete had to pick him up and carry him to his room; our son flailed his arms and legs the entire way up the stairs, drool dribbling down his cheeks and mixing in with tears. I had barely been able to force myself into the waiting town car.

Sighing, I pulled out my laptop at the airport and tried to read through a creative brief I needed to review. After reading the same paragraph eight times and not remembering what was in it, I gave up and wandered to the bar. After the day I'd had, a glass of Monte Bello would hit the spot. But when I got to the small self-serve counter, I realized I'd have to make do with a glass from the bottle of unknown red sitting by itself.

I helped myself to a wineglass, filled it too full by the standards of any wine snob and returned to my chair. The wine was bitter and too warm, but it was better than nothing.

As I swirled the wine in my glass, I looked around me. For the most part, the lounge was pretty quiet, with a few lone business travellers speckled throughout its seating pods. Every one of them had his or her nose buried in a laptop or smartphone, and none of them seemed interested in what was going on around them.

Several rows away, sitting next to one of the glowing lamps, a tall man with silver hair punched away at his keyboard. At almost the same moment my eyes found him, the man looked up and momentarily gazed out the window.

I froze. I was staring at my father. The very same father I hadn't seen or talked to in almost three years.

When I could finally muster up the ability to control my actions, I forced myself to switch seats so my back was to him. I spilled some of the nameless red wine on my light blue scarf as I moved, and internally cursed my father's name for ruining my favourite winter accessory. I gulped at the bitter wine and tried to think of a plan. I didn't want to see him, that much was for sure, and I feared he would be on the same flight as me.

As a global jetsetter, it wouldn't be unusual for my father to be going to New York City. He had an apartment there, after all, and was likely meeting one of his too-young companions so he could take her for dinner at Le Bernardin and drape her in jewellery from Tiffany's. The whole thought of it made me want to gag.

After my mother died when I was seven, my father changed dramatically. It took six weeks for him to emerge from the dark and dismal guest bedroom so he could end his leave of absence from work and finally greet the dawn, only to decide that his career in law was over. He quit practising, despite the fact it was always something he loved, and further outsourced his life by hiring a second nanny to help keep me fed and clean during the day. The night nurse stayed with me while I slept, and the tutor he'd hired helped me with my schoolwork.

With a full-time support system in place, and a previous inheritance that guaranteed he wouldn't have to worry about the decision to walk away from his life, Todd Blakeley was free to gallivant around the world, leaving the only reminder of his beloved wife behind.

Me.

It got worse as I grew older, his trips becoming longer and more frequent. He always returned with extravagant gifts, shipping home the bigger ones, which often greeted me at the door long before he arrived home. He must have convinced himself that a good dad would make it home for the holidays, because he forced himself to fly in just before Christmas Eve every year. Except for four.

At first I cherished the rare moments together, taking in every minute with him as I begged him to play with me or let me sit on his lap. But in my later teen years, I started to like it when he just stayed away. His trips home from whatever ski lodge or golf resort he had been at were usually accompanied by some woman who didn't want to be there. And I'd grown in independence. I didn't *need* him to be there.

After I graduated from university, my involvement with him stayed about the same. We rarely spoke, and when we needed to connect about something, it was mostly over email. He never let me know where he was in the world, except for when he'd show up unannounced to shower his grandchildren in extravagant presents they didn't need.

Our conversations during his awkward short visits were curt, almost tense. And we never, ever, spoke about my mother. I knew I contributed to a lot of the tension during those visits; I'd never forgiven my father for abandoning me when I needed him most, and even my years of therapy couldn't help me feel warm and fuzzy when I was around him.

The biggest bomb came when he unexpectedly showed up on Christmas Eve, three years prior. We were just about to leave for church, when he literally fell through the door, dressed as Santa and reeking of single malt Scotch. He carried a sack full of unwrapped gifts, including matching orange T-shirts for our children that read "Grandpa Loves Me." As he passed the gifts out, disgracing his dignity with each garbled word, I thought about the irony in the words on the T-shirts; my father didn't know how to love. He knew only how to buy presents.

"Just like old times . . . right Asheeey? I looove . . . uh . . . what was I going to say again? Oh. Right. I love Christmas . . . with you. You my little girl, sweetie Ashley. Forever . . . ," my father had slurred, wrapping his arm around me and dragging me down with him. Literally. His heavy frame sunk into my shoulders, making me collapse on the kitchen floor underneath his drunken body. In front of my children.

I immediately kicked him out and slammed the door, silently begging for my children to forget such a horrific display of alcoholism.

I didn't hear from him after that. He was sending me the loud and clear message that we were officially estranged—which I had no problem with given that he'd never been there for me anyway.

Now, three years later, I was going through much bigger problems with Nate, and the last thing I needed was another encounter with my father. I slipped out of the Maple Leaf lounge to the bustle of the general airport and called Pete on my cell-phone to tell him my news.

"You'll never, *ever* believe who's here. My *father*! Can you believe that?! I mean, seriously. What are the odds?"

"Really? Are you sure about that, Ash? Did you . . . did you talk to him?" Pete's voice seemed puzzled. Almost uncertain, like he didn't believe me.

"Yes, of course I'm sure. It's my father. Right there in the airport lounge, working on his laptop."

"His laptop, Ash? I've known your father a long time, and I've never seen him with a computer. How close were you to him?"

"I don't know. Maybe twenty feet away or so?"

"That's pretty far. To be sure, anyway. And you haven't seen him in three years. Honestly, it probably wasn't him."

"I know, but . . ." My voice trailed off as Pete's hesitation began to play on my certainty.

"Don't sweat it. There are a lot of guys who look like him out there. Go get on your plane. And try to relax before you hit the chaos of your week. It sounds to me like it will be pretty insane with all of those meetings." His insistence won, and I started to second-guess my previous conviction.

"Maybe you're right. My plane is boarding anyway so I guess I should run. I'll text you when I land."

"Sounds good," Pete replied. "And, Ashley? Don't worry about your father. I know how upset he makes you. Just focus on your meetings this week and then come home to us. We love you, you know."

I smiled, trying to let Pete's words make me feel better. But unfortunately for me, all it did was remind me that I needed to be away all week from a family who actually *wanted* to be around me instead of jet-setting off to the next adventure and leaving me behind. It had taken me a lifetime to find it, but I was finally in a family that was built on loyalty and love.

When I took my seat on the plane, I pulled my laptop open and forced myself to focus on the creative brief I still needed to review. I managed to get through half of it before the flight attendant gently reminded me that I would need to put it away for takeoff.

As I zipped up my red bag, the silver-haired man from the airport lounge scurried onto the plane, narrowly making the flight. He smiled at me as he passed, like he was apologizing for holding up the plane, and I realized immediately that he wasn't my father at all. Just a man who looked an awful lot like him.

As I returned the man's smile, feelings of relief fused with confusion, and I tried to convince myself that what I *wasn't* feeling was disappointment. But if I was honest with myself, I knew that a small part of me had hoped to see my father. To run into him. To talk to him — even hear about how he was. To find out about what he had been doing for the past three years. No matter what he had done, or *not* done as the case might have been, he was still my father, and I missed him.

I closed my eyes, squeezing out the tears and quickly wiping them from my cheeks. I told myself that I didn't need my father anymore. I was the parent now, not the kid. And I was a *good* parent. I was there for my children — even if work trips occasionally took me away from them.

As the plane took off, leaving Toronto behind me, I tried to bury all images of my father. Somehow Pete knew that man wasn't my father, and I didn't know how he'd done it. Maybe his instincts about my reaction to Nate's situation were correct, too?

24

When I arrived in New York, I quickly settled into my hotel room at the Waldorf and was asleep within minutes. The phone rang far too soon the next morning, and I answered it with a sleepy, "Hello?" before I realized it was the automated wake-up call telling me that it was six o'clock and time to get up.

I laced up my running shoes and hit the downtown streets of New York just as the sun was peeking over the buildings. It was my long-standing ritual on the first day of every business trip; I would trade in time typically spent at the breakfast table with my family for the chance to get some exercise and clear my head. It was quality "me time" before my crazy and hectic work day officially kicked in.

I ran up 51st Street to 6th Avenue, and past the AJ & Emerson New York office where all of my meetings would be held later that day. By the time I got to MoMA, I had fallen into my stride and let my stress from the day before erase itself with each step.

Once I'd finished my run and gotten ready for the day, I grabbed my usual latte from the Starbucks near the Waldorf and managed to resist the pumpkin scone that seemed to be calling my name. I knew my back-to-back meetings would be filled with catered baked goods, and I had a dinner meeting booked for that night at a restaurant that promised a rich meal with lots of wine.

My day flew by without a moment to pause. I didn't even stop for lunch. When I wasn't in the Amex meetings, I had other people I needed to meet with from the New York office, or conference calls with my team in Toronto.

I made it back to my hotel just in time to freshen up and change into something more my style. Amex was one of our more formal clients, and I quite often wore business suits when I met with them.

I quickly swapped my dark suit for a pair of skinny jeans, a cream-coloured top, and my favourite Smythe blazer. I spritzed on perfume and put on a pair of pumps before running out the door, and added a fresh coat of lip gloss as I waited for the elevator.

After I'd hailed a cab and asked the driver to take me to the West Village, I texted my colleague, Brad, to let him know I was running a few minutes late. As two long-time AJ & Emerson employees, Brad and I had known each other forever, and we tended to meet for dinner when I was in the city. Brad headed up the AJ & Emerson New York creative team, and it was good for us to both collaborate and commiserate when we could. And as a single guy living in the big city with more accountability during the daytime than at night, Brad could usually meet me for dinner when I was in town.

"*Hey* you!" Brad greeted me with the wide, white smile our

female clients loved. As the maître d' led me to him, Brad rose out of his chair to kiss both of my cheeks. He brought me in for his usual bear hug and, as he squeezed tight, the faint smell of his familiar cologne tickled my nose.

"It's so great to see you," I said, laughing as Brad squeezed tighter. "And to be here, finally. Where's that wine list, already?"

"No need, my dear. I've already ordered a bottle of your favourite. And, look! What do you know? Here it is, right on time." Brad pointed at the waitress who was approaching our table carrying a bottle of red.

"How does this look, Mr. Andrews?" she asked, presenting the wine.

"Great, thank you." Brad swirled the wine the waitress poured, then tasted before giving his nod of approval.

"You must come here often, Mr. Andrews," I teased him when the waitress left. "Does everyone get such special treatment?"

"Well, what can I say? The food is good. Clients love it here. And no one's cooking for me at home so it's better than the burned crap I'd surely make."

I laughed in response. "Makes sense to me. I'd likely do the same." I sipped at the wine, happy for the familiarity of my favourite Borolo and secretly pleased that I had such a good friend who knew my tastes so well.

"So? How did the meetings go today?" Brad asked, helping himself to a piece of bread.

"They went well. We covered a lot, actually. More than I thought we would, which is good."

"Glad to hear it," Brad replied in between bites. "And how's the Toronto office these days?"

"Great, as always. It's such a good team, and my associate creative directors make my job easier. They could practically run the creative shop."

"Come on now, Ash. You know *that's* not true. Please . . . AJ & Emerson Global would practically shut down without you."

"*Now* you're exaggerating."

"Maybe a little bit, but it would certainly be a huge hit for us if you left."

I laughed at Brad's flattery. He'd always had a knack for making people feel good about themselves.

"Speaking of AJ & Emerson Global," Brad continued, "has Cole made any headway in convincing you to move here already? This place would be rockin' with you and I working together every day."

"Funny you should ask: he actually *did* mention it in passing again today. But Jack would have a fit. You know that. Plus, there's no way I could move my family here. We're settled where we are. And, Nate, well . . . I'm not sure that would be best for him right now."

"Aww, Nate. How's my little tyke doing?" Brad asked, grinning at the mention of my son. He and Nate had become fast friends when I'd had Brad over for dinner the last time he'd been in Toronto. "And why do you say that about my little guy? He'd love this city! Who wouldn't?"

"Maybe one day . . ."

"But not now?" Brad tilted his head to the right and set his glass of wine down. He looked me straight in the eyes. "Anything you want to talk about, Ash?"

I shook my head no, my eyes filling with tears. I looked down, hoping Brad wouldn't notice. I longed to talk to someone about it. Someone who *wanted* to talk about it. Who would understand. Maybe even make it better. Or make it go away completely.

"You sure, Ash? The colour just drained from your cheeks." Brad took my hand from across the table. "We're more than just colleagues. We're friends, too. You can talk to me about anything."

Two tiny tears dropped onto the white linen napkin on my

lap. I wasn't a crier, and I was embarrassed to be letting my emotions show. But what was going on with Nate was big. Real. And for a mother who loved her son like crazy, it was also very scary.

"Sashimi?" our waitress asked. She had sneaked up behind me and startled me with our appetizer. She put down the wasabi and ginger, and then placed the sushi in between us to share.

Silence punctuated our first few bites. I tried not to feel uncomfortable, which was unusual for Brad and me. But I knew he'd spotted my tears and was likely wondering if he should keep asking if I was okay.

When his next question wasn't about my emotional state but rather my opinion on securing digital rights as part of talent negotiations for broadcast media, I realized he had decided to opt out of counsellor duty. And that worked just fine for me. I didn't want to get into a long conversation with Brad about how worried I was about Nate. Even though I certainly needed someone to talk to, I knew that person wasn't Brad.

Two hours later, as dessert arrived, my phone was still buzzing obnoxiously in my bag. For the majority of our dinner, I'd ignored it for fear of losing the groove in the conversation that Brad and I had finally found, but there was something about the way it wouldn't quit that made me feel like I should give in.

I picked up my phone and slid the arrow right to unlock it. Seven missed calls and thirteen text messages from Pete. I scanned to the last one and my heart clenched: *"Where ARE you? Call home ASAP. This is an emergency."*

I grabbed my purse and coat and excused myself from dinner before walking outside to call my husband. "Pete? What's wrong? Why so many calls?"

"You don't know what's going on? Didn't you see my other messages?" Pete's voice was frantic.

"No . . . I just saw your last text saying to call home

immediately and I phoned you right away. What's going on? You're scaring me."

"It's Nate. He left. Again. Only this time . . . only this time, we really can't find him. He disappeared while I was making dinner. He was there one minute, and then suddenly he was gone. All I did was go into the pantry to grab some pasta. It had to have been less than thirty seconds. And as soon as I realized he wasn't there, we started looking. We've looked everywhere inside our house. We've driven all over the place. We've searched and searched but . . . we can't find him. Anywhere."

My pulse quickened. The heat of fear I'd felt before crept its way back up my neck. I knew I was actually living out the imagined scene my incessant worry had forced into my mind so many times in the weeks leading up to that moment. I bit the inside of my cheek and tasted blood. I wanted to ask the million questions that were filling my head but I was speechless, completely muted by fear. I couldn't bring myself to say one word.

"We've called the police . . ."

The *police*?

Pete's words got fuzzy after that. All I could hear was the word *police* in my mind. I heard it over and over and over. The more I said it in my head, the more it started to sound funny.

"The police . . ?" I finally muttered out loud.

"Yes, the police. That's what I keep telling you. They're on their way over now. Should be here any minute. Tay came by and took Grace to her house because she's hysterical, as you can probably imagine. She was freaking out and I couldn't calm her down. I thought it would be better if she weren't here when the cops get here. So Tay picked her up."

"Has Grace eaten dinner yet? You need to make sure Tay feeds her."

"*What*? Huh? Ashley . . . *what*? What kind of question is that?" Pete spit into the phone. "I'm talking about how Nate is *gone*. We can't find him. Anywhere. I've been driving the streets and going everywhere I can think of for over an hour now. And I can't find him. And now it's dark."

I knew Pete was right. Given the situation, it was a weird question to finally ask, but in the moment, it was as if Grace's dinner was the only thing I could control.

"Ashley? I have to go. The cops just got here."

"No! Pete, wait. I need to know about Nate . . ."

"I'm sorry. I have to go," Pete interrupted me mid-sentence. "I'll tell you everything when you get home, but right now my time is best spent answering the questions the cops have. So they can start looking for Nate." Pete paused and gulped so much air I could hear it over the phone. I sensed the severity of the situation had really set in for him. "Oh shit, they have to start looking for Nate. The police are going to be looking for our son . . . how did this *happen*? After all that we've been through, how could I have let him go missing? Again?" The panic that I'd been feeling for so many weeks suddenly entered Pete's voice. We were finally on the same page.

"They'll find him, Pete. They have to."

"Just come home, Ashley. You need to come home. Right now. Okay?"

I nodded, tears streaking down my face. As I clicked off my phone, I hailed a cab and, within seconds, was tearing across the Queensboro Bridge on my way to LaGuardia.

25
Nate

My lungs hurt and I cannot breathe but it doesn't matter because I need to keep running and I need to run faster even though my ankle sometimes hurts a little bit because I'm running so fast. I cannot stop no matter what anyone says.

Even Noah. I thought about going to his house. But I know he would have told me to stop running. He doesn't like to run. Only ride bikes. So I decided not to go there. I ran past his blue house that is four doors down from mine to the end of the street. And then I turned right and kept going.

But now I really wish Noah was with me because I need to have him help me find my mommy. We need to find my mommy and I need to find New York because that's where Daddy says

Mommy is and we need to find her before the elephants get us because they are chasing me and I don't know where Noah is so I don't know if they have already killed him and the elephants are scaring me and they are growling behind me and are like shadows dancing everywhere and they make fun of me and they say they will hurt me and then kill me and I think they might have already killed Noah and that makes me so scared so that is I why I do not like the elephants but they keep following me anyway so I need to run faster.

Something bad is going to happen.

I just know it.

I know it because the angry elephants have come down. They have come down from the sky. And now they are chasing me. They have come to get me. And Mommy. They are going to chase her too because they want to kill her. They want to kill both of us.

So I need to run faster.

As fast as I can.

I need to find Mommy.

26
Ashley

I barely remembered to message Brad to let him know that I had bailed on our dinner. I thought about letting him know what was going on, but a tiny nagging feeling prevented me from sharing the specific details; I simply mentioned that a family emergency had come up, and asked him to let everyone know that I had to fly back to Toronto right away.

Brad's response came immediately: *"No problem. I'll let everyone know. Are you going to your hotel to get your stuff first?"*

"Oh shit. My stuff. Of course . . ." I muttered out loud. I hadn't even considered getting my suitcase from the hotel. I thought about asking the cab driver to turn around, but I didn't want to waste any more time. Instead, I called the hotel and arranged for my things to be packed and shipped home to me.

When I got to the airport, I rushed to the counter to see if I could switch my flight. I hoped my gold status from flying so frequently would help get me home faster.

"You're in luck, Ms. Carter." The airline employee smiled, holding onto my passport. I suspected she had picked up on the panic that was smeared all over my face. "The last flight out is at 9:50 p.m., and since you don't have to check a bag, I think you'll make it."

I thanked her before grabbing my passport and boarding pass. I ran in the direction of security, and got there twenty minutes before my flight boarded. A long line of waiting passengers loomed in front of me.

The security employee standing at the front of the line must have noticed how antsy I was. She got off her stool and walked in my direction. "Where are you going and what time is your flight?" she asked, reaching for my boarding pass without the slightest hint of a smile on her face.

"Toronto. The 9:50 flight."

The employee's eyes bored into mine. She hesitated slightly, but then signalled for me to follow her. She led me to the front of the line.

"You can't leave it this late . . . you'll miss your flight," the employee scolded me. She shook her head as she handed me a bin to put my purse and shoes in.

"I know . . . it's my son. It's an emergency. I just found out that I have to go home . . ."

The woman shrugged her shoulders and waved me through nonchalantly, as if she'd heard this excuse a million times.

When I got to the gate, I sank into an empty chair far from anyone else. I longed to have someone I knew with me. I was going crazy without an update, but didn't want to bug Pete while he was talking to the police. And I knew he would call me as soon as he knew something.

I sat in my chair, desperate for Nate to be okay. I put my head in my hands and prayed as hard as I could, begging God over and over to let the police find our little boy. My heart, pounding in my chest as it had never done before, was making it next to impossible to keep my composure.

Three minutes before they called us to board our flight, my phone rang.

It was Pete.

"*Please* tell me some good news. Have you found him?"

"No news. I'm sorry, Ash. The police just finished ransacking our house. I told them he wasn't in there, but they wanted to be sure. The two cops that came searched everywhere. All of our closets, the garage, our shed . . . everywhere. He's not here."

"So now what?"

"I filled out a Missing Person Questionnaire."

I gulped. Sucked in air. "A . . . a Missing Person Questionnaire? Really? What did you tell them?" My stomach was in knots, and my heart was going so fast I could feel it in my throat.

"I gave them a full description of what Nate looks like, what he was wearing when he left the house, stuff about his dental records. That kind of thing." Pete's voice sounded weak on the other end of the phone. Like he was already defeated.

"So what are they going to do now?"

"They're hitting the streets to start looking for him. I told them all of his favourite places to go . . . parks, the school, the rinks where he plays hockey. Basically all the places that I've already looked, but they want to double check the obvious spots."

"And do they have a picture of him?"

"Of course. Three."

"Oh no. This can't be happening . . ." My throat became tighter, threatening to take away my ability to breathe. I couldn't accept the fact that my baby was out on the streets. By himself. That the police were looking for him. That they now considered him to be a missing person. It was too much to take in.

"The cops asked that I stay here in case Nate comes home," Pete continued. Something in his voice sounded almost apologetic. "Because there's a good chance he'll come home. He's got to . . ."

"I know." I inhaled sharply, thinking through my next few words that I needed to ask my husband. I had to know about how Nate was behaving before he left. I tried to be delicate with my questioning. "Pete? What happened tonight? Was he acting strange again?"

On the other end of the phone, there was only silence.

"Pete . . .? Was Nate acting strange tonight?"

"I guess so . . . yeah . . . he was, I guess. He was acting really strange, actually." Pete's voice was soft. Barely above a whisper.

Taking a deep breath, Pete relived what had happened earlier that night. How Nate had been acting overly hyper and was bouncing off the walls. And how he had continually talked about monsters from the moment he got home from school. Pete said Nate seemed to be obsessed with what he described as big, shadowy elephant monsters that were all around them.

Nate swore up and down that the monsters were going to hurt them. At first, Pete thought it was because Halloween had been a couple of weeks before that, but Nate refused to drop it. He couldn't seem to get over it, and kept talking about how the monsters were going to kill them. And that they needed to find Mommy because only Mommy could save them.

Hearing that my son needed me so desperately, my heart completely broke. I hadn't been there to help him. I had abandoned my son in his time of need, just as my father had abandoned me.

I was an awful parent.

"What did you say to Nate? When he was telling you all of this."

"At first, I thought if I distracted him it might calm him down. So I asked if he wanted to help me make the pasta. He said yes, but when I came out of the pantry with the noodles, he had simply vanished. He was nowhere to be found. I started looking through the house, and noticed the front door was wide open. It's freezing outside and we didn't leave the door open, so I knew instantly Nate had left the house."

I felt like I was collapsing into myself and needed someone to hold me up.

Pete continued, "Grace and I jumped in the car and scoured the neighbourhood. But he was just . . . well, he was just gone. It was like he vanished into thin air. We looked everywhere."

"Did you tell all of this to the police officers?" I asked Pete.

"Yes . . . of course I did."

"And what did they say about it?"

"About the monsters? They brushed it off as standard nine-year-old stuff. That he was likely still scared from Halloween. They see it a lot, apparently."

When Pete had finished the tale of what had happened, silence filled the line. And my fear turned to anger. *Why* hadn't Pete listened to me when I told him something was wrong with our son? If he had, Nate wouldn't be missing. And we could have gotten Nate the help he needed.

And why hadn't I pushed more? I should have insisted that Pete listen to me. I should have taken Nate to see a doctor sooner. I should have booked the appointment, regardless of what anyone else said. I should have listened to the whispers that only I could hear. I had known something wasn't right. Instead, I'd let Pete convince me Nate was just a kid. That he didn't need help. And I'd ignored my intuition.

Pete and I, together, had abandoned our son in his time of need.

We were *both* awful parents. And Nate was missing because of it.

"Last call for Ashley Carter, Flight 1210 to Toronto . . ." A staccato voice interrupted my thoughts. I could see a short, snarly woman standing behind the check-in desk barking into the microphone, looking in my direction. She must have been calling all passengers to board but I hadn't heard her during my conversation with Pete. I was the only one still sitting in the chairs at the gate.

I told Pete I had to board my flight, and that I'd call him as soon as I landed.

The woman irritably held her hand out to take my passport and boarding pass, but her face somewhat softened as she saw my tear-streaked cheeks. She smiled at me, as if to imply everything would be okay, and then closed the gates behind me as I started down the jet bridge.

I took my seat and prepared for takeoff, knowing the short flight to Toronto was about to become the longest hour of my life. I barely made it through, and tried to ignore the other passengers whispering about me and nudging their heads in my direction. I hadn't stopped crying since I got on the plane, and no one knew whether they should ignore me or ask if I needed help.

Lucky for me, everyone chose the former and I was left alone to weep into the hard plastic of my window cover. Telling a stranger my story wasn't going to help, and I didn't want to talk about it with anyone except my family.

As soon as we landed, I called Pete from the plane and found out there was no news. On the other end of the phone, his voice sounded hollow and distraught; it was almost like talking to a stranger.

With nothing more to talk about, we hung up the phone, and I stared out the window, watching the crew begin to unload the luggage.

It was dark out. *Really* dark out. And my baby was out there by himself.

When the plane doors finally opened, the people in front of me cleared a path and let me off first. I suspected they'd heard me speaking to Pete, and knew that my son was missing.

The flight attendants waved goodbye kindly. One nodded her head in a knowing fashion. Their lips were pursed together in awkward smiles that were as identical as their uniforms, and it was clear they all felt uncomfortable but sympathetic.

When I finally made it home, I found Pete sitting at the kitchen table with his forehead resting on top of his crossed arms, which were folded on the table. The house was silent. He was clutching his phone. When he heard me walk through the door, he jumped up out of his chair and raced towards me too quickly, ploughing into me and suffocating me with his grip. He clung on tightly. We both did. Neither of us wanted to let go.

"Ash . . . I just don't know . . . what are we going to do? How could this have happened to us?"

I shook my head in response, unable to answer. Fresh tears stung my swollen eyes. I was convinced I'd left all of my tears on the plane and was surprised to feel them once again nip at my puffy lids.

Pete continued, "I'm sorry, Ash. I'm so sorry. I should have listened to you. You knew something was wrong. And I could see it in him tonight. Finally. But then he was gone. It was too late . . ."

It was too late . . . Pete's words hung in the air like the thick smog of a humid day in July. The enormity of the situation closed in on both of us.

Pete finally felt what I felt. And he knew what I knew: that we were dealing with something far larger than either of us could likely comprehend. And as my husband hugged me closer, the scariest part of everything we were dealing with settled into our bones. It wasn't what we knew, but what we *didn't* know: we had no idea what was going on in Nate's little brain, or what it might cause him to do. Worst of all, we didn't know whether or not it was too late to do anything.

Even after Pete's tight embrace began to relax, the raw fear did not dissipate. We parted, our eyes locking for a few moments before I let my glance go beyond my husband to the fridge at his back. There, hanging by the Golden Gate Bridge magnet my father had given us, almost as if it were staring at us — mocking us, even — was the angry-looking elephant that our son had created.

27
Nate

The elephants are still chasing me and so I need to run even faster than I was running before except I cannot really remember how fast I was running before because I feel like my brain will not slow down.

I am laughing now because I wonder if my brain is working faster than my running legs or if it is the opposite and I think that is really funny for some reason. I do not know why. I laugh for a minute but then I make myself shut up because I am worried the elephant monsters will hear me laughing and my mommy is not there to make them go away.

I need to find Mommy before the elephant monsters get me. I see them flying all around me and they are growling like lions and they have dark grey shadows behind them that look like the dark grey shadows in the movie I watched with Noah right after Halloween. I need to tell my mommy about the shadowy purple growling elephants because she will help me and make me feel better. She always makes me feel better in a way that no one else can.

So I need to find her soon.

I need to find her soon.

Mommy tells me she takes a plane to New York and I know that you get on a plane at an airport so all I need to do is find an airport and then I can go to her. I have no idea how to find an airport but I know I need to find someone who will tell me so I need to look for a teacher because teachers are all very smart and they can tell me how to find an airport. It doesn't even need to be a geography teacher because I think all teachers will know where New York is.

I stop.

I listen.

The elephant monsters start growling again. Loudly. And they are showing their mean, sharp teeth. They are scaring me so badly. They are flying all around me.

I start running again.

I run and I run and I run and I run and I run.

The streets are dark and covered in leaves. Wet, yellow leaves that have fallen off the trees. It is windy so they are blowing all around me. The houses are all bumped up against each other and some of them have lights that look like warm, melted butter pouring out of them and suddenly I want to go into one of those houses but I will feel bad bringing the elephant monsters with me so I know I cannot go into them.

My lungs still hurt. They are burning. But I cannot stop until I find Mommy and she takes the elephant monsters away from me.

At the end of the street I see a school and I know that it is a school where big kids go. Julia goes there. She's Auntie Tay's daughter and Mommy told me she started grade nine this year. Maybe she is in the school and can help me or if she is not maybe I will find a teacher and for sure they will know how I can get to New York and how I can find my mommy.

I run to the school as fast as I can and pull on the door. It is locked. I pull on the other door and it opens. I walk inside and it makes me less scared to be inside because I do not think that monsters go to school so I really hope they are staying outside and leaving me alone until I can find Julia or a teacher and then I can go to New York to find Mommy.

The halls are empty. All I can see are rows and rows and rows of lockers but there are no students in front of them like I see on *Glee*, which is my favourite TV show because my mommy loves to watch it so that means I love to watch it too.

I find a door and go through it. At the front there is a large stage with no one on it but there are people filling all of the seats who are cheering and waving and have big signs above their heads. I look at the people screaming and cheering and waving signs and I notice it is all the people from my class. I see Tyson and all of his friends who always make fun of me and Tyson yells at me and calls me stupid and tells me to go on the stage so he can tell me I am stupid in front of everyone and I don't want to go but I know I have to.

I *have* to.

I walk towards the stage to the steps and start to walk up. I feel jittery and I am breathing hard and I do not want to go on the stage but I know I have to because Tyson told me I have to and if I do not he will push me into a corner and pull my pants down and call me a hyena just like he has done to me so many times before.

I make it on stage and look out to everyone looking at me but they all look a bit blurry and it is hard to tell if they are really there or not. I look at all of the people watching me and pointing and laughing and I see Tyson sitting in the middle of the aisle with his arms crossed. He is snickering.

I know what snickering is because my daddy was writing an article for a newspaper and he wrote about snickering and then he told me that it is when someone is laughing but only kind of laughing and they are trying to hide it a bit. So I think Tyson is snickering because he is only half laughing and I wonder if it is because he is worried that Mrs. Brock will give him trouble again but I do not see Mrs. Brock and I think that is weird because all of the kids in my class are sitting in chairs and pointing and laughing at me.

I know they all hate me. All of the kids in my class hate me.

I stop looking at the kids in my class and look to the side of the stage and see all of my hockey team and all of my coaches and realize they are laughing and holding signs and screaming just like Tyson and all of the kids in my class. Even my coaches are laughing at me. Pointing, and calling me names.

Auntie Tay is there as well but not Julia. I try to talk to Auntie Tay but she turns sideways and suddenly she isn't Auntie Tay anymore and I am so confused and so scared and I want my mommy.

But she is not here.

She is in New York.

28
Ashley

Just before midnight, two police officers returned to our house. I watched them park in our driveway from the family room window, where I had been perched for the previous twenty minutes. My heart constricted as they got out of the car, and I forced myself to breathe.

In and out. *Breathe.* In and out. *Breathe.*

I could do this. I *had* to do this.

Incomparable angst shot through every nerve ending in my body, prickling the bottoms of my feet with each step as I lunged for the door. Pete was right behind me, and he gripped my shoulder as I opened the door to greet the police officers.

"May we come in?" the female police officer asked abruptly but warmly. Her name tag read Constable Matthews.

"Yes . . . yes. Of course," I responded. I opened the door wider, and felt the cold wind from outside whip into our front hallway.

"Sorry we're so wet," Constable Matthews apologized, stepping into the house. The two polices officers had wiped their feet on the mat outside our door, but puddles still formed at their feet the minute they walked into our home.

"Have you found him yet?" I asked, ignoring her apology. The last thing I cared about was a wet house.

"No. I'm sorry, Mrs. Carter. We haven't," the other police officer replied gently.

"Then why are you here? Why aren't you looking for our son?" Pete snapped.

"We need to ask you some more questions. We think they will help us. And then we're going to call in more officers to expand the search. So we can keep looking for your son."

I nodded. "Yes, of course. That makes sense. Please, come in." I guided them to our kitchen table.

"Mrs. Carter, I'm Constable Matthews and this is my partner, Constable Baker," the woman began, taking out a black pen and notebook from her chest pocket. I couldn't help but notice her bulletproof vest. "We'd like to start with you, if that's okay. We've had a chance to ask your husband several questions, but we want to start fresh with you in case there's anything we missed."

"Yes, of course. By all means . . . ask me whatever you'd like."

Constable Matthews launched into the same questions they had asked Pete. For the most part, I assumed I told them the same answers, given that Pete sat across the table from me nodding his head in a way that suggested he'd already covered what I was telling them.

"And he doesn't have a cellphone, correct?" Constable Baker asked.

"Right," I responded. "No cellphone."

"What about Facebook or Twitter? Any accounts we could access? It might help give us leads regarding where to look," Constable Baker continued.

"No," I shook my head. "He's only nine. He's not allowed to have a Facebook or Twitter account. We monitor everything he does."

"And what about his behaviour? Has he been acting strange at all lately?"

I paused, unsure of what Pete had told them.

"It's okay, Mrs. Carter. You can tell us," Constable Matthews urged gently.

"Yes, well . . . Nate . . . he . . . uh . . . he's been acting a bit unusual lately. Doing things we don't normally see him do." My mind flew back to the night Nate stole the gum. I was slightly torn on whether to tell the police officers that my adorable son had turned into a thief. But I knew I had to tell them everything if it would help them find him.

"What types of things, Mrs. Carter?" Constable Baker urged.

I started by telling the police officers about Nate moping around the house and losing interest in things he had previously loved, such as hockey. I told them about how he acted strangely in class, jumping around like a hyena, and how he hit his head after he fell off the desk. I mentioned the panic attack, the sprained ankle, and even how he had sneaked out in the middle of the night to go to the park. Eventually I even told them about the stolen gum. Once the floodgates were open, I told them *everything*.

Both constables nodded their heads as I poured out the new information, and furiously scribbled notes into their memo books.

"Thank you, Mrs. Carter. This has been enormously

helpful," Constable Matthews said after she'd finished writing. She glanced up and looked straight at me. "I'd like to ask you more questions about the moods you described Nate having. Did it ever seem like he was depressed? Do you know if Nate might be suffering from some kind of mental disorder or illness?"

Upon hearing her questions, the world seemed to halt in front of me. I froze, taking in her stigmatic words, which were suddenly dancing all around me, like they were pointing and making fun of my son.

Having the police officer link mental illness to my son's name — out loud — was like getting smacked in the head by buried inner truth. While others surrounding us and watching our family from the outside had hinted at depression and delicately suggested that Nate's odd behaviour wasn't normal, I'd never considered an *actual* mental disorder.

It couldn't be that . . . could it? My sweet son couldn't be . . . crazy?

Yet, it was in that moment, with two soggy police officers and an angry-looking elephant on the fridge staring at me, waiting for an answer, that I saw the truth clearly for the first time: the innate infallibility that had bubbled just below the surface of my conscience for Nate's entire lifetime. Every maternal instinct I'd inherited since the birth of my son told me that Nate was living with mental issues we needed to deal with. But my ferociously protective nature had concealed what was right in front of me. What I had known all along . . .

I had ignored what my gut was telling me. And the contrast of the two . . . the juxtaposition between listening to motherly instinct and the need to protect a child from stigma and a lifetime of battle had ultimately caused the intense inner panic I'd been feeling for way too long.

With Nate still missing, there was no time for overthinking an already complicated situation. I knew the best thing I could do was answer the police officer's questions as simply and honestly as I could.

"I don't know for sure, Officer, but I think that maybe he does . . ."

29
Nate

It is raining. I am outside again. I had to leave the school when a person carrying a broom came up to me and asked me for my name. He wanted to know why I was in the school by myself. He wasn't blurry like everyone else.

I wanted to tell him my name and ask him for help but I got scared that he would take me back to the monsters. So I kicked him in the shins as hard as I could and ran as fast as I could out of the school and away from him.

The man carrying the broom tried to chase me but I am super fast so he couldn't catch me. My daddy says I am the fastest runner ever and that I am even faster than Spider-Man but not Superman because I can't fly.

The rain is pouring onto my face and suddenly I feel really cold. My mommy would say it is called *chilled to the bone*. I am soaking wet. I need to go inside again.

I see a building in front of me with a blinking sign that looks like a Christmas decoration. It says "Ian's Billiards and Bar" on the bright blinking sign. Beside it there is another bright blinking sign that says "OPEN." It is red. I guess that means I can go in.

When I get inside there are big men everywhere with long sticks in their hands and they are all drinking beer. That is what my daddy drinks in the summer when people come over for a barbeque.

I crouch down in the corner beside a chair and watch the men. They are all laughing and saying words I know I am not allowed to say. One man keeps saying the F-word over and over again and I know my mommy would not be happy to know that he is saying it in front of me. We are not allowed to say that word in our house.

My legs start to feel all prickly from crouching beside the chair for so long. But I cannot move because if I do the men might take me back to the monsters and I know they will not help me find the airport or New York or my mommy.

A man in a red shirt asks me my name. He comes right up to me and asks me where my mommy is, and then says something to the other men that makes them laugh. Something about my mommy hookin' on the corner. But I don't know what hookin' means, so I don't find it funny.

They talk about calling the cops but decide not to. I hear them say something about being afraid of getting busted by pig sniffers for the skunk in their pockets.

And then they just ignore me.

The bar smells like throw-up and the floor is sticky, and I don't like it in here. But if I go outside the elephants will get me, so I have to stay here.

I slide back down into my spot beside the chair and watch the mean men with their long sticks and try not to think about the cold, wet clothes sticking to my skin.

I just keep watching.

And then I start to shiver.

30
Ashley

"So you think it's possible, then, that Nate is suffering from some sort of mental disorder or illness? That there's the chance he might hurt himself or someone else. Mrs. Carter, I need you to confirm this." The question was clear as crystal, and pointed directly at me.

"I . . . uh . . . I don't know for sure. But . . . maybe, I guess?" The police officer continued to stare at me. It was clear she wanted a more specific answer. "I mean, yes. My answer is yes. I do think it is possible that Nate could hurt himself. He doesn't seem to be making much sense lately. But I don't think he would hurt anyone else. He's too kind for that," I answered weakly. I looked down into my tightly clasped hands to avoid Pete's gaze.

I could sense that he was clenching his teeth, even from across the table.

"Has he ever been diagnosed with anything we should be aware of? Or gone to see a doctor for symptoms that might suggest he needs help?" Constable Matthews interjected. The questions coming from the cops were becoming more pointed. Increasingly urgent. Like rapid fire.

"No. Nothing like that yet," I responded.

Pete remained quiet.

"What about your families? Is there a family history of mental illness?" Constable Matthews asked.

"No. Nothing." I responded.

More silence from Pete.

"Mr. Carter? Anything in yours?"

Pete didn't respond. I looked across the table to see fear and uncertainty reach his eyes. He seemed torn about what to say next.

"Mr. Carter, it's important you tell us everything you know," Constable Baker said firmly. "Your son's life could be at stake. Every minute counts."

Pete shifted uncomfortably in his seat, then answered the officer's question. "Yes . . . Todd Blakely . . . Ashley's father and Nate's grandfather . . . he's bipolar. He was diagnosed with the disease two years ago and has been in and out of psych wards a lot since then."

Heat raced to my cheeks as I struggled to keep up with what Pete was saying. My *father*? Bipolar?

With Nate missing, it was all too much to take in and I began to feel faint.

"Mrs. Carter? Are you okay?" Constable Matthews asked. "Perhaps you could use a glass of water."

I nodded my head, and Pete jumped up to grab a bottle of water from the fridge. He twisted off the cap and handed it to me, silently apologizing with his eyes when they met mine.

I took a long sip and closed my eyes. Forced myself to inhale slowly and begin to dissect the pieces of the puzzle Pete had just revealed.

"My father . . . he's *bipolar*?" I looked at Pete for his response, but couldn't miss the glance exchanged by the two police officers. My question made it clear that this was new information to me. Pete had clearly known about it for a long time.

"We'll let you two talk about this. We're going to go look for Nate. We've got everything we need now, and we'll get a bigger team of officers out on the street to look for him right away." Constable Baker stood from his chair and pushed it into the table. "This new information about possible depression in Nate and a past medical history of bipolar disorder in the family escalates the urgency a great deal. I'll need to notify the sergeant. Ultimately, it will be his call, but I suspect he'll bring in a search commander and set up a mobile command post right away."

"Wait! I'm coming with you!" I shrieked, standing up and lunging for the police officer. I grabbed Constable Baker's arm as he was walking away and pulled him back towards me.

"Mrs. Carter? I know this is hard for you, but you need to let go of me. Now, please." Constable Baker firmly shrugged his arm out of my grasp.

As soon as my unexpected aggression registered with my brain, I dropped his arm. Judging by what was happening to my own actions and voice, I wasn't recognizing anything around me. There was too much going on for me to actually process anything.

"I'll tell you what," Constable Matthews interrupted. "Mrs. Carter, why don't you come with us? You can ride along as we look for Nate. It might be helpful to have you there, and I can guess you aren't going to do well sitting and waiting. But Mr. Carter, we need you to stay here. In case your son comes home."

Pete begrudgingly nodded in agreement. I grabbed my jacket and was out the door before he could consider asking to switch places. There was zero chance I was actually going to stay at home waiting while my son was out on the dark streets by himself, and I was too furious with Pete to even be in the same room as him.

The news of my father being bipolar, and how Pete knew about it when I didn't, had smacked my brain with more surprise and concern than I would have thought possible. But it was nothing compared to losing Nate, and I couldn't stop to think about why Pete hadn't told me. I couldn't focus on anything — or anyone — but my son until I knew he was safe.

Once in the back of the cruiser, I sat as close to the window as possible, peering out into the black night. The car window was icy to my touch, and it was still raining outside. Fresh tears streamed down my cheeks as I thought about Nate out in the dark. All alone and scared.

I looked up at the almost-full moon, barely distinguishable through the threatening, inky clouds. My mind flew to a conversation Nate and I had had a few years before, on one of my favourite days with our family.

Nate was about six years old, and we were by ourselves, lying on the dock of a cottage we'd rented. We were looking up at the stars. Overstuffed with toasted marshmallows we'd just roasted over the blazing fire Pete had built, Nate and I were enjoying some alone time and taking in the balmy August night.

"Mommy?" Nate had asked. "Why does the big moon look bumpy?"

"It's a great question, Bean," I'd replied. "Those things that look like bumps are called craters. And craters are big, gigantic holes."

"Gigantic holes? Like bigger than this *lake*?"

"Some of them, yes." I chuckled under my breath.

"How do they get there?" Nate was fidgeting beside me, but kept asking questions.

"Well, sometimes there are these huge flying things shooting through space at super-fast speeds."

"Faster than *Superman*?" he asked, his voice rising towards the end of the question.

"Yes, faster than Superman," I said and laughed. I gave him a squeeze. "Anyway, these super-fast things are called asteroids. Or comets. And sometimes they crash into the moon and create those massive craters. Which are the giant holes. And some of them are so big we can even see them just by looking up. Isn't that cool?"

"Uh huh. That *is* cool." Nate snuggled closer into me. I put my arm around him and he rested his head on my shoulder. His hair smelled like the lake and dirt but filled me with comfort as I remembered all of the fun we'd had in the water earlier that day.

"Mommy? How come they don't crash into Earth?" Nate asked.

It was another good question, and I wasn't sure I even knew the answer. As an arts major, science wasn't exactly my forte. "Hmmm . . . I'm not really sure, to tell you the truth. But we could look it up tomorrow and find out together. What do you think?"

"That would be good. I like finding things out together."

"Me too, Bean." I pulled him closer. Squeezed him tighter.

"Mommy? Will we always be together?" Nate had asked. He sat up and I could barely make him out, peering at me through the dark. My heart melted.

"We'll be together lots, Bean. As much as possible. But sometimes we might be apart from each other. Just for a little while."

"Like when?"

"Well, like when you're at school and I'm at work, for example." I paused, watching Nate's reaction. "Or, when you get older, and you might want to go for a sleepover at a friend's house, or at Cub Camp. Wouldn't that be fun?"

"Nah . . . I don't want to sleep over anywhere. I want to stay with *you*." Nate lay back down, returning to our snuggly position.

"You might not always feel that way, Bean. But I'll tell you what. You see that moon up there? That really big, crater-filled moon? Well, I happen to know that no matter where you are . . . or where I am . . . that moon will always be in the night sky. So if you're ever lonely, or not with me for whatever reason, just . . . look up. Find the moon, and know that I'm looking at that same moon, and thinking of you."

"Okay, Mommy . . ." Nate's voice trailed off and I knew he was getting sleepy.

I sat up and gently carried my son to the warmly lit cottage to tuck him into bed. I kissed his forehead good night. When I turned off the light in the room he was sleeping in, the bright glow from the full moon outside filled the room. It shone directly over of the cottage, its light streaming through the open window of the bedroom. As I stood in the doorway, watching Nate sleep in the cozy moonlight, my soul filled with warmth and peace.

Years later, sitting in the back of the chilly cop car, peering out the window into the cold, dark night and looking for my lost son, I couldn't have been further from what I felt that night. But one thing was the same. That full, crater-filled moon high in the sky.

I glanced up, taking in the shadowy glow of the moon and thought of Nate. My son. My baby. I watched the moon's shine play peek-a-boo with me through the dark clouds surrounding it. Like it was teasing me, just to see if I'd keep watching.

I held my glance, staring at that moon, and wondered if Nate, wherever he was, was looking at it too, and thinking of me.

31

We continued to circle the city, but Nate was nowhere. And we weren't finding any clues as to his whereabouts. We showed his picture to anyone we saw. But in the wee hours of the morning, most people were at home, sleeping soundly. At first, I had gone with them, but I knew they thought I was too anxious. Too forceful in my approach, and it wasn't helping anyone. Instead, they'd asked me to stay in the car while they approached people with Nate's most recent picture. In the meantime, I frantically called every person I could think of.

As I waited for the officers to finish talking to a group of teenagers who were hanging out at a park, Constable Baker's words raced through my mind.

"Mrs. Carter? Is there a chance Nate might hurt himself or someone else?"

I shuddered. No matter how hard I tried to get the words out of my mind, I heard Constable Matthews's voice over and over and over. The recurring words intensified my panic.

The police officers returned to the car, jerking open the door and snapping me back to reality. "Did you find anything out?" I asked anxiously. I felt as though I'd asked the question a hundred times that night.

"I'm afraid not. Although we did scare the pants off them with a warning about drinking underage," Constable Matthews answered. "I bet they're barely sixteen. I always wonder . . . where the hell are their parents?"

"Do you need to take them home?" I asked weakly. I needed them to keep looking for Nate, but was empathetic for the kids' parents. I imagined their mother pacing at home and worried about her own children.

"No, no . . . we gave them a serious warning and told them to head home. They seemed to be scared enough to just do it. We're committed to finding Nate, Mrs. Carter. The whole department is doing everything possible to find your son."

"I'm really grateful for that. Pete and I . . . we're so scared." The fresh tears I expected did not come, and I wondered if I had literally cried myself out of them. "And please, call me Ashley. I should have told you that hours ago."

"Okay, then. We'll do that. Do you need anything, Ashley? Water? Coffee?" Constable Baker asked.

"No. I just want to keep going. I need to find him."

Just then, my phone rang. It was Tay.

"Tay! Have you heard anything?" I asked frantically.

"No, hon. I'm sorry. I was just calling to check in and see how you are. And to see if you've found him yet."

"No, we haven't. And I'm so scared." The tears returned. Tay's voice sounded like home, and it made me even sadder.

"I know, sweetie. I know . . ."

"How's Grace?" I asked. "Is she freaking out?"

"She was, but she's finally fallen asleep. We had hot chocolate to try to make her feel better, and she's sleeping with Julia." Tay's voice was smooth. Somehow calming. "And Braeden's out looking for Nate as we speak. We rallied a group of people, and they're all out looking for him. We'll find him, Ash. You need to keep believing that."

"They're all out looking for him?" Gratitude flooded through me. We needed all the help we could get.

"Yes. Almost everyone you and I called. There have to be twenty of them, at least. We're all here for you, sweetie. There are a lot of people looking for Nate. We'll find him soon."

I tried to believe Tay. I knew she was right. I needed to remain positive. I had to have faith. Nate needed me to never give up, and I wouldn't. I couldn't.

After I'd hung up the phone, I called Pete to let him know that a neighbourhood search team had been championed by Braeden.

"I need to join them, Ash. I'm going crazy here waiting. I can't do it for one minute more."

"Yes, you can. You have to. What if Nate goes home? Pete, you don't have a choice."

"Yeah, I guess you're right . . ." Pete's voice trailed off.

"Why don't you call your sister? Maybe Kaitlyn could keep you company over the phone while you wait," I suggested. "Have you called her yet?"

"No. I don't want to bug her this late. Besides, there's nothing she can do and I don't want to alarm her."

"Don't be ridiculous. She's your *sister*. Of course she'd want you to call her. Just do it. Please. It will make me feel better knowing that you aren't going crazy by yourself over there."

I paused at my choice of words. They stung once I heard them out loud, suddenly sounding clichéd and horrible. I'd never stopped to think of them in that way, but the phrase "going crazy" suddenly hit way too close to home. Not only because of the possibility of what Nate was going through, but also because of my father.

I pushed the thoughts of my father from my mind. I forced myself to think of Nate. To focus on my son so we could bring him home.

At two o'clock in the morning, we stopped by the mobile command post that had been set up. It looked like a large motor home, but the inside was filled with cops, computers, and coffee.

"Are you Mrs. Carter?" a friendly man asked when we walked inside.

I nodded.

"I'm Oliver . . . the search commander assigned to Nate's case. We're doing everything we can to find him."

"Thank you." I tried to smile at him but couldn't muster up the energy.

"And I've got good news for you. We just got a great lead. We recently found out that Nate was at a pool hall about two hours ago. One of the patrons had seen him, and took pity on him after he'd left. We've searched the entire pool hall from top to bottom, and Nate is no longer there, I'm afraid. But we're close. And we aren't stopping tonight until we find him."

"A *pool hall*? Which one?" While I was shocked that my nine-year-old son was at a pool hall by himself, the flood of hope that shot through my veins trumped all other feelings. My son was still alive two hours ago. It had to be a good sign.

"Ian's Billiards," Oliver responded.

"Ian's Billiards? Isn't that . . . isn't that really far from our house?"

"Yes. Very far. We're not sure how he made it there, but the patron's description matched him perfectly. I had two officers pay him a visit at home with Nate's picture, and he confirmed that it was Nate he saw."

"Why wouldn't he help him?" I cried. "Why did he wait to call?"

"We don't know for sure. We suspect he was doing something illegal himself and was likely afraid of bringing attention to himself. Turns out he had a guilty conscience, though, which is good for us. It's our best lead yet, and we know he's still around here."

"Still around here?" I asked. Was the search commander talking about . . . *kidnapping*? He couldn't be. Not Nate.

Oh God. Please, please . . . not Nate. Please, God, keep him safe. He's just a little boy.

"We're going to keep going. We're searching all around the pool hall, Mrs. Carter. We've got cops going up and down streets, knocking on doors and asking for any clue that might find him."

I nodded and looked around for a chair. I was beginning to feel faint.

"Here, Mrs. Carter. Why don't you sit down?" Oliver grabbed a folding chair from one of the desks, and gently guided me into it.

"You need some rest, Ashley. Why don't you let us take you home?" Constable Matthews asked. "You can be with your husband, and we'll update you the minute we have any more information about your son."

"No. I'm not doing that," I replied, more forcefully than I intended. Taking a deep breath, I continued gently, "I'm sorry . . . I know you're looking out for me. But I won't go home. I need to stay out. For Nate. No matter what, I will not give up on my son. I just can't."

Constable Matthews nodded, looking at me sympathetically, and I knew she understood. I wondered if she had children of her own. And what she might be thinking or feeling to witness another mother looking for her child.

"Why don't you call your husband to let him know about the good news, and then we'll keep going. I understand why you want to stay out. You can do whatever makes you feel comfortable. We'll find Nate together. Okay?" Constable Matthews smiled at me, filling me with a quick burst of renewed energy.

Her response and the way she looked at me suggested that she was, indeed, a mother. That her stomach was in knots, just as my own was.

As I pulled out my iPhone to call Pete, I took comfort in Constable Matthews's compassion. It made me feel better to know that an empathetic mother was on my side during the horrific ordeal. Nate wasn't her son but, as a mother, she felt my panic. Shared in my dread. And if she was experiencing even one millionth of what I was feeling, I knew she'd never let them stop looking for my son.

32
Nate

It's cold. Really, really cold. I can't stop my teeth from chattering and I don't know where I am or how I got here.

I'm so scared.

I keep hearing my name being called all around me. I think it is the monsters who won't leave me alone and they're going to hurt me really badly. I'm so scared I feel like I can't breathe. I don't know how to breathe.

It is really dark and I don't like the dark and the dark makes me more scared because the monsters like the dark and they are all around me. They are like shadows. Really scary shadows.

I'm so afraid.

It is really smelly and I'm beside a garbage can filled with rotten stink. I don't like it at all but I feel like if I climb into the stink the monsters will leave me alone because they won't like the smell either and then I will be saved and then I will be able to breathe again.

I walk towards the big stinky bin and trip over something but I don't know what made me trip and I hit the ground and both my hands instantly hurt because I hit something sharp. I think I am bleeding. I sit down and start to cry but then I force myself to keep going because I need to get into the big stinky bin so the elephant monsters will stop chasing me and I won't be scared anymore.

It's so dark but I feel a little ledge that I can use to climb. I keep climbing and think I might make it to the top but then I slip back to the ground.

I am crying because I am hurting and scared but I need to keep going. I need to get inside the big bin so the monsters will not get me.

I try again and finally make it to the top of the bin and fall inside. It is wet and slimy and stinks more than anything I've smelled before but I feel better because it is dark and quiet and the elephant is too huge to get in here and I feel safe.

I finally feel safe.

33
Ashley

I sipped at the bitter coffee Oliver had handed me. It was luke-warm and tasted burnt and old. I tried to ignore the fact that brewed coffee past its prime also hinted at a search that had been going on for far too long.

It was four o'clock in the morning. We still hadn't found Nate. And no other clues had come in since the anonymous tip from the pool hall. Police teams were out in full force, and Oliver was in the process of working with the sergeant, a man named Ross whom I hadn't yet met, to decide if we should leverage the media to help find Nate.

"Yes! Oliver, *yes*! Please . . . let's do whatever we can to help find him!" I noticed Oliver shoot Officer Matthews a pointed look, to which she responded by nodding her head and steering me clear of his conversation.

"Look, Ashley, we're okay with you staying here because we know you need to be here. But you have to let the search commander and his teams do their jobs, okay?" Her eyes searched mine.

"I know. Constable Matthews . . ." I responded.

"Hey, we're like old friends now. Please, call me Sarah."

"Okay."

"Why don't you come and sit down? Take a rest for a minute. I'll sit with you."

I nodded and followed her to two chairs in a corner. I pulled my coat tighter around me to prevent myself from shivering in the chilly RV, and finished the black coffee. At least it had caffeine in it.

"It's a big decision. Whether to alert the media or not. We've got to make it soon if we're going to hit the morning news, but there can be negative consequences as well."

"Like what?"

"Well, we think there's a good chance we'll find Nate. In the majority of cases similar to this one, the child is located quickly and unharmed."

"You call this *quickly*?" I asked Sarah sarcastically. I regretted the clipped sound of my voice the minute I heard it.

But Sarah was understanding enough to be patient with my rudeness, and answered calmly, "Yes. If we find Nate soon, like we're hoping, and it turns out we didn't need media support, there are other things to consider."

I stared at her. She wasn't making any sense. What could be more important than actually getting Nate home?

"Ashley," Sarah began gently. "We think we're close. Given everything we know, we believe Nate is likely hiding somewhere, and we'll find him soon. Daylight is coming, and that will help us a great deal."

"But why wouldn't we want extra help from the media? Just in case?"

"If Nate's absence is made public, everyone will know about it. And that could make reintegration hard for him. And for you, and the rest of your family. We don't know anything yet, but if it turns out that Nate does require medical treatments for mental health issues . . . well . . . then that information will likely be public too. You will lose control of what, and who, finds out very personal information about your son."

"Are you saying I should be embarrassed? That I should be embarrassed about my son?" I asked her with a sharpness to my voice. *Or my father?* I thought to myself. *Should I be embarrassed about my bipolar father?*

"No, Ashley." Sarah shook her head. "I'm not saying that at all. But you and your family . . . you could have a long road ahead of you. Yes, we absolutely want to find Nate, and we're doing everything we can to find him as soon as possible. And we believe we will find him soon. But we also want to protect you from any unnecessary harm. It's a balance, and a delicate choice. One that Oliver won't make lightly. I've worked with him many times on different cases, and you should trust him. He's the right person to be running this search."

I nodded. I knew she was right, but so many thoughts were swirling together in my mind that I could no longer be logical. Nothing seemed to be making sense anymore, and I felt like my own sanity was being stitched together by nothing more than a few isolated bursts of determination and will. I was running on empty, and wondering how long I could keep myself together.

"*Oliver!*" a woman with short brown hair called out. She was sitting at the laptop farthest from Sarah and me. "I just got word that we found a shoe matching the clothing description."

I stood up quickly and felt Sarah holding onto my arm. "Nate's shoe?" I croaked. My voice sounded like a scream in my mind, but came out as something barely louder than a whisper.

A mash-up of emotions, encompassing both panic and relief, raced through my entire body. Hot prickles crept to the surface of my neck, making me feel even more raw and vulnerable.

I was frightened about what the woman was going to say next and, for the first time since I'd found out Nate was missing, I wanted time to stand still. I was scared about what I'd find out about my son, and I needed to prolong the feeling of hope that I'd been clinging to since his disappearance. I had to live within the quick, isolated moment of believing he was okay, that he was alive, before anyone could tell me anything different.

34

"Nate's shoe?" I repeated in a louder voice, feeling faint. I swallowed hard to diminish the chance of throwing up the rancid coffee that had started to bubble in my stomach. "Where was it?"

Oliver looked in my direction and held his index finger up to his lips, gently signalling for me to be quiet in a kind and sympathetic way.

"Do you have anything more, Ana?" Oliver asked the woman, walking over to her. "Was there anything with it? Any signs that Nate had been there?"

Ana shook her head. "Just the shoe, Ollie. About three blocks from the pool hall where he was last seen."

"Can I see the shoe?" I yelped. I knew Oliver and Sarah

wanted me to be patient, but there was no way I could stay quiet. "Please . . . I can tell you if it's his or not. I bought the shoes he was wearing just last week."

"I know this is hard, Ashley," Sarah said gently, trying to steer me away from Oliver and Ana. "But let's let Oliver figure out what's going on with the shoe they found. He'll talk to us when he's ready. We don't want to get in the way of figuring things out as quickly as possible."

"But . . . but *I* know Nate's shoes. I can tell them if it's his or not. *Please, Sarah.* Tell Oliver to show me the picture."

As if on cue, Oliver crossed the room and handed me a picture of the shoe they had found. "Here, Ashley. Take a look. It's a size six."

There was no mistaking it. The orange and blue lace-up shoe was lying on its side, a few inches from a giant puddle. The bottom was tipped up just enough to reveal the orange zigzag pattern etched onto the black sole. The picture Oliver held was dark, clearly taken with someone's phone, and there was mud caked onto the sides of the shoe. But it was definitely Nate's.

I nodded my head and collapsed into Sarah's waiting arms. Oliver took that as his final prompt to order his entire team to the immediate location where the shoe was found. "Knock on house doors and ask for people's co-operation. Look in people's garages, backyards, side yards . . . whatever. Find him, people. Let's go!"

I watched the search command centre come alive with new energy, and the officers who had checked in for updates returned to their police cars and sped off with lights flashing.

I called Pete to tell him the news. "So is this a good sign . . . or . . . not a good sign?" he asked after answering the phone on the first ring.

"I'm not sure. I guess it could be a good thing. Right? Especially since Oliver doesn't suspect foul play or anything like that? If they found Nate's shoe . . . well, then hopefully that means he's nearby and they will find him soon."

"Yeah . . . I guess you're right." Pete's voice didn't sound like he was convinced. I forced myself to ignore it.

I asked Pete if he'd talked to his sister. He hadn't. It wasn't shocking given my husband's stubbornness, but I felt sad for him that he was at home by himself, forced to deal with the terror and loneliness alone. At least I had Sarah and Oliver, and the woman I now knew as Ana. Their presence provided a bit of comfort, despite the fact they had all been complete strangers to me only hours before.

"Ashley?" Oliver had walked up behind me and tapped my arm. I covered the mouth of my phone, and focused my attention solely on Oliver.

"We found Nate."

"You found *Nate*?! You found our son? Oh . . . thank *God*," I shouted, dropping my phone and attacking Oliver with a bear hug.

"Yes, we found Nate," Oliver responded, picking up my phone and handing it to me. I held it up so Pete knew what was going on as well.

"Ashley? Ash!" I heard Pete call out from my phone. His voice was muted and distant. "What's going on?"

I returned the phone to my ear and explained what I'd learned, then put him on speakerphone so he could hear Oliver's update as well.

"Where is he?" I asked Oliver. "When can we see him?"

"He's in an ambulance, en route to the hospital. Sarah will take you to meet him there." Oliver took the phone from me and gently grabbed hold of my upper arms. He turned me towards him and firmly held me in place to keep me from dashing out the door. "Ashley, you need to know that Nate's in pretty rough shape. I think he's going to be okay, but he's fairly banged up. And the officer that found him said that he's not making a lot of sense. He keeps saying illogical, random things. You need to brace yourself for that."

"I don't care what he's *saying*," I yelled. "Just let me see my son. Please, Sarah, can you take me to Nate?"

Sarah nodded her head and held the RV door open. I climbed in the front of the cop car, and we rode to the hospital in complete silence. My eyes did not stray from the road in front of me, and it felt like the longest drive of my life.

"Can't you go faster? Please?" I asked. Sarah looked at me for a second, then hesitated slightly before nodding. She put on both her lights and sirens, and we raced through the city. We arrived at the hospital just as Pete was running in.

"Ashley. Oh, thank God," Pete cried, taking me into his arms. "I've been so scared. It's been a nightmare . . . I'm so relieved that it's over."

I nodded, pulling Pete's arm towards the hospital and into the Emergency Room. I barely noticed Sarah following behind us.

"You have our son!" I cried at the triage nurse when we arrived at the counter. "Nate Carter. A little boy. He's nine years old. He's been missing all night, and was just brought in by ambulance. *Please* . . . please, can we see him?"

The nurse took one look at my desperation and stood up, signalling for us to follow her through the double Emergency Room doors.

When we walked into the flurry of doctors and medical teams, I could already hear him screaming. His little voice, deafening in volume but full of vulnerability and fear, filled the room. I couldn't place exactly where it was coming from, and it was getting louder.

As we rounded the bend of the hospital corridor, we saw him. Our tiny son, who at only nine years old and still an innocent child, was flailing his arms and legs with more strength than I'd ever seen him show. He was crying and begging the doctors and nurses to leave him alone. To let him go.

"Nate!" I dropped my purse on the floor and started to run to my son. But before I could reach him, Sarah pulled me back.

"Stay here, Ashley," Sarah said firmly. "He won't be able to see you now. I know it's hard, as a mother. You want to go to him. To help him. But you should stay here. You *need* to stay here. That's what will help him the most right now."

Despite Sarah's firm grip on my arm, I somehow managed to escape. I pushed her away and continued running towards my son. I bulldozed my way through the medical team standing alongside his bed, holding him down, and tried to take Nate into my arms.

Half a second later, Nate elbowed me in the face.

The blow felt like it had come from a two-hundred-pound man. I immediately crumpled to the floor, crawling into Pete's arms when he rushed in to scoop me up and move us out of the doctors' way.

"It's okay, Ash. Shhh . . . shhh." Pete spoke softly, not taking his eyes off our son. "We'll let the doctors do their jobs. It's okay. Nate's safe now. That's all that matters."

"No! Nate needs us. We're his parents. I'm his *mother*, for fuck's sake. He needs *me*." My voice was getting louder. I was bawling hysterically and on the verge of hyperventilating.

Pete held me tighter. I sensed that my husband was restraining me in the same way the doctors were holding down our son.

Nate weighed barely sixty pounds, yet the team of adults trying to restrain him was having trouble. His arms and legs flailed everywhere, walloping those standing nearest to him. Two nurses struggled to get his arms and legs into restraints.

"He's too small," the shorter of the two nurses called out. "His wrists keep slipping. I can't keep him in the restraints!"

"Let's give him two milligrams of Lorazepam," one of the

doctors ordered loudly, looking at the nurse struggling to get Nate's arms in restraints. She immediately fled the violence and came back with a long needle, which she jabbed into Nate's upper arm.

The doctors and security team continued to hold Nate down, while Pete and Sarah held me back. Within moments, Nate's agitation began to diminish. Ten minutes after that, our son was peaceful. He looked like a completely different kid, quietly dozing, with his frail little body looking too small in the big hospital bed.

"Your son's sedation should last for several hours," the ER doctor explained quietly. "I'm sure you have a lot of questions for us, and we have a lot for you as well. But why don't you take some time to be near your son now, and we'll chat later. We've got a bit of time. Does that sound okay to you?"

I nodded, inching towards Nate's side and taking a seat beside him. Despite the fact that he smelled worse than anything I could have imagined, I buried my face into the side of the hospital bed. I didn't want to leave him alone.

With Pete standing behind me, his hand placed firmly on my shoulder, I wept into the hospital bed. My tears and sobs were uncontrollable. I cried because of what our family had been through that night, and the uphill battle I knew we were about to climb.

No matter how I tried, I couldn't stop the tears from rolling down my cheeks and onto Nate's smooth little hand. I pressed his limp fingers to my face as I wept, the dirt from his hand stamping my face and leaving my cheeks stained with the grime he had found while combing the streets alone. Underneath the dirt, the welt on my temple began to puff up.

Sarah left quietly, saying something about being in touch later to find out how we were. I heard her words but couldn't absorb what she was saying, and didn't have the mental capacity to even say goodbye or thank her for all she had done for me.

Twenty minutes later, the nurse who had administered the needle crept through the curtains and told us she needed to check on Nate. I nodded, but didn't move an inch as she made sure Nate was okay.

She worked quickly, pausing to smile in a sympathetic way every few moments. When she was done, she gently patted my back the way my mother had done years ago, and left.

Pete went to call Tay and give her another update on Nate, but I was going nowhere. With my feet planted firmly on the ground, my hand gripping his, I stayed beside my son.

I couldn't let go. Nor could I shake the electric fear that coursed its way through my soul as I braced myself for what might happen once Nate's medication wore off.

35

Just as the sun began to peep over the hospital, the ER doctors decided to move Nate to the psychiatry ICU wing. They wanted him to be under constant observation and given one-on-one nursing attention. They encouraged Pete and me to go get something to eat in the cafeteria, and join them on the eighth floor when we were ready.

"No," I said flatly. "I won't leave my son."

"Mrs. Carter, I understand you've been through a great ordeal," a new doctor sympathized as he stood on the other side of Nate's bed. He had greying hair at the temples, and an affable smile. I remembered him introducing himself when he walked into the curtain-lined room, yet I had already forgotten his name. "But you're going to need to keep your strength up for your son. You need to eat, and you'll need to sleep, too. You will be in a much better position to help Nate if you take care of yourself."

I shook my head. "I can't. I can't . . . leave him. I was so scared. I can't leave him again."

The doctor exchanged glances with Pete, who quickly jumped in and offered to go get us both something to eat. "I'll grab something quick and meet you on the eighth floor, Ash. Then you can stay with Nate. Okay?"

I nodded, wiping away yet another stubborn tear that had insisted on falling, and grabbed my bag. I followed silently as two new nurses whisked Nate's bed into the elevator.

The grumpier looking of the two nurses punched the elevator button with unnecessary force, and we rode upwards in silence. I was uncomfortable going with them, and slight feelings of embarrassment crept to the surface. I couldn't determine whether it was because I had been unreasonable, ignoring the doctor's advice to take a break, or because I felt shame in being there. I ignored the latter, feeling guilty for even letting thoughts of embarrassment for my son creep into my mind.

I kept my eyes glued to the numbers that took turns lighting up as we made our way to the eighth floor. After what seemed like an eternity, the door finally opened and we took awkward turns leaving the elevator.

"Maya? This is the nine-year-old boy we called about. He came into the ER agitated and was given two milligrams of Lorazepam about two hours ago. Which bed?"

"Seven," the nurse behind the desk replied. She remained glued to her seat as she pointed down the hall. "We're ready for you."

I followed Nate's rolling bed as the nurses wheeled him to the empty spot in a single hospital room. An immediate sense of relief hit me as I realized he wouldn't have to share a room with a crazy person, which was immediately followed by a flush of redness to my cheeks as I realized the nurses with me probably thought that *Nate* was the crazy person.

"Your son will stay here for a while. Until he wakes up at least," the crustier-looking nurse explained. "He'll be under constant observation and will be assigned a nurse, who will look after only him. Okay?"

I nodded. Slowly, I walked towards the only chair in the room and practically collapsed into it. I was surprised by how weak I was.

"If you need anything right away then just ring the bell. But your nurse should be in soon, so only use it if there's an emergency. Not sure who you have, but she'll come find you."

I nodded again as the nurses got ready to leave the room. Through the uncovered window that provided a clear view into the hallway, I watched them return to the nurse's station. They spoke to Maya for a few moments, then disappeared into the elevator.

Alone with Nate, I watched him sleep. My eyes were fixated on him, as though I was mesmerized. With what seemed to be a gentle smile on his lips, he looked so peaceful. Like it could have been any of the normal days when I'd crept into his room to kiss him goodbye before rushing out the door to an early morning breakfast meeting.

I pulled the chair closer and tentatively took my son's hand in my own. I squeezed it. Gently at first. And then a bit more firmly.

There was no response. Not even a flicker. It was as if Nate was in a coma. Or worse.

The thought scared me, so I squeezed harder. I was half hoping he'd wake up. But I was also scared of what would happen when he did.

"Mrs. Carter?" A nurse holding Nate's chart walked into the room. She had a tender smile and a warm hand as she shook mine to greet me. "I'm Addison, Nate's nurse. You can call me Addy. I'll be with him all day, and will be constantly monitoring him. We expect Nate to wake up in about four or five hours, but it could be longer. Especially since he came in after a night of no sleep."

I nodded. Again. It felt like it was all I was doing, but I couldn't seem to find words. I didn't know what to say.

"Are you alone?" Addy asked me.

I shook my head.

"Is there someone coming?"

I nodded my head.

"Who, Mrs. Carter? Is it your husband?"

I cleared my throat. "Uh, yes. My husband. Pete. He should be here soon."

"Great. I'm glad you'll have some company." Addy smiled at me. "I'm going to check Nate's vital signs and make sure everything is okay. You can stay or take a walk in the hall. Whatever you'd prefer."

I sat, watching Addy as she wheeled a machine into the room and placed the clip on Nate's index finger. When she did, I practically felt it being attached to my own, just as the nurses had done to me so many times in the hours following his birth; I'd held my darling newborn son in one arm while offering up the other so the nurse could take my temperature, blood pressure, and heart rate. It seemed like only yesterday.

"Nate looks good," Addy said when she was done. She snapped Nate's chart closed when she finished writing. "I'll leave you alone for a bit, but I'll be right outside if you need me."

"Thank you," I said quietly. "I appreciate you being so kind."

"Of course, sweetie." Addy crossed the room and crouched down beside my chair. "I know this is hard, Mrs. Carter. I've seen it many times. But Nate is in good hands now. And he's safe. The rest of the stuff you're worrying about? Well, we'll just take it one hour at a time. Together. Okay?"

I looked down. Tears dropped from my cheeks onto my folded hands.

"Can I get you some water? Or coffee? Something to eat, maybe?"

"Pete . . . my husband. He went to the cafeteria. He should be here soon. I'm surprised he isn't already, to be honest."

"Would you like me to wait with you until he gets here?"

"No . . . it's okay. Thank you, though."

Addy nodded and stood. Her knees cracked, the sound startling in the quiet room. "Call me if you need me, Mrs. Carter. For anything."

"Call me Ashley."

"Okay, Ashley. As long as you promise to call if you need me." Addy patted my knee before walking towards the hospital room door. She opened it to the horrible sound of yelling in the distance. First, a man with a deep voice, roaring ferociously and screaming profanities at the nurses, telling them to leave him alone or the CIA was going to take him to jail. Then came an escalating scream from a woman, a high-pitched soprano drowning out the man's tenor vulgarities.

I squeezed my eyes closed, trying to shut it all out, and started to pray.

36

Someone gently tugged at my shoulder. I was groggy and completely unaware of where I was until I finally managed to blink my bleary eyes into clarity and saw Pete standing in front of me in Nate's hospital room.

"Hi sweetie," Pete said softly. I stretched, then grabbed Pete's wrist to look at his watch. It was just after eleven a.m. Pete and I had slept for most of the morning. After he'd brought us both breakfast, Pete had located another chair and we'd fallen asleep, side by side, next to Nate's bed, our heads propped against each other's. My neck felt stiff and cricked as a result.

"Sorry to wake you, but your iPhone has been going off like

crazy for the past hour and I'm wondering if there's anyone you need to reach out to?"

"What? Oh . . . right. Work is probably wondering what the hell happened to me."

"Yes, probably."

"What about Tay? Have you talked to her?" I needed to know how Grace was doing. It was far more concerning to me than work.

"Yes. Several times, actually. We agreed that she'd tell Grace and anyone else who asks that Nate was found and is in the hospital for monitoring. That we're with him, and we aren't sure of next steps yet."

"That sounds good, I guess." I had no idea what to tell people, but everyone needed to know that Nate had been found and was safe.

"Grace desperately wants to come here," Pete continued. "Tay is holding her at bay for now. But we need to figure out what to tell her and when to see her."

"I know."

"Do you want to call and talk to her? I talked to her early this morning after I spoke to Tay, and it made me feel better. I know she wants to talk to you. She mentioned it several times while I was speaking with her."

"I'll call her after school."

"Okay."

We sat in silence and watched our son. Beside me, my phone went off. I started to reach for it but quickly retracted. I didn't know what to say to whoever was trying to reach me.

"Pete?" I asked hesitantly. "I don't want to fight. I'm too exhausted. But I need to know . . . I need to ask you about my dad."

Pete looked directly at me with sadness in his eyes.

When he didn't respond, I continued, "How can he be

bipolar? And how do you know about it? And why didn't you tell me?"

"It's a long story, Ash. I'm not sure now is the right time for it."

"I think it's the perfect time. All we have right now is time. And I have no doubt the doctors will be asking about it soon anyway."

Pete nodded his head. "Can I get a coffee first? Do you want one?"

"No. I need to know. Now, Pete. You owe me that."

"I know. You're right."

I waited for him to continue, but he stopped talking. I could practically hear the hamster wheel spinning in his brain as he tried to figure out where to begin.

I urged him on. "The last time I saw him, or heard from him, was that horrible Christmas. I thought that was the last time you had heard from him, too. Why don't you start there? You know, at the beginning?" Immediately, I wished I hadn't tacked on that last sentence; it was more sarcastic than I'd intended.

"Okay. That makes sense." Pete took a big breath. "After you kicked your father out on Christmas Eve, I didn't hear from him for a very long time. I thought he was pissed off at being kicked out on Christmas, and had decided to get out of our lives for good. I know that's what you thought, too."

"Yes," I agreed. "You're right about that."

"About two years later, just before Christmas, I got a call from a hospital in Florida. It was a psychiatrist, calling to speak to me about your father."

"Go on."

Pete took a deep breath and continued, "Months before that, in the summertime, your father had been at some party and had hit the booze pretty hard. Then he did cocaine."

"Cocaine? What? My *father* did cocaine?" My voice rose with every word.

"Yes. Cocaine. I have no idea if he had been doing it a lot or if it was his first time. But, on that particular night, he did it. A lot of it. And eventually he started acting crazy. At first, everyone at the party thought it was the coke making him act all weird. But he got worse and started screaming and throwing things. Apparently, he threw a bunch of wine glasses against the wall, and even punched one guy in the head, claiming the guy was an undercover cop and was going to bust them all for drugs."

"Was he? The guy he punched, I mean. Was he an undercover cop?"

"No. He was just some guy at the party. But your dad was convinced he was a cop. He was just paranoid, I think. And then it got worse, and your dad started thinking *everyone* was a cop. No one knew what to do, and no one wanted to call the real cops because they were scared of being busted for the coke."

"Pete? How do you know all of this?" I interrupted him. I was struggling to keep up. "Did the psychiatrist tell you all of this on the phone?"

"He told me some of it. But not a lot. He was very careful not to step over the line of confidentiality. Your dad told me most of it, once I talked to him."

I took a breath and bit my lip, trying to avoid lashing out at my husband for keeping a secret so big. Too big. It crossed well over the line of what a husband should keep from his wife. But I needed him to continue. I had to know what happened to my father. So I continued biting my lip and forced myself to remain silent.

"Well, no one called for help. They were too scared, I guess. So your dad left the party. He went to a bar and drank far more than he should have. He told me that he hadn't slept in days. Apparently, he felt he didn't need to. His brain was on some crazy fast speed, and it wouldn't let him sleep. And I think his lack of sleep, combined with the drugs and booze, made him really lose control. It all snowballed really, really fast."

"What happened when he left the bar?"

"He never did. I think that, at first, everyone thought he was the life of the party. He knew no one there, yet was talking to everyone. He sat down at people's tables, introduced himself and never stopped talking. He says he remembers feeling safe there at first. But then the paranoia came back and that's when it all went to hell."

"What did he do? What happened?"

"He doesn't remember much. But he found out later that he jumped behind the bar and started throwing bottles everywhere. Liquor, beer, wine. You name it. They smashed everywhere. He must have slipped on the floor because he fell on the glass and cut his hands open. Messed them up pretty badly. He had damage to his tendons and nerves. Took a long time to fix up and, even now, his hands aren't completely normal."

My head was spinning.

"Your dad didn't feel it at the time. Or didn't care, anyway. Because he jumped back up and threatened the bartenders, accusing them of being spies for the Russian government. Someone must have called the cops because they showed up soon after and took him to the hospital."

I swallowed hard, unsure of whether or not I wanted to know what came next. But like a traveller who sees a bad accident on the highway, I couldn't shake myself from needing to know what happened. "So then what?"

"He was in there for months. He had a hell of a time finding the right cocktail of meds that worked. And he went through all kinds of therapy alongside the meds. I also think he had no desire to leave. That part's my own theory, but I know your dad felt like he had no one to turn to. He felt like he had alienated and offended all of his friends and family in the years leading up to it. And sadly, there was no one there when he fell hard. Or, at least, that's how he told me he felt anyway."

"What about me? He could have called *me*!" I cried. The

guilt bubbling up in my throat was beginning to suffocate me. "I'm his daughter, for fuck's sake. Why wouldn't he call me? I would have helped him." I was crying openly by that point. Pete left the chair he was sitting in and crouched down beside me. He pulled me into his arms.

"It's okay, Ash. Really. It's okay. Your dad's okay now." Pete stroked my hair as he tried to calm me down. "He wasn't ready to call you. I'm not sure that he is even now. It's one of the reasons I didn't tell you before now. Your father loves you deeply. But he wasn't ready. He wasn't ready to talk to you about it. And he made me promise I wouldn't say anything until he was ready."

"Have you seen him?"

"No. I've talked to him a lot on the phone. But I haven't seen him."

"And you've known for about a year?"

Pete nodded. "Yes. About that."

"And you've lied to me. For a *year*?" I clenched my fists and pounded them into Pete's chest. He grabbed my hands and held them tightly.

"No, Ashley. I haven't lied to you. I just couldn't tell you. Please, baby. See my side of it. I thought I was doing the right thing. I wanted to protect you. *And* your father. He wasn't ready for you to know, and he begged me to not say anything. He kept saying he wanted to tell you himself. Please, baby, see my side of it . . ."

"And what side is that, Pete?" Darts of hatred coursed through my body as I spat the words at my husband. Pete not telling me about my father went far beyond keeping a secret; keeping silent about the information had created massive barriers in recognizing what was likely going on with Nate. And for that I was more livid than I'd ever been in my life.

"Ash, you've got to know that I was in a really tough spot with all of this. When I first found out, it was Christmastime. I didn't want to ruin that for you. Our family was so happy. *You*

were happy." Pete's eyes begged for forgiveness. "I remembered how much the Christmas fiasco from two years before had
impacted you. How much it had devastated you. And I couldn't
bring myself to tell you. I just couldn't. I told myself that I would
wait until after the holidays, and then figure out what was best."

"*You* determined what was best for *me*?"

"Well, yes. I really thought it was best. I didn't want to ruin
your Christmas. I thought that a few extra days weren't going to
hurt anyone. Nothing was going to change in the week or so that
I waited."

"But you didn't tell me a week or so later."

"I know. Because I ended up talking to your dad shortly
after, and he begged me to wait. He said that he wasn't ready.
That he didn't want you to know yet."

"But what about *me*, Pete? Didn't you think that I had a right
to know?"

"I don't know," Pete replied honestly. "I was put in the
middle of it the minute your dad's psychiatrist called me, but
ultimately it was up to your dad to decide when you found out.
And I was worried about your dad's health, and didn't want
to push him too hard if he wasn't ready. I had no idea what he
would do. Or if it would make him go crazy again."

"And what about your son? Now your *son* is the one who's
gone crazy. So where is your loyalty now, Pete? How do you feel
about not telling me about my father? Because, clearly, you
couldn't draw an obvious conclusion. Even when it was right
in front of you, smacking you in the face." My eyes flashed and
fire ignited in my cheeks as I struggled to keep my composure.
"For some reason, even though you knew my father was bipolar,
you couldn't even begin to see the signs in Nate. Even though it
should have been obvious to you. I had no idea about my father
. . . and yet it was *me*, and not you, who knew there was something wrong with our son. And all you've done this whole time is

try to convince me I'm overreacting. That there's nothing wrong with Nate. And that I'm being extreme."

Pete remained silent, not meeting my eyes. I had never seen so much sadness or guilt in his eyes. And I had never been so angry with him.

"Well, how's this for extreme, Pete? I don't know that this is something I can forgive. I don't know if we can *fix this*. And I don't know if I want to." I grabbed my bag and headed for the door. I knew Nate had several hours before he woke up, and I was in desperate need of fresh air. I walked ten steps down the hall before I angrily snatched my vibrating phone out of my bag and whipped it in the garbage. I laughed outwardly after I did it, the sound coming out of my mouth more like a snort than laughter. But I found it funny that I'd done something so out of character in such an anomalous moment — and that I'd likely be mistaken for a patient in the ward instead of a visitor.

Yet throwing my phone away with all of its irritating work calls and messages had instantly made me feel better. A lot better. So I just walked away.

37

After I'd gone for a walk outside of the hospital, the weight of the anger that had attached itself to my shoulders slowly started to lift. I inhaled deeply, squeezing my eyes shut, and let the crisp, cold air fill my lungs and nip at the insides of my chest.

I stood there, focusing on my breathing, just like they'd taught me to do in my prenatal class. After a few moments, I opened my eyes. Everything was blurry after squeezing them shut for so long, and my eyes needed to acclimatize to the sights around me.

All around, people were rushing about. Everyone was in a hurry. It was clear people were late for appointments. In need of test results. Trying to exist within the chaos that hospitals present.

A little girl about four years old, wearing a green jacket and plaid mittens, skipped down the sidewalk alongside a man who I assumed was her father. She was holding his hand, and radiated so much joy that I thought she would burst. The balloons the man carried said "It's a boy!" I imagined the little girl's mother holding a tiny, newborn baby on the fourth-floor maternity wing, singing softly and welcoming her newest family member to the world.

"Are you excited?" the man asked the little girl as they passed by me. "Don't forget to call him by his name. Do you remember what we named him?"

"Yes, Daddy. It's Steven. We named him Steven. But I'm going to call him Stevie."

"Okay, honey," the father laughed, bringing his daughter in for a little hug. "You can call him Stevie."

When the father and his little girl had passed, a horn honked angrily and I turned my attention to the street. Taxicabs formed a row directly out front, waiting for their next fare. The drivers of the cars looked bored. Tired. Grouchy. The looks on their scrunched faces mirrored what I was feeling. I thought about getting in one of the cabs and taking a drive around the city for a bit. Away from the hospital. Away from life.

But I knew I couldn't do that. No matter how much I needed to escape, I couldn't abandon my son. I needed to put him first.

Instead, I kept walking. Eventually I made my way back to one of the benches outside of the main hospital doors. I sat down and leaned forward, placing my elbows in my lap and propping my head up with closed fists. The bench was cold, and the iciness of exposed metal snaked its way through my pants and attached itself to my legs.

About fifteen feet away, I watched a man in his early forties push a delicate woman in a wheelchair towards the hospital doors. She was so short that she barely made it above the top of the wheelchair. On her head, she wore a pretty pink hat with a matching winter coat that looked like it was two sizes too big.

I noticed her slowly raise a frail hand in an attempt to get the man's attention. I could tell it took her more energy than she had just to raise her finger.

The man stopped and bent down to put his ear next to her mouth so he could hear her; I doubted her voice was barely more than a whisper. The man listened attentively, nodding his head to let the frail woman know that he understood.

I knew I was being rude, staring at them as I was, but I couldn't take my eyes off of them. The woman was so pretty, even in her feeble state, and it was obvious how much the man cared about her.

After a few moments of hushed conversation, and a tiny smile from the woman that looked like it took as much energy as raising her hand had, the man continued pushing the woman towards the hospital.

Something about the way the man pushed her wheelchair — and how he had looked at her when she was speaking to him — told me with absolute certainty that the man was her son. A son who had been raised so well he didn't think twice about taking a hiatus from his likely successful and thriving life to take care of his ailing mother . . . because it was the same mother who had spent *her* glory years rocking her son to sleep when he was a baby, even though her entire body ached from lack of sleep.

For the grown man, the woman he was pushing in her wheelchair had been the healer who had sat up all night with *him* when he was ill. The educator who spent endless hours helping her son with his math homework at the kitchen table. The taxi driver who took him to his early morning hockey practices every weekend. And the worrier who stayed up well into the wee hours of the morning, waiting for her teenage boy to come home, just so she knew he was safe.

The man wasn't taking care of his ill mother just because he wanted to. Nor was he doing it solely out of obligation. The man was caring for his mother because somewhere deep inside of him lived an unconditional love that was so powerful he didn't have an option. Simply put, he was all in, and completely committed to his family.

Standing there, watching the woman and her son, induced a shift in my attitude towards everything that was going on with my own family. While not even realizing they were doing it, the man and his mother had reminded me that, after all the complicated layers have been peeled away from the complex onion we call life, what's really left is the unconditional love for those we care about most. It's the connection that keeps us tied to them. Helping them. Forgiving them. No matter what else has happened.

Unconditional love keeps us moving forward, I thought. It's altruism that offers no bounds and is completely unchanging. An affection and allegiance to the people in our lives — the very same people who likely drive us the craziest — with whom we've either been tied to by blood or have chosen as lifelong companions. With no limitations and no exceptions, unconditional love is stronger than reason. More powerful than choice. And it provides us with a dynamic, unexplained energy that lifts us up in the most difficult times, and bonds us to the family members within our complex world of challenge and uncertainty.

The man pushing his mother in her wheelchair was standing by her. Walking alongside her, no matter how big her battle had been, or would be in the future. He was committed to her. No matter what.

And I was committed to my family. To my husband and, most importantly, my son. My immeasurable loyalty to Nate had never been in question. But I had thought about walking away from my husband.

Nothing was going to change the fate that had been handed

to us as a family. We were in the battle together, no matter what was thrown at us. I was angry at Pete for not telling me about my father's illness. He shouldn't have kept it from me. But he did it to protect me, as well as my father. He did it because he thought it was right. I couldn't let a mistake that was made based on my genuine best interests get in the way of the altruistic ties that were meant to bind us together as a family.

As a mother who loved her son more dearly than life itself, I wouldn't let anything get in the way of Nate's health, whether physical or mental. I simply had no choice. It was the unspoken vow that had wrapped itself around Nate and me the moment I held his six pound, twelve ounce body for the first time, moments after his birth.

My son deserved the world. A world filled with opportunity and health. And he certainly deserved two parents fighting for his recovery, together, as a united couple.

As I walked through the hospital doors, anxious to get back to Nate, a nagging thought continued to play through my mind: if I believed so strongly in loving family members unconditionally, what did that mean for my father and me? He and I had been officially estranged for three years, and he hadn't been a parent to me since I was seven.

After so many years of my father and me co-existing within the complicated heartache, disappointment, and abandonment that had been my childhood, I didn't know if there was the same chance of forgiveness with him. Or if I even really wanted it to happen. Even if he was sick.

It was hypocritical, yes. But with everything going on with Nate, thinking through my issues with my father was too much. Dealing with the news of his illness would only serve as a distraction from my focus on Nate. And nothing, no one, was going to take me away from being dedicated to making my son better as quickly as possible.

38

When I reached Nate's floor, I slowed my pace as I walked by the paper garbage directly outside the nurses' station, and peeked inside to see if my iPhone was still there.

It was gone.

"Is this what you're looking for?" a voice piped up from the office behind the nurses' desk. "I figured you'd return for it."

I snapped my head up, embarrassed to be caught looking in the garbage, and was greeted by Addy waving my phone.

"I, uh, I guess I lost it . . ."

"No need to explain. I saved it for you. You know, just in case you wanted it back." Addy winked as she handed my phone to me.

"Thanks. I guess my actions were a little excessive," I said. I could feel the heat of embarrassment rush to my cheeks. Obviously, I would need my phone. If not for work, for keeping in touch with close friends and family to update them on Nate.

"You seem like a busy lady. Your phone hasn't stopped going off since I retrieved it. Anyone I can call for you?"

"Er . . . no, thanks. It's okay. I can call them."

Addy was about to respond but was cut off by a man in the room across from us. He was wailing loudly, and escalating in volume with each word he said. Except for his deep voice, he sounded like a toddler who was throwing a temper tantrum.

Addy recognized the overwhelmed look in my eyes as the screaming continued. "Here, Ashley, why don't you come back to our office and have a seat. We can sit and chat for a bit. Nate's not going to wake up for a long while. I expect him to sleep until at least dinner."

I smiled gratefully and followed the nurse into the office.

"What about Nate's school? Have you called to let them know he won't be in today?" Addy asked.

"Damn it! Of course . . . Nate's school. It's Tuesday. Where's my head?"

"Spinning. And that's normal. You're not thinking straight right now, but not many people would be. Don't worry about the school . . . you can call them in a bit. I just didn't want you to forget."

"What should I tell them? I have no idea what to say to people about all of this." I could hear the panic lining my voice as I said the words out loud.

"Why don't you just say that Nate's sick and you don't expect him to be in for a few days? It's all true, and it buys you some time to process all of this."

I nodded, thinking through what I was going to tell everyone. How could I begin to admit my son was in a psych ward? That he was most likely mentally ill, and we had no idea when, or if, he would get better?

I shuddered at the thought of the stigma and continual bullying that was going to attach itself to my son. The black mark that had been cast on so many people living with a disease that was no fault of their own had created a cruel world for them to live in. I couldn't stand the thought of the nastiness my son would endure from both kids and adults alike who had no idea that he was just a sweet little boy who, underneath everything else, had a heart of gold.

"Ashley?" Addy interrupted my thoughts. "I was asking about your work. What do you do?"

"Me? Oh, uh, I head up the creative department at an advertising agency here in Toronto."

"Sounds like a big job."

"Yeah. It is. I love it, but it's a ton of work."

"And what about your husband? Where does he work?"

"He stays at home with the kids. He has for several years now. It's one of the ways we make it work."

Addy nodded her head, showing she understood. "My husband and I both work shift work. But I've gone down to part-time so we can be more flexible with our kids' schedules. You do what you have to do for your kids."

Her last sentence struck me hard. I knew she was talking about more than just schedules.

"Oh crap. What am I going to tell my work? I can't go back now, and so many of them won't understand. Very few people have kids in my office," I said out loud, suddenly anxious about managing my career on top of everything that was going on. "And what's going to happen? How long will I need to be here? How am I going to *work*?"

"Let's just take it one day at a time. For now, tell your work the same thing you're telling Nate's school. Your son is sick, and you need to be with him for a few days. That's it."

"They're going to know . . . Nate, he was missing all night. Tons of people were trying to find him. They know he's in the hospital."

"So tell them he's in the hospital. You don't need to go into details. And if they ask what's wrong and you're not sure what to tell them . . . or when . . . keep it simple for now. Just tell him that Nate has to get some tests, and you're waiting for the results. People don't need to know the whole story. And if they speculate, well, then they speculate. You can't control that. With all you're focused on, I'd say it's the thing that matters least."

I nodded, absorbing what Addy was saying. She was right, of course, and it helped to hear it.

"Thanks. I appreciate you talking me through this. If you'll excuse me, I have to make those calls. Then I'd like to get back to my husband and son."

"Of course. I'll leave you alone so you can have some privacy. In fact, I'll go check on Nate and see how he's doing." Addy rose from her chair and patted my back. Just like the caring nurse from the ER had done. It was a simple gesture, but it made me feel better. It reminded me of my own sweet mother, who used to care for me so tenderly.

I called Nate's school and sent emails to Jack, Ben, and Brad. Just as Addy had suggested, I kept it simple and told them I'd be away for a bit, taking care of my son. I instructed Ben to take my place and work with Jack and Emily to figure out what meetings he needed to be in.

Instantly, I got an email back from Brad. I held my breath, preparing myself for the questions about Nate's disappearance. Instead, his response was gracious and caring.

We're thinking of you and your family, Ashley. You take care of them, and we'll take care of the rest here in New York. ~Brad

When I read his reply, I remembered that I hadn't shared any details of Nate's disappearance with Brad. He knew nothing more than that I had needed to leave New York. And he didn't ask any questions, for which I was extremely appreciative.

Ben's response was similar, saying that he'd rise to the occasion and send emergency emails only.

Unfortunately, Jack's response wasn't as considerate or understanding. I could see straight through the rhetoric.

> What's going on, Carty? Sorry to hear you're going through whatever it is. Doesn't sound fun. Let us know if we can help in any way. And take the time you need, but remember it's busy here and we'll need you back soon. Ben will do for now, but he's no you. And we need YOU. ~JP

"Not as much as Nate needs me . . ." I muttered out loud. Without my job, we'd have no income. Or drug plan, which I was sure we were going to need.

Despite the temptation to reply right away, I decided to ignore Jack's email until the following morning, and return to my son. Addy's words had etched a spot in my memory, and I remembered her advice of taking it one day at a time.

So Jack could wait for a day. It was my son who needed me most.

39

When I returned to Nate's room, Pete was chatting with Addy as she took his temperature and monitored his condition.

"Hi," I greeted them quietly. "How is he?"

"The same. Everything looks good, and the meds are forcing him to sleep. As I said, he'll be knocked out for a while. Why don't you go and grab something to eat? Maybe a shower and some fresh clothes, too. There's nothing we can do while he sleeps, and I have no doubt getting out of here for a while will make you feel better."

I hesitated. I knew Pete was waiting for my answer, and would go with whatever I felt comfortable with.

"Go on," Addy continued. "Really. I'll call you on your mobile if he wakes up, and you can come right back."

"Well, okay. I guess I can go. As long as you promise to call us if anything happens or the minute Nate wakes up."

"I promise."

"We'll just be gone for an hour or so. Two hours, tops. You don't think he'll be awake by then, do you?"

"No, I don't."

"Pete, is that okay with you?"

He nodded, rising out of his chair. Walking towards the door, I suddenly turned and asked, "Addy, when are you here until?"

"I'm here until seven o'clock. We've got lots of time." She smiled warmly and ushered us out the door.

When we got to our car, Pete sat on the driver's side but didn't turn on the car. "Ashley —" he began.

"It's okay," I said. "I know you thought it was the right thing, not to tell me. And I'm sorry my father put you in that situation to begin with. Honestly, it's such a typical thing for him to do . . . thinking only of himself and not the position it would put you in. Or how it would make me feel."

Pete bit his lip. I could tell he was refraining from saying something, but I didn't have the energy to pursue it.

"The only thing I don't understand is why you didn't see the connection between what you knew about my father and the signs we were starting to see in Nate." I was delicate with my words, careful to keep my voice calm and uncritical.

"I don't know," Pete answered honestly. "Looking back, I guess I should have. Especially when you were telling me every day that you were concerned about Nate's behaviour. But I never linked it to what your dad was going through. I never even knew kids could go through something like this. Mental illness is for adults, isn't it?"

"Apparently not," I said sadly.

"I'm so sorry, Ashley. I really thought Nate's hyper behaviour was because he's a kid. Kids get hyper and do weird stuff. It's just how it is. I didn't know. And you were so worried about it that I was completely focused on convincing you he was okay. I guess that, indirectly, I somehow also convinced myself."

"And what about the depression?"

"He's been through a lot. We all have. All the bullying that he's been through has made it tough even for you and me to deal with, and we're adults. I guess I just thought that he was acting miserable because he was sad about it. Just like we were."

I nodded. I had no energy to talk about it any further. "Look, Pete, I'm exhausted. We're both exhausted. And we have a huge mountain in front of us. Let's just move forward as a team. We need to do that. For Nate's sake."

"I know. I agree with you. But we also need to do it for *our* sake. I love you, Ash. And you need to know I'd never do anything to purposely hurt you or this family. You know that . . . right?"

I nodded, wanting him to stop talking. I loved him too, but I was so tired I could barely see straight or string a sentence together.

Pete leaned over to give me a kiss on the cheek before starting the car, but I pulled away. I had meant what I'd said about needing to be a team, but somehow couldn't be near him in that particular moment. It was all still too complicated for my exhausted brain to fully process. I needed a bit more time.

Pete pulled out of the hospital parking lot and started towards home. And as we drove through the familiar streets close to our neighbourhood, I relished the silence that was as awkward as it was peaceful.

40

When we got home, Pete put on a pot of coffee. I went upstairs to brush my teeth, anxious to rid myself of the pasty layer of grime that had formed throughout the long night.

I stepped into the shower and let the hot water pound onto my back. I turned it up, practically scalding my skin as a result. Then, a tiny bit hotter. The intensity of the heat felt good, forcing my mind to focus on something different than the fear and pain I couldn't otherwise shake.

When I couldn't take the heat any longer, I turned it down and let the spray from the shower hit my face. With no one to see me cry or judge my tears, I sobbed, ultimately giving into exhaustion and sitting on the floor of the shower. I curled up into a ball and wept.

After I couldn't take any more, I got out of the shower and wrapped myself in one of our thick, white towels. Puffy-eyed and sopping wet, I stared at myself in the mirror. The face that peered back at me was so different from the one I had seen last; there was a purple welt on my temple from where Nate had hit me, and my eyes were bloodshot from crying so much. I could barely even recognize the person I had become overnight. My face, swollen and red from the shower, looked almost distorted, and my eyes appeared haunted by fear.

Water from my shoulder-length blonde hair dripped onto my shoulders as I continued to stare at myself, feeling almost drunk. My bloated eyes were making things seem blurry, and I was so over-caffeinated and in need of food that I felt jittery and faint.

When I was finally able to peel myself out of my towel, I went to our walk-in closet and changed into comfy jeans and a warm turtleneck. I shuffled down the stairs and into our kitchen, to let Pete know he could have the shower.

I grabbed more coffee and sat at the kitchen table to call Tay. I needed to talk to her myself. To give her my own update, and see how Grace was doing.

"We're good, Ash. Don't worry about us. The kids are all getting along well, and we can be a big, happy family over here for as long as you need. Don't worry about us."

"Thanks. You have no idea how much I appreciate it."

"Grace has calmed down now that she knows Nate is safe. But she has a lot of questions. She keeps asking to see you. Do you think you'll be able to see her at some point soon?"

"I don't know. I want to, of course. And I'll call for sure. But I'm not sure I'll be able to see her today. They think Nate will wake up around dinner, so I want to be there by mid-afternoon at the latest. And she's in school until then." I felt guilty for not going to see Grace, but I couldn't leave Nate. I was being pulled by the opposite poles of my children.

"Do you think I could bring her to the hospital?"

"No. I don't want her there. Not yet, anyway. Nate hasn't woken up yet, and it's a bit of a scary place. I think it would be too much for her. She can't be there until I've figured out a way to let her know what's going on in a way that she will understand."

"Okay. So then what should I tell her?"

"Tell her I'll call her later on tonight. That I miss her and love her, but that I need to be with Nate right now."

"And what do you want me to say about Nate?"

"Just that he is sick, and he'll be okay, but he needs to stay in the hospital for a while so the doctors can monitor him and better understand what is going on with him."

"She's a clever kid, Ash. She's going to figure things out sooner than you realize. You need to think of a way to be more honest with her."

"I know."

We said goodbye, and I downed the rest of my coffee before grabbing my coat and heading to the car to wait for my husband. The toast Pete had put in front of me before going upstairs remained untouched. I wasn't hungry. And I couldn't stay in our kitchen any longer. Everywhere I looked I saw the police officers who had been there less than twenty-four hours earlier . . . where they had stood, where they had sat . . . and it instantly took me back to the fear that had flooded through me when Nate was missing and I thought there was a chance we might not see him again.

With Nate found, I just needed him to get better. To be healthy. Normal, and completely recovered.

But I didn't know when that would happen. Or if it even *could* happen. So despite the fact that Nate was no longer on the streets by himself, and was now lying safe in a hospital bed, I was still deathly afraid that we might not actually find my son.

41

Nate finally woke up the next day. He hadn't stirred for over twenty-four hours. Pete and I had both slept in the hospital room, a favour called in by Addy before leaving her shift. Family members weren't usually allowed to stay, but because Nate was so young, and still sleeping, the hospital had made an exception.

Just before seven a.m., Nate opened his eyes. The straitjacket had been removed long before, once the meds had knocked him out, and Nate began to shift in his bed, lifting his arms to touch his face.

"Nate? Baby? It's Mommy. I'm here. Daddy, too. We're here for you, sweetie. Are you . . . are you feeling alright?"

"Mommy? My throat. It hurts. I'm thir-thir-thirsty," Nate

croaked. Pete instantly left the room to get some ice chips. Addy had warned us that Nate's throat might be dry when he woke up, less from the meds and more from the dryness of the hospital.

Pete returned with a cup full of ice chips, and I helped feed them to Nate. He seemed perfectly normal, as though he weren't really sick and was just a bit weak from the flu. He tried to sit up, but lacked the energy he needed. Pete pressed the button to lift the bed.

"Look, champ. One of the coolest things about being in the hospital is the super-awesome bed. You can press a button and it helps sit you up," Pete said, continuing to press the button. I shot him a look and shook my head. I had no idea if we should be showing Nate things that he could "play with" while he was there. But then again, I didn't know what we should be saying or not saying.

"Hospital?" Nate asked. "What do you mean?"

"You're in the hospital, Bean. You gave us quite a scare last night. We couldn't find you for a while, but the nice police officers helped us find you, and we brought you to the hospital to make sure you are okay."

"I'm not at the hospital," Nate responded, matter-of-factly.

"Where do you think we are, honey?" I asked.

"We're at the zoo. In a holding tank. The zookeeper is making sure we're safe. All of us. You. Me. Daddy. Noah." Nate spoke slowly, as if trying to force out each word.

"Safe?" I asked.

"Yes. From the elephants. They want to kill us. They're mean. With huge teeth. And they growl, kind of like lions." Nate paused, looking exhausted. Neither Pete nor I knew what to say.

"Honey, Noah is not here. It's just Daddy and Mommy." I had no idea if I should be going along with what Nate was seeing or if I should tell him the truth.

"*Yes*, he is," Nate continued, appearing frustrated. "And the elephants are going to hurt him if he doesn't stay safe. And they want to hurt you, too, Mommy. That's why I had to find you. I had to find you in New York. Because the monsters were going to get you. To hurt you. Maybe even kill you."

"I . . . uh . . . I see. That's awful."

"Can't you hear that?" Nate asked in a groggy voice. I strained to hear, but there was nothing.

"On the radio? Can you hear it? They're talking about me. The zookeeper is being interviewed on the radio, and he's talking about *me*. On the radio! Can you hear it? Listen . . ." Nate seemed almost excited.

Pete and I paused, listening for the sake of our son.

More silence.

"See? He just said that I'm finally safe from the mean elephants! The ones that fly all around in the sky and want to kill us," Nate continued. He had a sudden burst of energy, and seemed frustrated that Pete and I couldn't seem to keep up or understand what he was saying.

"Okay . . . what else is he saying?" I glanced at Pete. For the time being, I decided to go along with Nate's delusions to try to avoid any agitated behaviour.

"That they're going to lock up the elephant monsters. To keep us safe. They're doing it all for us. Isn't that nice of them?" Nate's response was starting to slow, and he slinked further into his bed.

"Mommy? Can you pull the sheets up on me? I'm cold." Nate's eyes were beginning to close. I pulled the covers up over him, just as I had always done when he stayed home with the flu, and motioned for Pete to go and ask the nurse for an extra blanket.

"I'm glad you're safe, Mommy. I'm happy that you and Daddy and Noah are . . . here. That we're at the zoo . . . together . . ." Nate's voice trailed off as he went back to sleep. We were at the hospital, but my son was happy that we were at the zoo. He was so very sick.

I was tucking him in as best I could when Pete returned with a blanket. Following directly behind him was Addy, who had returned for another shift.

"So, our boy woke up, did he? That's great!" Addy said, greeting me with a smile. "How long was he up for? And did he just fall back to sleep?"

I nodded in response. "He was awake for about five minutes, but he was really groggy and then seemed to need to sleep again."

"That's perfectly normal. I suspect he'll be really sleepy for a while. Likely a few days."

I nodded, trying to muster the grit to admit, out loud, that my sweet and innocent boy was convinced monster elephants were about to kill us. And that we were in a zoo, seeking protection.

"He, uh, he's talking about flying elephant monsters still," I said through a wavering voice. "He . . . he thinks they're going to kill us."

Addy responded without missing a beat. "Was that what he was fixated on when he was going through the extreme psychosis?"

"Yes," Pete replied. "He talked about that a lot before he left the house. You know . . . when he went missing."

Addy nodded. "It's not a surprise he's still delusional and experiencing psychosis. Did the night-shift nurse tell you about Dr. Aldridge?"

I shook my head. The nurse who had replaced Addy through the night hadn't been anywhere near as good as our new favourite nurse. We'd barely talked to her when we'd returned to the hospital, and then we'd tried to get some sleep.

"Dr. Aldridge is a psychiatrist who specializes in mental illness in children. She came to check on Nate yesterday while you were gone."

"Oh! We missed her?" Guilt filled the pit of my stomach as

I realized I should have stayed at the hospital. I didn't need a shower. Or sleep. Or food. I just needed to be there for my son.

"It's okay, Ashley. Don't think for a second that you should have stayed here on the off chance that Dr. Aldridge visited Nate," Addy said warmly as if reading my mind. "She said she would be back today. She also ordered more Lorazepam in case his agitation persists. So when Nate wakes again, if he's still upset we'll give him some more. Pills this time, though. No more needles, unless he refuses the meds."

"More meds?" My mind was reeling. In the wild and rabid state of the ER the first night we had been there, there had been no time to discuss giving Nate a shot of Lorazepam. And he had clearly needed something. But the thought of starting down the path of an overly medicated boy made my stomach churn.

"We'll see how he is when he wakes up. One day at a time, right? And sometimes, one hour at a time." Addy smiled at us. "How are you both today? Ashley, are you feeling any better than you did yesterday?"

"Me? Oh, I'll be fine," I responded.

"Did you sleep much last night?"

"Not really. I appreciate being able to stay, but the chair wasn't the most comfortable sleep ever, and I've got a lot on my mind." I refrained from saying that it wasn't just the chair that had been uncomfortable. The all-night screaming from other hospital rooms had also kept me awake.

"And Pete? What about you?"

"I'll be okay." Pete's answer was short. Vague and imprecise.

"Okay, well I'll leave you two alone. Let me know if you need anything at all, and I'll be back to check on Nate in a bit."

Addy left the room, and I followed suit a few moments later. I headed to one of the courtesy rooms they reserved for private phone conversations. I picked up the receiver and dialed Tay's number.

"Hi," I said, when she answered the phone. "It's me."

"How's Nate?"

"Not great, to be honest. I don't really want to talk about it right now, though. I'm worried about Grace."

"Yeah, I know. She was pretty upset when she got off the phone with you last night," Tay responded gently. I knew she wanted to be honest with me about what was going on with my daughter, but was sensitive to doling out more worry when I was buried under the stress of what we were dealing with at the hospital.

The night before, I'd had a long conversation with Grace, and I'd stuck to the story that I'd asked Tay to tell her. But it hadn't gone well. Just as my always-knowing friend had predicted, Grace was unsatisfied with the explanation and desperate to know the whole truth. She was a bright girl, and accused me of knowing more, but I was adamant in my quest to protect both her and Nate.

"Grace, honey, I really want to be with you again too," I'd told her during our conversation. "But you're the big sister. And you need to be brave at Tay's house. For your brother's sake. You won't be there for long. I promise."

"You don't mean that. You don't love me! You aren't even *here* with me. You love Nate more than me. You don't even *care* about *me*," Grace had retorted back emphatically. While I normally dismissed my daughter's drama with annoyance, her words, at that moment, had broken my heart.

"Sweetie, just because I'm not with you doesn't mean I don't love you. I love you and Nate equally. Always. And absolutely the same amount. Even when we're not together. And I love *you*, Grace Marie Carter. Very, very much." I was pleading with a twelve-year-old to understand the situation, which was unfair given that even I couldn't grasp what was going on.

There was silence on the other end.

"Grace, I promise we'll be together as soon as possible. But, right now, Dad and I need to be at the hospital so they can find out why Nate is sick."

Again, no answer came from Grace.

"So can you be the big sister?" I asked her. "And be very brave? For your brother's sake?"

"Whatever."

"Grace, please . . . if not for your brother, then can you do it for me?"

"I *said*, whatever." Grace's clipped voice sounded wounded.

She'd dropped the phone quickly after that, saying she had to go do her word problem assignment. Always the bright girl who frequently used her cleverness to manipulate a situation, she'd deliberately chosen math as her exit strategy. She knew there was no way I'd refute the need to do homework.

"Ashley? Are you still there?" Tay asked. Her voice on the other end of the line snapped me back to the present. "I asked if there was anything I can bring you today."

"Oh, sorry. No thanks. We're good. We can grab food in the cafeteria. And I don't think they allow visitors outside of the family in here anyway." I had no idea if that was true or not. I felt terrible about lying to Tay but, more than that, I felt guilty for making up an excuse to keep her away because I was too embarrassed to let my lifelong, always-understanding best friend visit us in the psych ward where my son had been admitted.

The truth was that I didn't want Tay to see the place where the crazy lunatics stayed when they were too delusional to exist in society. The place where schizophrenics went when there was nowhere else for them to go. The place *my son* had to stay because it was where he belonged, so the doctors could help him get better. And to make him "normal" by the standards of the society we all live in.

The moral compass that I'd followed my entire life, which had always fostered the complete acceptance of everyone for who they were, was in disarray. Of course, there was no chance I'd not accept Nate for everything that made him *him*, including any demons that might have jumped into his brain because of a chemical imbalance that was as uncontrollable as the colour of one's skin. Or one's sexuality. Or being diagnosed with cancer.

But my pendulum was quickly swinging from the steadfast belief in a fused world of unique human beings to the side that flourished in the comfort of segregation and protection. When it was a minority person outside my family who needed acceptance and inclusion, I never stopped short in taking every measure possible to help them feel comfortable. Yet what I hadn't stopped to realize before was the raw fear and overwhelming anxiety felt by a person when it is their turn to be integrated into "normal" society. I had in no way begun to realize the truth behind what it would feel like to be *the one* — or the mother of *the one* — who needed to suddenly blend in with our not-yet-fixed prejudiced world of cruelty and bigotry.

I had been unaware of all of this. And as I tried to temper my overwhelming need to isolate my son and protect him from others, I realized there was nothing blissful about my ignorance.

42

Throughout the rest of the morning, Nate had stirred and woken a few times, but had always been groggy and would quickly fall back to sleep. While he remained fixated on being at the zoo with Pete, Noah, and me, he wasn't overly agitated, and we were able to hold off on giving him any more Lorazepam.

Shortly after lunch, Dr. Aldridge walked into the room. She brought with her a positive energy that filled the room, and she offered Pete and me a warm smile as she introduced herself and shook our hands. I could see why Addy had said everyone loved her.

"I hear you've had a rough couple of days," Dr. Aldridge sympathized. "Pretty scary too, I imagine."

"Yeah, it's been tough. But thank God we found Nate and he was okay."

"Indeed. He's a very lucky little boy. And he's in good hands now. Addy's one of our best nurses, and I can tell that she already cares a great deal about your son. I just spoke with her and she updated me on how Nate has been since I saw him yesterday."

Beside us Nate stirred, thrashing his head from side to side, as if to warn us that he'd soon wake up. Dr. Aldridge cleared her throat. "It's not surprising that your son is still delusional and talking about monsters. We know there's something going on in his brain that's causing him to experience the psychosis that's making him say those things. You have to remember that, in his mind, the elephants really exist, and he can see them all around him. It would be a very scary thing for a nine-year-old. So we're going to work hard to figure out what's going on, and provide him with the best treatment possible to make him well."

"Will he need more meds?" I asked.

"Likely," Dr. Aldridge replied. Her answers were honest and direct, which I appreciated. "But let's not get ahead of ourselves just yet. What we need to do first is figure out what's causing the psychosis."

"Wouldn't it be bipolar disorder?" I asked. "Do you know that my father has it too?"

"Yes. I saw that in Nate's chart. I can see why you would say that, given bipolar disorder is genetic. And it could very well be what's causing Nate's psychosis. But first we need to rule out everything else."

"So it's psychosis that Nate is having at this point? That's how we refer to all of this?"

Dr. Aldridge nodded as she glanced in Nate's direction and observed how he was stirring in his sleep.

"What causes it?" Pete asked.

"To be honest, it isn't fully understood. It can definitely be caused by a mental illness, such as bipolar disorder. But there are other contributing factors as well. A stressful event may trigger a psychotic episode, for example. Or psychosis can be brought on by drugs like marijuana or LSD, although I don't suspect this in the case of Nate simply because of his age. It could also be brought on by another medical condition. There are many causes."

"Does it happen to a lot of people?" I asked. I felt myself holding my breath, hoping that Dr. Aldridge would tell me it happened all the time. My misery needed company.

"More than you might think. About three in one hundred people will experience a psychotic episode at one point in their life. Some will have only a few episodes, or it could be one episode lasting just a few days or weeks. Others will experience symptoms more frequently, and some will have the condition for life."

"So Nate could be okay? This could be a fluke?" I asked, praying for Dr. Aldridge to say this could all just go away.

"It's a very small possibility. But with a family history of mental illness, we need to be certain of what's going on."

"So what should we do now?" I asked.

"Unfortunately, there is no specific test for psychosis. It's more a matter of recognizing the behavioural and thought disorder patterns to make the diagnosis," Dr. Aldridge explained. "I'd like to do a full physical examination on Nate, including a thorough history evaluation and blood tests. Based on what we find, further diagnostic tests may be warranted."

"What kind of history evaluation? We can begin pulling the information you need if it will help."

"We'll need to know his full family history, as well as a complete medical overview. Things like recent or past head trauma, and possible neurological symptoms like headache patterns or visual disturbance. I'd also like to know about any previous medications Nate has taken. Really, I need to know everything about your son. I'd even like to know about his dietary history, and how Nate eats on a regular basis."

Pete and I both nodded, and I grabbed a pen and pad of paper from my bag to start taking notes. I was already struggling to keep up.

"What kind of blood tests will you do?" I asked.

"The initial tests will focus on the most common organic causes. We'll do a CBC, or a complete blood count, in order to measure the concentration of Nate's white blood cells, red blood cells, and platelets. I'm going to order a liver function test to measure his liver enzymes, and also look into Nate's thyroid function. The blood tests will cover a lot, actually. Right down to things like Nate's vitamin B_{12} and folate levels so we can exclude nutritional deficiency."

"Okay, just give me one sec." I scribbled on my pad of paper at arm-numbing speed.

"It's great to write things down. I always encourage the parents of my patients to do so. I know all of this can be very overwhelming," Dr. Aldridge said. "But don't worry if you don't capture everything. We're here to help you with whatever you need. I can answer any questions you might have, and Addy is always here to help explain things again, if needed."

I put my pen down and searched Dr. Aldridge's eyes. She was so genuine and kind in her approach, and I instantly trusted her. "Is my son going to be okay?" I asked.

"Mrs. Carter, we're going to do everything possible for Nate. We're going to work hard to find out what's going on, and then we'll work together to give him the best possible treatment."

It was a vague answer that I'd heard far too often on TV shows and movies. Dr. Aldridge's direct answers had flown the way of the cuckoo bird when I'd asked for her to look into a crystal ball, but I knew she was just being honest with me. Of course she couldn't predict the future. No one knew if Nate was going to be okay: we had no idea what was wrong with him.

All we could do was take every step that was needed to try to figure out what was wrong with him, and then work towards making him better.

Dr. Aldridge continued, "Once we've ruled out all organic causes, I'll begin to do a psychiatric assessment on Nate. We'll all need to work together on this, including Nate. It's one day at a time around here." Dr. Aldridge tucked a strand of dark hair behind her ear and gave us a big smile. "Now, if you'll excuse me, I have a few other patients to see. Do you have any other questions for me before I go?"

"Is this psychosis . . . is it normal to happen to someone so young?" Pete asked.

"It's unusual to see psychosis in someone as young as Nate. And it's often a bit trickier than dealing with adults. The fantasy lives of children, and issues of developing language and cognition, impair diagnostic accuracy. Particularly when differentiating between something like bipolar disorder and other mental illnesses, such as schizophrenia. Which we can't rule out either."

Schizophrenia. I shuddered at the mere mention of it.

"But it does happen to children as young as Nate?" Pete probed again. He was fixated on Nate's age, and I couldn't help but wonder if he was fishing for an answer to support his previous denial of anything being wrong with our son. I needed Pete to wholeheartedly support me in our quest to identify what was really going on.

"Yes, it can. It happens at all different ages, although diagnosis typically happens in the late teens or early twenties."

"So Nate is really young for this?"

"Yes, he is, Mr. Carter. But he *is* experiencing psychosis for some reason. And we know there *is* something going on with your son. Nate's actions are not normal. I know it's all very scary, particularly given Nate's young age, but finding out what's going on as soon as possible is a good thing. Because it means we can help him sooner. I've seen what happens when a child's mental illness is not treated: every part of their life suffers, including relationships, school functioning, extracurricular activities, and so on. Early treatment with proper medication and therapy will help Nate become a fully functioning, stable kid. It means the difference between a balanced, healthy life and one that is so out of whack it becomes all-consuming and prevents them from being successful in all walks of life."

I nodded, taking in what the doctor was saying. She made a good point, and I felt better speaking with her. I knew Nate was in good hands.

Once Dr. Aldridge left, Pete and I sat in silence, lost in thought as we watched our sleeping son. Eventually, I forced myself to take advantage of the calm before the storm by responding to some emails, including Jack's from the day before. I told him that I'd be available when possible via email and conference calls, but that I didn't know when I'd be back in the office. I had no idea how he would respond, but I had no choice in taking a physical leave of absence.

I was just hitting send on Jack's email when Nate started shuffling anxiously in bed, jolting from his sleeping position and screaming wildly. He thrashed from side to side, crying out in what seemed like pain, and spitting through his wailing words that the elephants were trying to kill him.

I froze in my seat. Pete jumped up and tried to hold Nate down, for fear that he might hurt himself. Or us.

"Go get the doctor!" Pete gasped right before Nate elbowed him in the face. I knew instantly he'd have black eye.

I jumped up and pulled the buzzer to call the nurses' station, but Addy had already seen what was going on through the window. She rushed in and was immediately followed by a medical and security team who shouted at us to step away from our son before they jumped directly into the chaos of thrashing arms and legs.

Our nightmare had started up again, and I watched in terror, crying into Pete's shoulder and praying for it to all go away.

And it did, moments after the next shot of Lorazepam was plunged deep into our son's leg.

43

Our drugged-up son slept through all of Dr. Aldridge's medical tests. His blood was drawn by Addy on multiple occasions, and he didn't even flinch. I doubted that he even felt it.

An on-call doctor whom we hadn't previously met came to listen to Nate's heart and lungs. He examined his abdomen and did as much of a physical assessment as he could to a sleeping body.

A psychologist named Isa, who worked closely with Dr. Aldridge, came and interviewed us about every aspect of Nate's life. We talked directly in front of our son about everything the doctors needed to know, including his history of odd behaviour. How he'd run away on more than one occasion. How Nate had started doing weird things, like stealing. Or how obsessed he often became with random things, like gum. We told Isa about Nate's sleep patterns, and we explained how, on so many nights, our son refused to go to sleep. How we always found him up in his room doing strange things. Nate didn't hear a word.

Dr. Aldridge came to Nate's room to ask Pete about my father's condition, and my husband revealed everything he knew, including the name of the Florida doctor to whom he had talked at the beginning.

We talked about all the bullying and everything we'd been through as a result. We told her about all of the times Nate had been sad, and we rated his moods on a scale of one to ten, trying to distinguish between gloomy and depressed. I tried to recount what I could, but everything seemed to be blurring together.

We told Addy about what Nate liked for dinner, and what he refused to eat. What his favourite sports were. What happened the time he had an anxiety attack in the hospital. The questions were exhausting and never-ending. No aspect about our son's life was left uncovered.

A few hours later, the blood test results came in, and Dr. Aldridge came to discuss the findings. Everything appeared to be normal, right down to Nate being properly nourished.

"So what do we do next?" I asked Dr. Aldridge as I took Pete's hand under the table. We were sitting in one of the quiet courtesy rooms.

"I'd like to start giving Nate a low dose of a drug called Risperidone. It's an atypical antipsychotic that has proven to be effective, and I believe it will help Nate begin to think clearly and function normally again. Essentially it will help restore the balance of certain natural substances in his brain."

"Does he really need it?" I asked.

"Yes, I believe he does. It will help to stop the mania and delusions he's having, and will allow me to really speak with him, so we can continue investigating what's going on with him and begin to move forward."

"But might this just be the start? If it doesn't work, or if Nate has side effects, then we need to move onto different drugs? Or stronger drugs?" As a mother who subscribed to her fair share of parenting magazines, I'd read the articles on overly medicated children, and was petrified of getting into a vicious cycle of drugs that we couldn't get out of. There were so many horror stories.

"You're right. Finding the right medication does take a certain amount of trial and error. And this might not be the right drug for Nate. But it's what I believe we should start with." Dr. Aldridge's eyes were warm and compassionate, and her voice was clear and firm.

"What are the side effects?" Pete asked. I looked at my husband and noticed for the first time how tired he looked. His eyes were bloodshot and puffy, and his right eye was turning black and swollen thanks to Nate's elbow. "Can you tell us, honestly, what we're in for if we give our son this drug?"

"Yes. Of course. I want you to make an informed decision," Dr. Aldridge responded, "The main problem with Risperidone is that it commonly causes weight gain. It can also lead to hand tremors and restlessness."

"Is that it? Is there anything else?" As Pete listened to the doctor, he pulled at the stubble that had begun to form on his jawline.

"There's more. Sometimes dizziness, drowsiness, fatigue, muscle stiffness, nausea, constipation, increased appetite, which is often what contributes to the weight gain. Dry skin, nervousness. Sometimes it leads to difficulty concentrating . . ." Dr. Aldridge's voice trailed off, and she paused before continuing, "I know it's a big decision. And all of this is very overwhelming. I've brought you some things you can read, if you're interested. It covers a lot of ground, and if there's anything else you're wondering about, I'm always here to talk."

"Would you do it?" I asked, cutting her off. "If it were your son. Your child. Would you give them the drug you're recommending?"

"Yes, if I were in your situation, I would," Dr. Aldridge said simply. "I know the risk of side effects is scary. And no one would ever want any of them for their child, including me. But I'm prescribing this medication for Nate because I believe the benefit of Risperidone is greater than the risk of the side effects."

I nodded, picking up the jam-packed, glossy brochure from the table. What she was saying made sense to me. Given our current state, we needed to pick the best bad solution. A plan that offered a likelihood of benefits that outweighed the risk of harm.

"What do you think?" I asked, turning to my husband, who was now leaning onto the table and burying his forehead in his hands. He suddenly seemed smaller to me. Almost like he had been crumpled by a life that had quickly become too complicated.

Pete looked into my eyes. When he did, I lost sight of the bloodshot puffiness of an overly tired man who had been hit in the face by his son, and simply found truth. "I want to do what's best for Nate. If Dr. Aldridge believes that it is Risperidone, then that's what I think we should give him."

I nodded. "Okay, then. Let's do what you feel is best, Dr. Aldridge. Let's give him the drugs you've recommended."

Dr. Aldridge explained she would begin working with Nate as soon as the Risperidone started to kick in and he was thinking more clearly. He needed to be able to carry on a conversation. She wanted to talk to him about all he had experienced and felt over the past few months. She'd exhausted our side of the story, but it was really his version that was more important.

"How long do you think it will be before we see an improvement?" I asked.

"It might take up to six weeks to see the full effect, but he could start feeling a lot better much sooner than that. As soon as he can carry on a conversation with me, I'll begin to work with him."

"Six *weeks*?!" I cried. I felt like I'd been kicked in the gut.

"Yes, it could be six weeks. But it could be much sooner than that as well."

Six weeks would take us to Christmas. We couldn't wait that long for Nate to get better. And I couldn't be away from work for that long either.

"Six weeks," I repeated. "Is there anything faster?"

"This isn't a race, Ashley. It's about doing what's right for Nate. I know six weeks seems like a long time, but it might not take that long to kick in. We might begin to see significant progress right away. And I'll be working with Nate throughout the six weeks, regardless."

"Dr. Aldridge is right, Ash. And six weeks is nothing in the realm of his lifetime."

I sighed. I knew they were right. But wasn't medicine supposed to be a quick fix? Like Tylenol to a headache? Or Gravol to an upset stomach?

"Will Nate need to be here the entire time? When can he go home? And what about school?"

"It will depend on how Nate responds to the drugs. If he's not agitated or dangerous or experiencing minimal psychosis, there's no reason he can't go home and come to the hospital to meet with me."

"And school?"

"That, too, will depend. Let's try not to get ahead of ourselves, okay? In the meantime, why don't you begin talking to Nate's teacher about what she'll be covering over the next few weeks? When the time is right you can begin to introduce school back into his life, whether that's at home or back in the classroom."

I nodded, tears springing to my eyes as thoughts of Nate falling behind in school entered my mind. I tried to stop my racing thoughts of what that might mean, and if he might need to repeat a year.

"Try to not to worry about it, Ashley," Dr. Aldridge said. "Based on what we've learned about Nate so far, it seems like he's a really clever kid and will be able to catch up quickly."

"I know. You're right."

"Of course I'm right. I'm a psychiatrist!" Dr. Aldridge laughed. I smiled in response, thinking that, although her light-hearted words were meant to be a joke, they were actually rooted in something extremely serious.

Dr. Aldridge *had* to be right. Because it wasn't just our son's education that depended on it but also his overall mental wellness.

And the rest of his life.

44
Nate

My legs hurt. Something is on them and I cannot move them. I try to lift one. It moves a little bit but not that much. So I try again. It moves a bit more. But it feels really heavy.

I open my eyes. Just a little at first. Then more. No one is with me. I am in a room by myself. But I can hear the elephant monsters screaming somewhere near me. They want to kill me. I am scared.

At least I know I am safe. It makes me feel better to be locked up in this room at the zoo so the elephants can't reach me. Even though they are so loud outside my room and they are very scary.

"Nate? Oh, baby. You're awake!" Mommy says. She runs through the door with Daddy. They run over to my bed.

"Mommy! Daddy! Don't go out there. Please! The monsters will KILL YOU! I DON'T WANT YOU TO DIE!" I scream. I start to cry. Just a little bit at first because I am trying to be brave. But then I start crying harder because I am so scared the monsters will eat my mommy and daddy. I do not want them to die.

"Champ, it's okay. Mommy and Daddy are safe," Dad says. He holds my shoulders with both of his arms and looks at me in the eye. "We were just with Dr. Aldridge for a while, and we're sorry we weren't here when you woke up."

"Are you feeling okay?" Mommy asks me.

I shake my head. I feel sick. Like I'm going to puke.

"Maybe you're hungry. There's some food for you here, if you want some?" Mommy stops holding my hand and walks to a table to get a tray. There is food on it. A sandwich. An orange. Something that looks like a yogurt. And apple juice.

"What would you like to eat, bud?" Dad asks me.

I stare at them. Don't they know the food is made with poison? I can't eat food that has been poisoned. That would be stupid.

"Would you like a sandwich?" Mommy asks me. She really wants me to eat so she must not know about the poison but if I tell her she will die. I can't remember why she will die if she knows but I know she will. I try to remember what will make her die but everything is so foggy in my brain. It feels like marshmallows. And it hurts. It hurts really bad.

"I'm not hungry."

"You need to eat something, Bean."

I shake my head. It hurts more.

"How about the apple juice then?"

I don't want apple juice. Or anything to eat. I feel like I'm going to puke.

I take the apple juice and throw it against the wall. That will teach them for trying to make me drink poison.

At first Dad looks like he is going to get mad at me. But then he just looks sad. He leaves the room and comes back right away with towels. He cleans up the mess on the floor. He still looks sad.

"How about some ice chips? Or water?" Mommy asks me.

"No."

"Do you want anything at all? Maybe I could go get you a cookie from the cafeteria?"

"No."

"I know . . . ice cream?"

I shake my head again. I do not want anything. I don't know what cafeteria she is talking about but I know there is poison there too.

"Maybe later, hon . . ." Daddy says to Mommy. He is talking softly to her. I watch him rub her back.

"Do you hear that?" I ask. "The radio. It's the radio again! The zoo has turned it back on. They're talking to me. They are telling me not to eat. And you should know why . . ."

"Why honey?" Mommy asks me.

"Because of the poi —"

Stop.

I can't tell her or she will die. I shut my mouth tight. I bite my lips so I cannot speak anymore.

"Why don't we talk about food later?" Dad asks. And I know he knows. *He* knows about the poison. "Let's get you up. You've been in bed a long time, champ. Might be good to walk a bit."

"WE CAN'T GO OUTSIDE! THE MONSTERS ARE OUT THERE AND ARE WAITING TO KILL US!" I scream. Why can't they learn? Why won't they listen to me? I throw my fists into the air but Dad steps back and I do not punch him. I'm glad he stepped back. I do not actually want to hurt Dad.

"Okay . . . it's okay, Bean. We won't go outside," Mommy says. "Can we walk around this room? Is that okay?"

I look at her and think about the question. I wonder if it's okay.

"Shhh," I say. *"Shhh! Beee quiet!"* I listen for the man on the radio to start talking. For him to tell me whether or not I can walk around the room.

The room fills with silence.

"Nate?" Mommy asks me after a few minutes.

"I said *shhh*." I try to kick my feet but they still feel heavy. I kick harder and my mommy steps away. She is finally quiet.

We keep waiting in silence. I do not know for how long.

We wait.

We wait.

Then, suddenly, the man's voice is back. He is talking over the radio, and says to me, *"Nate. Good boy for not eating the poisoned food. You are very smart. Stay away from the food. You will die if you eat it."*

"Did you *hear* that?" I ask Mommy. I start crying. I'm so scared because I think she heard the man on the radio. Because then she will know about the poison. And she will die.

Mommy shakes her head to tell me no.

"Oh *thank you*!" I shout. My voice is very loud. Even for me. But I am so glad. I am glad my mommy will not die.

"Nate?" The radio voice continues. *"You can walk around. Start now."*

I turn to look at Dad and tell him that I can walk around the room. It is safe.

Dad helps me get out of bed. I turn and hang my feet over the side. I feel really weak all of a sudden, but the man on the radio told me to walk around the room, so I have to. Dad lifts me off the bed and my bare feet touch the floor. It is really cold. Smooth.

I wiggle my toes to try to warm them up. I take a step. Then another. Daddy is holding one hand and Mommy is holding the other.

I feel woozy.

Wobbly.

Scared.

"You okay, bud?" Dad asks me.

I say yes, even though I'm not. Even though I feel so funny in my brain.

Dad lets go of my hand for one minute. I think he wants me to try myself. But that is when I fall down. Mommy tries to hold me up on her own but she must not be strong enough. Because all of a sudden I'm on the cold, smooth floor. I think my shoulder must have hit first because now it is hurting. I wince at the sharp pain.

Dad scoops me up and puts me back into bed. "Maybe we'll try again later, champ."

"He needs to eat," Mommy says, looking at Daddy. "He needs energy."

But I won't eat.

I don't want to die.

45
Ashley

I glanced down at the glowing clock on the car dashboard. Three fourteen. The school bell would ring in one minute, and Grace would likely be out somewhere between ten and twenty minutes after that, depending on how talkative she was at her locker.

I sighed and picked up my iPhone. I was taking Grace for a mother-daughter afternoon so we could spend time together. Given the number of hours I'd spent at the hospital over the past week, I knew she needed some alone time with me.

I scanned through my waiting emails to answer the most important ones. I always responded to Jack, as well as any others I felt were time-critical, including the urgent ones from Ben. Just as he'd promised, my associate creative director was only looping me in when absolutely needed, and I owed him the courtesy of replying to anything he felt was important.

"Huh, would you look at that. Only about a hundred today . . ." I murmured out loud. Despite the fact that I hadn't set foot in the office in over a week, my emails hadn't slowed down. I tried to wade through them on a daily basis, but felt the most stress in my day when I did. Things were happening at the office at lightning speed, and it was tough to keep up over email and phone.

I opened the last email from Jack, which had been sent twenty minutes earlier, and squeezed my eyes shut after I read it. He wanted to know when I would be back in the office, and was practically demanding that I tell him what was going on. I'd manage to skirt the issue over the past week, but my boss was growing less patient by the day and I knew it was only a matter of time before I would need a new plan.

I hit reply and told Jack that Nate was doing better, but he wasn't fully recovered and the hospital was still doing tests. I thanked him for his patience and understanding given the very difficult medical issue my family was going through, and told him I'd try to pop by the following morning to touch base in person.

I'd bought myself twenty-four hours to figure out what to do.

Almost instantly, Jack replied, saying he was in New York until the weekend, adding that he had needed to go because I wasn't there to go myself. Jack suggested Monday morning for our face-to-face meeting instead.

Perfect. Jack's trip bought me more time. And if Nate wasn't well enough for me to go in the following week, I'd call Jack and ask for more time. I was doing the best I could, trying to balance being there for my very sick son while managing a creative team of thirty from afar. In order for me to achieve the balance of two things that were as massive as that, it had to be on my terms. And on my schedule. If Jack couldn't understand that, then he could screw himself — and find another creative director to run his show.

Feeling better after my internal rant and rationalization, I responded quickly to the other emails that needed my attention. Less than ten minutes after the bell rang, Grace came skipping outside and climbed into the front seat.

"Well, that was fast!" I said, turning to give my daughter a big smile. "I'd say it was your quickest exit from school yet."

"Yeah, well I want to get my new shirts! I'm thinking we start at Aritzia, and then maybe hit up Forever 21, Hollister, H&M. Oh, and we *can't* forget Lululemon either. And maybe Abercrombie, too . . ."

"Hold on, Grace. I said you could get *one* new shirt. From *one* store," I replied, putting my arm around her seat to reverse the car.

"Yeah, yeah. I know. But we can still just shop at the others."

"Okay. That part sounds good. But remember: *one shirt*," I said, and laughed. "How was school?"

Grace quickly responded with all of the latest news, and my mind raced to keep up with all of the quickly changing, ongoing sagas of her almost-teenage group of friends. By the time we reached the mall, I was exhausted.

"So, Holts first?" Grace asked, switching gears from her talk about her friends.

"Sure. Whatever you'd like, sweetie." I pulled the car into a parking spot, and we got out to start our shopping.

Grace found her "perfect shirt" within five minutes of being at the mall, and begged to get it despite my continued warnings of her not being able to get another one.

Oddly enough, Grace stayed true to her promise of not asking for a second shirt, and we had a fun afternoon together laughing and chatting our way through her favourite stores. It was the most normal I'd felt in over a week.

As we snuggled into a cozy booth at dinner that night, Grace ordered her favourite spaghetti and meatballs and I decided to try the angel hair primavera.

"So how have you been, honey?" I asked Grace as she slurped her Coke. She shrugged in response.

"Is there anything you want to talk about?"

"I told you everything in the car."

"No, you told me all about your friends. And what's happening at school. And I loved hearing all about it. But I want to talk to you. I want to know how *you* are doing."

"I don't know," she responded, shrugging her shoulders again. I watched my daughter squirm in her seat as she waited for the next question. From behind me, the waitress appeared and set down some bread and olive oil. Grace immediately picked up a hunk of bread, tore it in two, and smeared them one at a time through a plate of city-famous olive oil.

"Mmm . . ." she said, chomping up the bread.

"Grace! Chew with your mouth closed, please."

"Whatever," Grace replied through an open mouth of food. She rolled her eyes.

"Pardon me?" I asked. My daughter was a lot of things, but she was rarely rude to me.

"I *said* whatever. Geez. Chill out, would you?"

"Grace Carter. You need to think long and hard before you say one more cheeky word to me," I said firmly. I watched her eat the bread. She had closed her mouth, but her eyes weren't leaving the table. And when her tears hit the plate sitting in front of her, my heart broke.

"Oh, Grace . . . honey, I'm sorry," I said, scooting out of my seat and switching sides of the table so I could sit beside her. "I had so much fun with you today, and I don't want to ruin a wonderful dinner with my only daughter. Let's start again, okay?"

Grace shrugged and wiped away the tears that were falling more quickly.

"Sweetie . . . honey, tell me what's wrong." I brought her in close to give her a hug. She suddenly seemed like she was about four years old again, when she had been small and quiet, and innocent to all of the world's hardships.

"I . . . I want to . . ." she sputtered as she tried to find the right words. "I . . . I'm scared. And I want to know what's wrong with Nate. I miss him. And I miss *you*!"

"I know, honey. And I miss you too," I replied, pulling her in for a hug. She was crying openly now, and it dawned on me that I couldn't remember the last time she had cried in front of me. Especially in public.

"When are you going to come home? And when is Nate going to come home so we can be a family again?" Grace asked, weeping into my shoulder. I hadn't slept one night at home since Nate was admitted into the hospital, but Pete and I had decided that he would return home to try to provide as much normalcy for Grace as possible. I thought that Grace sleeping in her own bed would help her, but it was clear that she desperately wanted Nate and me to return home as well.

"I'm not sure when we'll be able to come home, honey," I replied honestly. "But I know I won't be away forever. And I bet it will go by faster than you think."

"But Mommy . . . what's *wrong* with Nate?" My heart leapt hearing her say "Mommy." Nate still called me that, but Grace hadn't in many years. "Why can't I even see him? And why won't you tell me what's wrong with him? I know you know. Moms *always* know."

I took a deep breath. I knew there was no more hiding what was going on with Nate. Pete and I had talked endlessly about what we should say to Grace. About when we should tell her, and if we should talk all together or one-on-one. But we hadn't gotten past talking about how to have the conversations. We hadn't made any decisions.

Dr. Aldridge had recommended that we be honest and direct, in an age-appropriate way. And she had also cautioned us to be very mindful of what a big change it would be for Grace. She stressed that finding out about a sibling with a mental illness could be as life-changing as being diagnosed with the disease.

In the therapy sessions that Pete and I had started with Dr. Aldridge, she had been determined to focus on the entire family and not just Nate. She explained that quite often parents spend so much time thinking of the child who is ill that they often neglect to see that the disorder creates other, quiet victims. That the child's siblings hurt too but don't want to complain or make things any worse for their parents. So they often get ignored.

"Sweetie, Nate's sick."

"I know that part. How is he sick?"

"We really don't know yet. That's the honest truth. And we're doing a lot of testing to find out."

Grace dismissed my answer by rolling her eyes and letting out an infuriated sigh. Her arms remained tightly crossed against her body, and she refused to look at me.

I waited, knowing that a bit of silence often worked well when trying to get Grace to open up about something she was upset about.

When her eyes finally met mine, I was hit with a well-known glimpse of saddened aggravation. It was a look I'd never forget. In the moment my daughter's eyes met mine, she looked exactly like my father. And it took my breath away. I was flooded with emotions that hadn't visited me in many years yet at the same time had never left and were still very much a part of me.

The moment passed quickly, and Grace returned to her normal self. "Mom? Come on. I'm not a kid anymore."

She was right. I was skirting the issue. Again. My stomach was in knots at the thought of another one of my children hurting. The time had come. There was no more avoiding the truth. I got out of the booth and returned to my side of the table, where I could look directly at her. I reached out for her hand, and she gave it to me.

"Do you remember when you got sick a few years ago with scarlet fever?" I asked Grace.

"Does Nate have scarlet fever?"

"No, honey. He doesn't. But you know how you had a whole bunch of symptoms, so we took you to the hospital because we didn't know what was wrong with you?" I asked Grace. She looked slightly puzzled, so I kept going. "You had a really sore throat, and a funny red rash all over your neck and chest. Remember?"

"Oh right! And my stomach hurt. But not as much as my throat. I couldn't even swallow."

"That's right. So we took you to the hospital. And the doctors did a lot of tests, and told us you had something called scarlet fever. But we didn't know right away. We had to wait for your test results before we knew for sure."

"So what kind of things are wrong with Nate?"

"Well, uh, he's acting unlike himself. He's saying a few things that he doesn't normally say, for example."

Grace gave me a funny look. I knew I was botching it, but I had no idea how to begin to tell a twelve-year-old about mental illness. How was she expected to grasp the concept when even grown adults couldn't?

"When you had scarlet fever, there was something wrong with your throat. And you took the right medicine to make it better." I took a big breath. "In Nate's case, there is something that's not quite right in his brain. There's an illness there right now, just like there was an illness in your throat. And we're working very closely with the doctors to figure out exactly what is wrong, so that we can give him the right medicine and make him better."

"Does anything hurt him? You know . . . like his throat or something?"

"No, I don't think so. He feels a bit nauseated right now, and tired too, but other than that he's okay. He just says some funny things sometimes, because his brain isn't working properly. Just like your throat wasn't working properly."

"Oh. Okay. Well, is that it? You're telling me everything you know?" Grace asked.

"Yes. I'm telling you everything I know." I watched relief pass through my daughter's face. It was like seeing a physical weight being lifted from her shoulders.

"You mean he's not going to die?" Grace asked.

"No, sweetie. Not at all! Why would you think that?"

"Well, you couldn't find him when he was out on the streets by himself. And everyone thought he was going to die then, so . . ."

"Who told you that?"

"Julia. When I slept in her room. That first night at Tay's house."

My heart lurched, and I outwardly shuddered at the thought of my daughter being alone with Julia, thinking her brother was going to die.

"And then you found him. And that was good," Grace continued. "But everyone at school is talking about how sick he is and that he will probably still die anyway."

"They *are*?" I said, more to myself than to Grace. "Why would they say that?"

"I don't know. But that's what they're saying."

I scolded myself internally for not being more open with Grace sooner. With all that was going on with Nate, I hadn't even stopped to consider the fact that she had been left to believe the poorly drawn, gossipy conclusions that she was hearing. I hadn't even realized other kids at school knew about it, much less talked about it.

"Well, I assure you, it isn't true. Nate isn't well right now, but we've started giving him medicine that we think is going to help him get better."

"I'm glad he's going to be okay. And I'm glad you told me."

At that moment, the waitress set down our dinners in front

of us. She sprinkled extra cheese on Grace's pasta and pepper on mine. The big smile returned to Grace's face.

Once the waitress had left, we dug into our dinners. Grace was quiet for a moment, chewing thoughtfully. I wondered what was going on in her head.

"Mom?" she asked once she'd had a few bites. "I have one more question."

"Okay, honey. Anything you want." I braced myself.

"When can I see him?"

It was the only question I wasn't prepared to answer. Over the past week, Nate had slowly started to show signs of improvement. He was eating again, and far less agitated than he had been. The doctors had even moved him to the regular psych ward, which was less intense than the Psychiatric ICU where he'd been for the first few days.

But the medication hadn't fully kicked in, and he was still paranoid and delusional. There was no more talk of monsters or the radio, but Nate still said things that clearly demonstrated he wasn't thinking clearly.

After hearing what Grace had been thinking and feeling over the past week, I had no idea if seeing him might make things easier for her or more difficult. The whole ordeal with Nate had handed me the most complicated parenting uncertainty I'd ever experienced. I had no idea which answer was best.

"Mom? Did you hear me? I asked you when I can see Nate. I want to go and see him . . . and I know just who we can bring with us. You know, to make him feel better."

I looked my daughter straight in the eyes.

"Okay, Grace. We'll go tomorrow."

46
Nate

I'm bored. I'm sick of this room. I feel like I've been in it forever.

Dad is with me. He's sitting beside my bed and reading a magazine. He brought some stuff for me too. I guess that was nice of him, but I don't feel like doing anything. I'm too tired. And I'm tired of being tired. I'm so sleepy all of the time. Even right when I wake up.

And I feel sick, too. Like I have the flu and am going to puke, but I never do. And it won't go away. I feel like I've been sick for days.

"Hey champ," Dad says. "Why don't you read one of the comic books I brought you? How about that new superhero one I found?"

I shrug. I don't feel like it.

"Here," Dad says. He stands up and hands me the maga-zine. I take it and open it to the first page. It is a story about Spider-Man. I start reading. I can't believe it! The story is about *me*! Spider-Man is talking to *me* in the story! No wonder Dad wanted me to read it so much. He knew the story was about me.

I look over the comic book and give Dad a big thumbs up. He smiles at me and I laugh back. I love this book!

I start reading again, and Spider-Man is telling me that everything will be okay. That it is good I am eating my food again. It is no longer poisonous. But Spider-Man is telling me to be careful of the nurse wearing navy blue.

"That nurse. The one wearing navy blue. She'll hurt you if you're ever alone with her. She will kill you," Spider-Man says to me in the bubble above his cartoon head. "Do not ever be left alone with her. Or you will die. And I will not be able to save you."

My feet start to feel prickly because I'm so scared. I put the comic book down on my chest and look quickly around the room for a nurse wearing navy blue. I look everywhere I can, but can't see inside the bathroom. She could be in there, so I get out of bed and walk quickly to the door. I'm scared, but I force myself to look inside.

No one is there.

"What are you doing, bud? Do you have to go to the bath-room?" Dad calls out.

"No. I'm just checking for something."

"Checking for what?" Dad asks me. He's behind me. I lift up the toilet seat to see if there is a nurse wearing navy blue inside.

"Nurses. Wearing navy blue."

"Bud, I don't think they are in there."

I whip the shower curtain back, convinced there will be a nurse standing there, holding a knife. Or maybe a gun. No, probably not those. What would a nurse use to kill me? *Of course!*

A nurse wouldn't use a knife or a gun — that would create too much blood. They would just use drugs with poison in them.

I make a mental note to *not* take any drugs from a nurse wearing navy blue.

"Come on, dude. Let's go back to the room," Dad said. His voice is shaking. He looks sad again.

I follow Dad back to my bed because I don't want to tell him about the nurses who are going to poison me with drugs. That would only make him worry more. And I know Daddy and Mommy are already really stressed out and worried. I don't want to make it worse.

I climb back into my bed, and pick the comic book back up to find out what else I should worry about. Just as Spider-Man is telling me that I need to find codes in the book to know what else will kill me, Mommy walks into the room with Grace and Noah.

"Nate!" Grace cries, running to my bed. "I've *missed* you!" She jumps on top of me and gives me a big hug. I see Mommy smile at Dad.

"Mom says nothing hurts you," Grace said, stepping down from my bed. "Is that true? Does your throat hurt or anything?"

I shake my head. I'm happy to see my sister. And Noah too! I'm so happy Mommy brought Noah to see me. It's because she knew it would make me feel so happy to see him. It feels like it has been forever.

"Dude," Noah says, stepping forward. "What's up?" I know he's asking how I am.

"I'm okay, I guess."

"I brought you a new game for your Nintendo 3DS," Grace says, handing me a cartridge. "And Olson too! Look, Nate . . . it's your favourite teddy bear from when you were little."

"Sweet! Thanks," I say, taking the beat-up bear from her. I haven't seen him in a long time, and don't know where she even found him. I slept with Olson every night when I was six. And a bit when I was seven, but I didn't want Noah to know. "What's the game?"

"The new Super Mario Bros. U," Grace answers. "I bought it this morning with Mom."

"Awesome. Thanks!" I tear open the package. "Can I play it now?"

"Why don't you wait for a bit, Bean? We want to visit with you," Mom answers. I frown. I'm happy to see them, but I want to play my new game, too.

"Okay," I answer. "I guess."

"I brought you some other stuff," Grace says. "Here. I got you your favourite candy."

I take the bag Grace hands me and open it to find Sour Patch Kids and Nibs. I tear the Sour Patch Kids open and start eating the red ones first.

"Candy at ten-thirty in the morning?" Mom asks, laughing. "I guess it's okay. Just this once."

I dump the candy out on the tray, and Noah, Grace, and I eat it quickly. It's gone fast. I open the Nibs and we devour those too.

"So what's it like here?" Noah asks with his mouth full of Nibs. I wait for Mom to tell him to stop talking with his mouth full of food, but she doesn't. It's weird, because she always cares about that. I guess it is because Noah isn't her son.

"Some people are really weird. One guy makes chicken noises. There is a girl who never talks, ever."

"Totally weird," Grace responds.

"Tell us about other weird people," Noah says.

"They aren't *all* weird. Some are nice."

"Like who?"

"Well, I meet with this nice lady all the time . . . Dr. Aldridge. She's cool, I guess." I look around me, and then say quietly, "But not all of the nurses are okay. You have to stay away from the ones wearing navy blue. They will kill you."

Grace's eyebrows shoot to the top of her head. She looks confused. And a bit scared.

"Nate, honey, that's not true. The nurses here . . . all of the nurses at this hospital . . . they're here to help you. You don't have to be afraid of any of them."

"Yes, you do! Spider-Man *told* me! Not all nurses are bad, but some will really kill you. The ones wearing navy blue."

"The ones wearing navy blue, huh?" Noah laughs hard. "I'll be sure to stay away. I don't want to mess with anyone crazy."

"They'll kill me?" Grace asks. Her face is white.

"No sweetie," Mommy says. She turns so she can't see me, and looks right at Noah and Grace. She is talking quietly. "Remember what we talked about? Some things aren't true."

Grace nods. Noah shrugs. Mommy switches the conversation. "What did you have for breakfast this morning, Bean?"

"Dad brought me pancakes that he made at home. With chocolate chips. They were awesome!"

"Glad you liked them, bud," Dad replies. He smiles.

"How about a movie?" Mom asks. "Do you guys want to watch one together? I brought my iPad, and it's loaded with new movies." Mom takes her iPad out of her red bag.

"Okay. Nate can pick," Grace answers.

"That's very nice of you, sweetie," Mom says. She opens her iPad and puts it on my bed. Grace and Noah get in beside me. We're squished, but it's okay. I like being with my sister and my best friend again.

Grace leans into me and whispers in my ear. "You know why she wants us to watch a movie, right?"

I shake my head, barely able to hear her.

"Don't you get it?" Grace whispers. She gets louder with each word she says. "Mom and Dad want you to stop talking about crazy nurses wearing navy blue. Because then you can come home. So stop it. Just stop it already. Stop talking about the nurses wearing navy blue. I want you to come home with me."

47
Ashley

"I think that went fairly well, don't you?" I asked Pete quietly as he shrugged himself into his winter coat and got ready to leave. We'd made the decision to not miss Grace's practices because of what was happening with Nate. We knew we needed to keep our routine as normal as possible, so Pete was going to take on driving duty for Grace while I stayed with Nate.

"As well as it could have, I guess."

"I didn't really know what to expect. But I think it went okay."

"I guess that's one of the worst parts about all of this. You never really know what to expect with Nate. Some days he's okay, and others he's not."

"At least he didn't act too strangely," I responded. I turned to look at the kids. They'd just devoured the pizza Pete had gone to pick up for lunch, and Grace was showing Nate how to make it past the next level on her favourite iPad game, Subway Surfers.

"So cool!" Nate cried. "I didn't know you could do that."

"C'mon, you guys," I said, interrupting. "Dad's ready to go."

As everyone said goodbye to each other, I marvelled at how normal it seemed. They could have been parting ways on any regular day.

Once the others had left and Nate and I were alone, I asked him what he wanted to do.

"Subway Surfers!" he said. "I'm getting so good."

"Okay. You can play for a bit longer. And then we'll get ready to go to our meeting with Dr. Aldridge. We need to be there in about half an hour."

I opened my laptop and focused on getting through my pile of email. I had thirty minutes to plough through as much as I could.

I was just typing a response to Ben with feedback on the new creative he'd sent to me for approval when Nate started screaming. I'd never heard someone so frightened.

A nurse I'd never met before had just walked into Nate's hospital room, carrying his meds and a cup of water. Her eyes widened at Nate's bloodcurdling scream and she immediately dropped the water. It splashed everywhere and she slipped in it when she stepped forward, tumbling onto her back.

Nate kept screaming. "Nate, honey, why are you screaming?" I said as I rushed over to help the nurse.

"I'm sorry," the nurse cried, jumping up. "They told me he was fairly stable. I'm new to psych and wasn't expecting that."

The nurse unsuccessfully tried to gather her composure over Nate's screams. As I tried to figure out what had set off my son, I grabbed a towel off the end of the bed and started wiping up the water. The nurse reached for the tablets that had fallen and put them back in the cup, saying she'd be back after getting Nate a new cup of water and fresh pills.

As soon as she was gone, Nate stopped screaming.

I ran over to my son and took him in my arms. "Baby, what's wrong? Why did you do that?"

"That nurse. She's wearing navy blue. She's going to *kill me*," Nate whispered. His voice was shaking and he was breathing hard.

"Honey, no . . . she won't kill you. She's here to help you."

"No! Spider-Man told me so. In the comic book. I have to stay away from them. All of them. The ones wearing navy blue."

"She's gone now. It's just you and me. And babe, you need to take your meds."

"No!" he cried. "*Not* those ones. They're filled with poison."

"Sweetie, they're not . . ."

"Yes, they are! And I won't take them. No matter what." Nate pursed his lips and kept them tightly closed.

"Your meds will help you, Nate. It's why you're starting to feel a bit better."

"I'm not feeling better. Not at all! I feel sick all of the time. And my brain feels like it's mushy. I can't think properly. Sometimes I can't even read. It's like I forget how to."

I sighed, holding Nate tight. I decided to stop pushing for a minute. In my incessant need for information, I'd read all about kids not wanting to take their medication. It was for a variety of reasons, but most commonly for the side effects I knew Nate was experiencing. In many ways, it was a lose-lose situation. I understood why Nate didn't want to feel so crummy, but without the meds he would never be better.

Just as Nate's breathing returned to normal, the nurse came back into the room and Nate started screaming again. "Get out! Get out of here! I know what you want to do, and I won't let you!"

"It's okay," I said to the nurse. "Would you mind going, though? I'll come out in a bit and let you know what's going on."

The nurse nodded, setting down the cup of water and tablets before she left. Nate picked up the water and dumped it down the sink, then flew into my arms, sobbing.

I stroked his back and sang his favourite song, just as I'd done his whole life when he needed to calm down. *"You are my sunshine . . ."*

When he finally calmed down and I was convinced he'd be okay for a few minutes, I left his room to find the nurse.

"It's the colour of your uniform," I explained to the group of nurses who were behind the desk. Given the rotation, I didn't know any of them very well, and I missed Addy. "My son, he's afraid of navy blue scrubs for some reason."

"It's okay," a nurse named Cayenne piped up. She gave me a bright smile. "We're used to our patients being afraid of different things. Until the fear ends, we'll be sure to avoid sending in nurses wearing blue."

"Thank you," I said gratefully.

"Hello everyone," came a familiar voice from behind me. I turned to see Dr. Aldridge, and was thankful to see that she was dressed in regular clothes. Ones that weren't blue. "Is Nate ready for our session? I've been waiting for him."

Cayenne explained what had happened, and Dr. Aldridge nodded. "Let's chat with Nate in his room today, shall we? Less chance of seeing another nurse wearing the wrong colour."

I followed Dr. Aldridge into the room, and she asked Nate to chat with her for a bit. He climbed out of bed and opted for his beanbag chair that Pete had brought from home. I settled into the chair I had been sitting in all afternoon.

"Mrs. Carter?" Dr. Aldridge asked. "Would you mind going to get some coffee? Maybe come back in about an hour or so?"

"Oh, sure. Of course," I replied. I stood and walked over to Nate. "Will you be okay if I leave you with Dr. Aldridge for a bit?"

"Okay."

"I think we'll have a good chat," Dr. Aldridge responded

through her consistent warm smile. "But first we need you to take your medication. Will you take it if I give it to you?"

"I guess."

"That's good, Nate. I'll go and get some water so you can take it before we start." Dr. Aldridge picked up his tablets and left the room. She returned shortly holding a bottle of water. She had put the meds in different colour cup.

Nate took the medicine from Dr. Aldridge. She watched him to make sure he completely swallowed it. When she was convinced he'd taken the meds, she motioned for me to go.

As I left the room, Dr. Aldridge started the session. "Nate, tell me about how you're feeling today . . ."

48
Nate

"I'm feeling okay, I guess." But I am annoyed. Dr. Aldridge always asks how I feel. I want to tell her that I feel like shit, but I don't want Mommy to be mad at me for swearing.

"What do you mean by 'okay'?"

"Tired. Like I'm going to puke. And I can't think properly. Even though I want to, and I try really hard to think. I just can't."

Dr. Aldridge nods and writes something down in the book she brought with her. "And what about your mood? How are you feeling?"

"Okay, I guess. My sister and my best friend came to visit me today. That was good. I was happy to see them."

Dr. Aldridge nods again. She writes more words down in

her book. There is a pad of paper inside it. "Can you tell me about your sister, Nate?"

I shrug my shoulders. "I don't know. She's okay."

"Is she older or younger than you?" I give the doctor a funny look. Because it's a funny question. I know she knows how old Grace is.

"Older. Grace is twelve."

"Do you get along with Grace?"

"I guess."

"Is she nice to you?"

"Sometimes she's nice. Sometimes she's not. Mostly she just ignores me."

"And what about Noah? Can you tell me about him?"

"He's my best friend. He's always nice to me."

"What do you do together?" Dr. Aldridge asks. She finishes writing more stuff down in her book.

"I don't know."

"Are you in the same class?"

"No, but I see him sometimes at school. Mostly we just hang out at home. He lives on my street."

"What types of things do you do with Noah?"

"I don't know." I am getting bored by my conversation with Dr. Aldridge.

"Well, how about we start with today. What did you do when Noah was here visiting you?"

"We watched a movie. And played some video games."

"I see. Do you do anything else with Noah? When you're not in the hospital?"

"Yeah. We play outside. We go swimming. And ride bikes. And we play hockey. We are on the same team, but sometimes he's not there."

"How come?"

"He only plays when we need the help."

"Makes sense." Dr. Aldridge scribbles on her paper again.

When she finishes, she looks up. "The nurses told me you had quite the scare today, Nate. Can you tell me about that?"

I stop and wait. I watch Dr. Aldridge for clues to see if she's been sent by the nurses who wear the bad clothes.

"Nate?" Dr. Aldridge asks again. She keeps smiling. I decide it is okay, so I tell her all about what Spider-Man told me. What I needed to be careful of. Why I couldn't take the pills from the nurse wearing navy blue because it would have killed me.

"That sounds pretty scary." Dr. Aldridge stops for a minute and then asks, "How do you feel when you think about dying, Nate?"

I don't say anything. I don't want to talk about this.

"Do you want to die? Or do you ever think about hurting yourself?"

"No. Of course not. Why would I want to do that?" I shake my head. Sometimes doctors are so strange. They are supposed to be smart, but then they go and ask stupid questions like that.

"I'm happy to hear that. I wouldn't want you to hurt yourself." Dr. Aldridge stops talking. It's like she's waiting for me to say something. But I have nothing to tell her.

"How about school? Can you tell me about that? Do you like it?" Dr. Aldridge asks.

"I guess so."

"Do you like your teacher?"

"Yes."

"What's her name?"

"Mrs. Brock."

"What do you like about Mrs. Brock?"

"I don't know. She teaches me stuff. And she's nice to me, I guess."

"Do you have a favourite subject?"

"No."

This is a dumb conversation.

"What about the kids in your class? Do you like them?"

I shrug again. I don't want to talk to her about Tyson or any of the other mean kids in my class.

"Who are your friends in your class, Nate?"

"Can I play a video game now?"

"No. Not yet. I'd like to talk about your friends at school first. What are their names?"

"I only have one friend."

"Okay, what is your one friend's name?"

"Noah."

More writing. "But Noah isn't in your class, Nate. Do you have friends in your classroom?"

"But I told you . . . I still see him at school sometimes, even though he isn't in my class. I don't need any more friends."

Dr. Aldridge smiles at me. "Okay, then, why don't you tell me more about Noah? What is the best time you've spent together? Any favourites?"

"Yeah. Definitely. This summer, he came with us to the cottage. It was fun. I liked swimming with him. And fishing, too."

"Anything else?"

I shrug. "I'm tired. Can we stop, please?"

"If you'd like. But I do have a few more questions for you. Do you think we could keep going? Just for a little bit?"

I look down at my hands. "I guess so."

"Okay, Nate. That's good. We'll talk about a few more things, and then we'll stop. If you feel too tired, let me know and we'll wait for another day."

I wait for her next question.

"Can you tell me about any of the kids in your class who might not be so nice to you?"

"No."

"Why not?"

"Because I don't want to talk about them."

"Okay. I understand that."

Dr. Aldridge waits. She says nothing. I stare at her and cross my arms.

"Nate, I want you to know that if you ever want to talk to someone, I'm always here to listen. No matter what. And don't forget what I told you last time. Everything you tell me will stay just between the two of us. I won't tell anyone. Not even your mom and dad. Not unless you want me to."

I think about this for a moment. I wonder if I really can trust her.

"Do you remember how you told me the last time we met that you sometimes don't eat your lunch? That you throw it out when your dad isn't looking?"

I nod my head. I feel scared. I'm going to get into trouble for doing that.

"Well, I didn't tell anyone about that. Not one person."

"You didn't?"

"No, I didn't." Dr. Aldridge looks me straight in the eyes when she says it. It makes me believe her.

We sit quietly.

It feels like a really long time.

If I tell her about Tyson, will she let me go to sleep sooner? Or play video games?

"His name is Tyson. But there are others too. They are mean to me like the kids at my last school"

"Tyson? Who is that?"

"The kid in my class who is always mean to me."

"What does he do, Nate? Can you tell me about it?"

"I don't know. Stuff, I guess. He calls me names all the time. Like weirdo and cuckoo. And he tells me I'm ugly."

"That isn't very nice. It must be very hurtful."

"Yeah, I guess. And sometimes he steals my snacks, when he likes what I bring for my recess snack. Especially if it's Fruit Gushers. Those are his favourite. And a few times he punched me when I wouldn't give them to him."

"He punched you? Where?"

"In the cheek. Or in the stomach. One time it really hurt. He did it so hard. I felt like I couldn't breathe, and I fell to the ground. Then he took my apple juice and Fruit Gushers and ran off."

Tears fall down my cheeks and I am surprised. I didn't think I was going to cry. "But the worst part was that he didn't even eat it. Even though I know he loves Fruit Gushers. He threw them in the garbage and screamed at everyone in the playground to never eat a snack from a weirdo. That I probably do weird things to my food."

"That must have been very hard. Did you tell anyone?"

"Yes."

"Who did you tell?"

"Noah."

"Anyone else?"

I shake my head. I never tell anyone things like that, except for Noah.

"Why not?"

"I don't want them to know, I guess."

"Thank you for telling *me*, Nate. I know that must have been hard to do. And I'm here to help you, if you want me to. With Tyson or anything else that's going on in your life. You now that, right?"

"Yeah. I do." I scratch my head. It feels itchy. "Dr. Aldridge?"

"Yes, Nate?"

"Are you going to tell anyone about Tyson stealing my snacks and punching me?"

"No, Nate. Not unless you want me to."

"Okay, good. I don't want you to." I look down at my arms. They look funny for some reason. And I'm starting to feel like I'm going to throw up.

"Dr. Aldridge? Can I ask you something?"

"Yes, Nate. Anything you'd like."

"Can we stop now? I don't feel good."

Dr. Aldridge snaps her book shut and puts her pen in her bag before smiling at me and giving me a hug. "Of course, Nate. We'll start again the next time we meet, okay?"

I nod and crawl into bed. I don't remember falling asleep.

49
Ashley

"I think Nate's ready to go home," Dr. Aldridge said to Pete and me from across her desk.

"Really?" I asked cautiously. Nate had been in the hospital for just over two weeks and although I was desperate for him to return home to our family, I was also nervous to be without the constant support of the medical team at the hospital.

"I will still treat him, as an outpatient. And I should see him regularly. Twice a week to start, and then less frequently as Nate gets better. You should all continue to go to your support groups. But Nate's delusions have really started to diminish. He isn't showing signs of paranoia. And he's certainly not agitated like he was when he first came in. He's stable. I think he can handle it."

"What about school?" I asked hesitantly, my protective instincts kicking into high gear. I knew Nate would need to return to school at some point, but I was dreading the moment he would go back to the bullying.

"I have a suggestion for you about school. It's fairly new, but there's a solution that I think will work well for Nate. A new type of school has recently opened not far from here, called the Henry Lewis School Hospital. Basically, it's a child and adolescent day program that also offers schooling. It's a really great transitional program for kids like Nate who no longer need to be a part of the inpatient unit but still require more intensive treatment and would have a tough time being integrated back into a regular classroom. Nate would spend the day involved in individual and group therapeutic activities. There are teachers on site, and he would attend school at the hospital, and then return home each afternoon."

"Are there doctors on site as well?" Pete asked.

"Yes. Including me. There are three psychiatrists who work out of the day hospital. I could continue to work with Nate there."

"It sounds too good to be true!" I replied with a sense of relief. "It really sounds wonderful."

"It is. I strongly believe in this program. It focuses on combining things like individual therapy, family therapy, behavioural interventions, and medication management to facilitate keeping the child at home, in school, and in regular outpatient treatment. Nate's a perfect candidate."

"When would he start?"

"I've looked into availability, and we can get Nate in the week after next, if you'd like. Starting on Monday."

Pete and I both nodded eagerly.

"If Nate is to go home, there's one big thing we need to all be aware of," Dr. Aldridge continued. "The Risperidone has started to work, and is doing a good job of shifting his brain from an unbalanced world of mania and psychosis to reality. As we talked about before, though, every patient is different and it could take weeks before Nate sees the world for what it truly is. Nate doesn't need to be in the hospital anymore, but he *is* straddling the fence between the delusions he's experienced and what's actually happening around him. He's on middle ground right now, and while the psychosis has really been minimized, Nate still believes some of the things that are not true."

I nodded. I knew exactly what she was talking about. Beside me, Pete took my hand.

"We have no way of knowing when that will change," Dr. Aldridge continued. "It would be better if I were with him when he starts to realize everything for what it is. Because when he does . . . when he realizes things aren't as he's thought, it will be a very tough adjustment period. And he will likely mourn them, like a real-life loss."

"Is that why you asked us to bring in the pictures? To help get him to realize all of this?" Pete asked. Dr. Aldridge had sent us both an email the night before asking us to bring in family pictures from the past year.

Dr. Aldridge nodded, pursing her lips. "If you've got them, let's go to Nate's room. There's no time like the present to see if my idea helps . . ." Dr. Aldridge stood from her chair and we followed her into the elevator.

When we got to the room, Nate greeted us with a big smile. He was just finishing his session with Payton, the art therapist whom he had been working with for the past two weeks. He loved it, and Dr. Aldridge felt it was one of the treatments that was helping him the most. During her daily visits, Payton used various materials to get Nate to express his inner images, feelings, and needs.

"I was just leaving," Payton said. "I'll see you tomorrow, okay Nate? You can finish your clay project when you have some more time today. Sound good?"

"Okay!" Nate responded.

Once Payton had left, Dr. Aldridge pulled up a chair. "Your parents brought in some of your photo albums from the past year for me to take a look at. I loved seeing them. You've grown so much taller over the past few months . . ."

"I know, right?" Nate grinned. He looked proud.

"Want to see?" Dr. Aldridge opened the first album to a section about halfway through. The pages revealed pictures of our street pool party from over a year before. All the kids were in the pool, and Nate was jumping off the diving board, hamming it up for the crowd.

"Look what a great jumper you are!" Dr. Aldridge said, pointing to another picture of Nate. I remembered him jumping off the diving board and doing an impersonation of a frog like it was yesterday. "And here you are with your hockey team that fall. Lots of pictures of you scoring goals . . . you must be a very good hockey player."

"The best — right, Nate?" I said, smiling proudly. "He's the leading scorer on his team."

"That's great," said Dr. Aldridge. She slowly flipped through the photos.

"And here you are this past summer, Nate, riding your bike." Dr. Aldridge grinned, pointing to the pictures of Nate racing up and down the street.

Nate nodded his head, examining the photos. Dr. Aldridge continued to flip the pages, until Nate took over. He stared intently at the pictures, as though he was seeing them for the first time.

"Ah. Your trip up north from this past summer!" Dr. Aldridge said, pointing to a picture of our family sitting in front of the cottage we had rented. "You look like you're all having so much fun."

"Yeah. I guess." Nate's voice was very quiet. When Dr. Aldridge didn't respond, the room fell still.

"Nate?" Dr. Aldridge asked quietly. Pete and I remained

silent. We did not move an inch. "Is there something you're noticing in these pictures?"

Nate shrugged, looking very sad.

"Anything you want to talk about?" Dr. Aldridge asked in a voice barely above a whisper.

"It's Noah," Nate said almost inaudibly. Tears formed in his eyes. "He's not in any of these photos."

Dr. Aldridge waited for our son to continue.

"He's . . . he's not real, is he? My best friend Noah . . . he doesn't exist in real life. That's why he's not in the photos. Even though he was there with us. On my hockey team, at the cottage . . . he was there with me. I remember him standing beside me when we took the group picture in front of the cottage. But now . . . he's not in the photo."

"That is right, Nate. He isn't in the photos," Dr. Aldridge said quietly. She sat down on the side of Nate's bed, and looked my son straight in the eyes. Her voice was calm and clear. "I know Noah has been very real to you for a very long time. And this is likely difficult for you. But you need to know that your mom and dad and Grace . . . *they* are all very real. They *do* exist in real life. And they all love you very, very much."

Hearing Dr. Aldridge's words, Nate started to cry openly. I was desperate to go to him, but didn't want to interrupt the doctor's progress. Instead, I watched from the sidelines, my heart breaking a little bit more with each tear that fell down Nate's cheeks. I took Pete's hand, and he squeezed it tight.

"But . . . if Noah isn't real, then how do I know that? How do I know Mommy and Daddy and Grace are real? What if I find out tomorrow that they aren't real either? And I'm all alone?"

I couldn't take it any longer. I rushed to his bed, and pulled my son into my arms. Tears were coursing down both of our cheeks. "Sweetie . . . oh honey. Mommy and Daddy, we're right here. Feel my face. Give me a hug. I'm so very real, and I will never leave you. I promise you. We all love you so much, and we will always, always be here for you."

"Nate," Dr. Aldridge said softly. "You knew that Noah wasn't real because he wasn't in the pictures. Is that right?"

Nate sniffed loudly and wiped his wet cheeks with his hand. "Yes."

"But who was in the pictures with you? Who has always been in the pictures with you?" Dr. Aldridge asked.

"Mommy. And Daddy," Nate responded. "And Grace too."

"That's right. So you know that *they are real*. It isn't like Noah."

"But . . . but I'll miss Noah. He was my best friend in the whole world."

"I know, sweetie. And whenever we aren't with people we care about, it's very sad," I said, squeezing my son more tightly.

"Do you know what the good thing is, Nate?" Dr. Aldridge asked, gently interrupting me. "You've told me exactly what you like about Noah. Right? You like that he's fun. And that he likes hockey. And that he keeps your secrets. Well, the next time you make a new friend, and I know you will, you can use all of those things to help you figure out exactly who you want to be your absolute best friend. Does that make sense to you?"

Nate nodded but didn't stop crying.

"Why don't I give you some time?" Dr. Aldridge asked Pete and me quietly. "I know one of you will need to get back to Grace at some point, but I'd suggest you stay as long as you can with Nate tonight. We can plan on discharging him in the morning, after he's had a good night's sleep and I talk to him one last time. Does that work?"

I nodded. I was so grateful that between her and the medication, she had finally been able to get through to Nate and convince him that Noah wasn't real. He'd been talking about his made-up best friend for months.

When Nate's obsession first started, Pete and I had thought

Noah was just an imaginary friend. Grace had had two of them when she was slightly younger than Nate, and always insisted on bringing her two best friends, Chippia and Mippia, along for the ride. But Nate's fixation on Noah had lasted longer and was far more intense. And by the time the real psychosis kicked in, it was apparent what was actually going on.

With the doctor gone, I crawled into bed with my son and pulled him close. He had stopped crying, and was staring into nothingness. Any remaining sparkle that he'd had in his eyes over the past few months had completely vanished.

Lying there, Nate remained unresponsive. I pulled him tight, hoping for a squeeze, or even a shift in position. But I received nothing in return. Not even a twitch.

Nate's eyes were open but he lay still, barely breathing. It was as if his spirit had vanished along with Noah.

"Sweetie? Do you want to talk about it?" I whispered in my son's ear. Pete was sitting in the chair in the corner, quietly waiting. Watching. Wanting to help, but unsure of what to say. Unsure of what to do.

"It's okay, Bean. You can talk to me. I love you, and I'm here for you," I whispered. I said a silent prayer, asking for God to return my son to me.

Nate said nothing, but I didn't get out of the bed. If he wouldn't talk to me — if he *couldn't* talk to me in that moment — well, then, I would wait with him until he could. I was not going to leave my son.

Someone knocked gently on the door. Dinner. Pete quietly ushered them out of the room, signalling that we'd come and get it when we were ready. The attendant quickly left, taking the food tray with him.

The room grew darker. I didn't know if Nate was awake or asleep, although I sensed his eyes were open. I squeezed him tight to let him know I was there. To let him know that I wouldn't leave him. I knew what it felt like to be abandoned by a parent, and I would not do that to my son, particularly when he'd just found out the person he was closest to did not really exist. I couldn't imagine the horror of learning that someone so important to you wasn't just gone but, worse, had never even existed in the first place.

None of us moved from our positions in the room. Under the covers, I took Nate's little hand, still soft like a baby's, and gently squeezed. But I got nothing in return. Just the lifeless, silky hand of my broken-hearted little boy.

Pete eventually left the room, quietly and without saying a word to us. He wanted to get home to Grace.

Somewhere in the middle of the night, a delicate, hushed voice entered the room. "Mommy?" Nate whispered. His breath was hot against my ear.

I hugged him tighter to let him know I was listening.

"How do I know what is real?" He asked the question so quietly I had to lean in to hear him. "How do I really know that you are real?"

Squeezed beside my son in the dark hospital room, my heart broke. A sane adult with a logical approach to life would have difficulty processing such a complicated, life altering devastation. I couldn't even imagine what it would be like for the fragile mind of an innocent little boy.

In the darkness, I took Nate's hand and guided it to my tear-coursed cheek. I kissed his palm. "Sweetie, I am real. And I am here for you. Feel my cheeks. Hear my voice. Take hold of what you are feeling right now . . . just for a moment, sweetie, and try to feel with your heart. Don't think with your brain. And you will know, down deep in your soul that I am real. That I have *always* been here for you. I always will be. Nothing will ever change that, my dear, precious Nate. No matter what."

I pressed my eyes shut and waited for his response. At first nothing came, and I wondered if I had gotten through to him.

But then, finally, Nate nestled in closer to me. He took my hand. Returned my squeeze.

And there, in that dark moment with just the two of us, Nate came back to me. I was real.

50
Nate

.

I'm going home today. Dr. Aldridge is sitting in my room, trying to talk to me. But I still don't want to talk to her.

We are by ourselves. Mom went to get a coffee. Dr. Aldridge came to talk to me about leaving the hospital. She said she thinks it is a good thing that I'm going home. I don't care where I am. I don't want to be at the hospital. But I don't want to be at home. I don't want to be anywhere.

I want her to leave.

I do not want to talk.

"Nate? I asked if you are looking forward to being at home, with your mom and dad and sister. And all of your things. You even get to sleep in your own bed tonight."

If I talk, will it make Dr. Aldridge leave sooner? I try to answer her but I can't seem to speak. I don't know if it is my brain not working or my mouth. I try to think of the answer for a second and then realize I don't care. I do not want to speak to her.

"Is there anything about your house that you miss?" Dr. Aldridge asks.

No.

"Are there special breakfasts you like? Ones that you can't get here?"

No. I want you to go.

"Or maybe it's a special dinner you could have. I know you like spaghetti and meatballs. Would you like to have that for dinner tonight?"

No. I want you to get the hell out of my room.

"What about family movie night. You'll be able to start having those again. Are you looking forward to that?"

No. Get the hell out of my room, you dumb doctor.

"Nate, would you like to talk about Noah?"

Yes. Of course I do. You just told me Noah doesn't exist, and now all you want to talk about are dumb things like movie nights and my favourite dinners.

"Yes."

"Okay. Let's do that, then. How do you feel about what we talked about yesterday?" Dr. Aldridge asks me.

I shrug. I don't know how to tell her.

"It's okay, Nate. You can tell me." Dr. Aldridge waits for me to talk. When I don't, she says, "Why don't you think of just one word to use to describe how you are feeling about Noah. Can you do that?"

I nod. I know one word.

"That's great. I'd love to hear it."

"Sad."

"I can understand that," Dr. Aldridge says. "It would be very sad to find out that someone you thought was real does not really exist."

"I . . . I want to go back to how it was. When I knew Noah was . . . was real." I start crying again. I'm mad that I'm crying. Because I don't want to. But I cannot help it.

"Nate, realizing that Noah isn't real is a big step to realizing what is real around you and what is not. It's a big step towards you being better. And we've talked a lot about why it's important that you get better."

I nod. I wipe away my tears.

"You have parents who love you very much. And a sister who does too. And they'll help you continue to get better. Every day it will get a little bit easier."

"But I don't like being awake in the days. I feel . . . kind of funny. Not like I've ever felt before."

"Can you tell me more about it?" Dr. Aldridge asks.

"I feel tired all the time. But I can't sleep. And my mouth feels like I have wet cotton balls in it. So does my head. And my heart won't stop beating really, really fast. I don't like it."

"Those are all side effects of the medication you are on. And I know they're very uncomfortable for you, but we're hoping they will get better soon. And the most important part is that they are making *you* better."

"If the medication is making me feel like this, then I don't want to take it anymore. I want to stop."

"You can't stop, Nate. You need to take your medication, just like we talked about. Every day. It is very, very important. It will keep you healthy."

"I don't want to."

"Look at how much progress we've made, Nate. When I first met you, we would not have been able to sit here like this, talking the way we are now. And you were very, very scared at that time. The medication is helping to make you less scared."

"Will the medication make me forget Noah? I don't like that. I do not want to forget him."

"I know you're sad about Noah. It's understandable. And it's okay to think of him still. It's also important to remember that he's not real. But if you need anything at all . . . something that you would have told Noah before or shared with him . . . then you can tell your mom or your dad. Or me. We are all here to help you."

I look at Dr. Aldridge and tell her I know.

But really I don't.

Because I don't believe her.

All I know is that the medication is awful. It makes me feel sick. It makes me feel like I'm someone else. Not me. And if the stupid meds are making me feel sick, and making me forget Noah, I don't want to take them.

I just don't.

So I won't.

51
Ashley

"Are you comfortable, honey?" I asked Nate. It was his first night home from the hospital, and I was tucking him into bed.

He didn't answer me.

"I'm sorry you couldn't eat your spaghetti tonight," I said, my voice filling the silent room. Pete had made homemade meatballs for Nate's first family dinner at home, but our son had hardly touched his meal. He claimed he wasn't hungry, and told us the meds were making him feel so sick that he couldn't eat. We hadn't pushed it, and settled instead for his agreement to take his meds, which had been the first exhausting battle when we got home.

The second had been Nate's silence. He'd been stone quiet

since we got home. I had such high hopes for his return home, but his chronic silence was making everyone feel anxious and uncomfortable.

"Well, let me tell you, the sauce your dad made was pretty awesome. And the good news is there was a lot left over, so you can eat it whenever you're hungry. Maybe you could have some for lunch tomorrow."

Nate gave me a look that suggested he wouldn't want it. I decided to drop the subject of eating. "Is there anything you'd like before you go to sleep? Some water maybe? Or I could stay with you. If you want, that is. Or I could sing you songs, or rub your back?"

Nate turned over in his bed, clearly telling me to leave him alone.

Dr. Aldridge had warned us of the highs and lows we'd experience. I knew Nate was far from being better. And for a long while, we'd never know what to expect from him.

"Okay, sweetie. I'll leave your door open so that I can hear you. Call me if you need anything at all." I leaned over my son's back to kiss his cheek. It felt rigid, like he was clenching his teeth.

I left his door ajar and went downstairs. I found Pete waiting.

"Look what I found," he said. He was holding two of Nate's pills.

"What? Where?"

"In Nate's napkin. I was cleaning up after dinner, and decided to do a little checking. Just in case."

"Oh no. Really?" Our son not taking his meds was a nightmare. And I thought him taking them was the only thing that had gone right since Nate had come home.

"What do we do?" Pete asked. "Should we wake him up and make him take them?"

"I don't know . . . maybe?" With the mood our son was in, I had no idea what was best.

Pete started to walk up the stairs but I grabbed his arm. Something in my gut told me to wait until the next morning. "I don't know. Maybe we shouldn't. He's not doing well right now, and maybe the morning will bring a fresh perspective. Dr. Aldridge said it wasn't a huge deal if he missed one. We can sit him down in the morning and talk to him. After a full night's sleep."

"I don't know if that's a good idea. I'm scared about him going back to what he was like before."

"Me too. But I'm also scared to push him too hard. At least right now. He doesn't seem like he'd be able to take it."

"Okay . . . I guess. But we need to talk to him as soon as Grace goes to school in the morning."

"Agreed."

"And I think I should sleep down here tonight. You know, just in case he gets up or something. He can't get outside because of the alarm, but I don't really want him walking around the house either. I'm sure he could do a lot of damage."

"Yeah, I was thinking the same thing. I'll sleep with the door open so I can hear him, too. I doubt I'll sleep a wink tonight, to be honest."

Pete drew me in for a hug and kissed my hair, filling me with comfort. Given the battle we were up against with our son, it was good that we had each other.

52

The next morning, after Grace had left for school, we sat Nate down on the couch so we could talk to him about what we'd found. He seemed uncomfortable, visibly twitching, and his face was ashen.

I sat a tall glass of chocolate milk down in front of our son, knowing it was his favourite. He hadn't eaten breakfast with our family, and I was desperate for him to take in something.

"Nate, your mother and I want to talk to you about something we found," Pete began. He placed Nate's pills on the table in front of him. "Do you understand why it's important for you to take your meds?"

Nate immediately turned around in his seat so that he was

facing the back of the couch. As he buried his face in the fabric, I could see that his hands were twitching and it looked like he was in spasms. It was one of the common side effects Dr. Aldridge had warned us about.

I clenched my fists and drew them to my mouth, biting my knuckles. *We* were doing this to him. *We* were making him take his meds. *We* were causing him to twitch. And feel nauseated. And not eat.

Pete drove the conversation forward.

"Bud, what happened to you when you first went into the hospital was the scariest moment of our lives. And this medication, even if it's making you feel sick . . . well, it's keeping you safe. It's making you better. You need it to be healthy."

Nate whipped around, his eyes flashing with anger. "You don't get it, do you? You don't understand. It's making me feel like shit. It's making me feel like someone totally different. I don't even *want* to be healthy if it's going to make me feel like this. Because I'm not healthy. I'm sick. All of the time. I can't sleep. And I have this rash that's so itchy I scratch all night. And last night I puked three times, but there was nothing to throw up. Because I can't eat anything. I *hate this*. And I *hate you* for making me take it. And I won't. I won't take that stupid fucking medicine."

I sucked in air, horrified to hear my little boy talking this way. I'd heard him swear on occasion, but never like that. And never to us.

"I'm so sorry to hear that," Pete continued. "But none of us have a choice with this. You will be gone without it. You need it."

Nate crossed his arms, and Pete stared back.

Before I could interject, Pete stood up and crossed the room. He grabbed hold of both of Nate's shoulders and lay him onto the couch, straddling our son's torso and arms, pinning him down so that he couldn't move. Nate struggled with as much force as he could exude, but Pete's strength and weight far surpassed our son's. Nate's head thrashed from side to side, in protest of what Pete was doing to him. He tried with all of his might to force Pete off him, but our son didn't have a chance.

"Pete!" I cried. I didn't even know I was going to speak. I pleaded with him to stop, but couldn't seem to find it in me to get out of my seat. I was frozen, watching the horror unfold in front of me.

Pete ignored my pleas and held Nate's head still, his firm lock stopping our son's head from thrashing about. He grabbed the medication and chocolate milk from the table, and pinched Nate's nose closed with one hand, forcing his mouth to open, then popping the pills into his mouth.

"Pete, no! Please. Stop!" I cried, finally finding movement in my legs. I leapt out of my seat and grabbed at my husband's arms, using all of my strength to try to get him to stop.

Pete didn't shrug me off like I knew he could have, but managed to find the strength to keep going, even with me on his back. He poured the chocolate milk into Nate's mouth, spilling it all over Nate and the couch, and forcing our son to swallow the pills and milk to avoid choking. When Pete was convinced the pills were down his throat, he got off our son, who was coughing and sputtering through his fear.

Kicking Pete off the couch, Nate curled into the fetal position on top of the milk-soaked cushions, and wailed through tears I'd never seen before. I shot Pete a look that I hoped expressed the true revulsion I felt towards him; I couldn't believe he would do something like that to our son when he knew how important it was for Nate to trust us.

Pete stood and left the room, running up the stairs and mirroring the sobs that were coming from both Nate and me. I'd been married to Pete for thirteen years, and I'd never seen him cry until that moment. Not even when Nate was missing or in the hospital.

I placed my hand on my son's back, gently, to let him know

I was there and wouldn't hurt him. He responded, turning into me and showing the intensity of his fear by how tightly he hugged me. How powerfully he grabbed at my back. How tensely he gripped my clothes. How strongly he clenched his teeth. And, worst of all, how he couldn't stop his frail body from shaking in my arms.

53

"We need to change Nate's medication," Dr. Aldridge said matter-of-factly, after hearing about the severity of Nate's side effects and his refusal to take his meds. Pete and I were sitting with Dr. Aldridge in her office at the hospital later that afternoon, while Nate was downstairs working on that day's art therapy with Payton. "Remember when we talked about this being a big game of trial and error? If Nate isn't responding well to the Risperidone, we'll try something new."

I nodded, grateful to hear Dr. Aldridge's recommendation. I had been anxiously hoping she would say that, and had been prepared to beg her to switch Nate's meds if she wasn't instantly willing. The side effects and the hurricane of high-strung emotion and poor judgement that surrounded his refusal to take the drugs was tearing us apart. And it wasn't just Nate who was having a bad reaction.

"If Nate is struggling with the Risperidone, I think we should switch him to a drug called Aripiprazole. Like any medication, side effects can occur, but it's usually well tolerated. And if side effects do occur, in most cases they are minor and either require no treatment or can easily be treated."

"What type of side effects?" Pete asked.

"The side effects that sometimes occur with Aripiprazole are similar to the ones that are associated with Risperidone. Most commonly, it's headache, drowsiness or insomnia, fatigue, nausea, and restlessness. But Nate's risk of getting any one of these side effects is less than thirty percent, and metabolically it's quite good. I think it's our next best bet."

Pete and I nodded. We needed to get Nate away from the Risperidone.

"Now, how about you two?" Dr. Aldridge asked sympathetically. "How are you doing? Are you hanging in there?"

I didn't respond. I clutched the Kleenex I'd been holding since I'd walked into her office. Out of my peripheral vision, I could see that Pete was staring straight ahead with a blank look on his face. He didn't answer Dr. Aldridge's question either.

"Ashley? Pete? What's going on? It's important that you talk to me about how you're feeling and what's going on with your family. It's a crucial step in Nate's recovery."

I waited for Pete to answer. I wanted *him* to tell Dr. Aldridge all that had happened when he tried to physically force our son to take his meds. It was his wrongdoing. It should be his confession.

"Did something happen?" Dr. Aldridge asked gently. She looked patiently at us over her smooth mahogany desk, which was bare except for a few perfectly organized piles of paper. Behind her sat a framed photo of her beautiful smiling family.

She had two children of her own, who looked slightly younger than Nate.

"You could say that," I answered, giving in to my need to talk. Pete and I hadn't spoken since the conflict that morning, and my need to confront the issue was overwhelming.

"I'd like to hear from both of you about this, but why don't you start, Ashley?" Dr. Aldridge suggested.

I told Dr. Aldridge everything. As I recounted the story, I became more heated in my gestures and concern, and knew that I was practically accusing Pete of abusing his son by the time I was finished. It was completely unfair of me, but the floodgates to my pent-up raw emotions had been opened and there was no stopping them.

I waited for Pete to jump in and defend himself, but he didn't. Instead, he sat still as stone beside me, and said nothing.

"Pete? Do you have anything to add? I'd like to hear your thoughts as well," Dr. Aldridge coaxed gently.

"No. Ashley pretty much covered it. I did all that," Pete said quietly, looking down. He looked so sad. "And I'm so sorry. I didn't mean to hurt Nate. I would never, ever hurt him. I was just so scared that he wasn't taking his medication. I *need* him to take his meds."

Dr. Aldridge nodded compassionately. "I can understand that."

"But I don't know what happened there. Ashley is right. I didn't handle it well at all. And I hate myself for it. I want my son to trust me, and now he won't." Pete wouldn't look at me while he spoke, but I could see his face had turned white.

"Dealing with all of this is very complicated for everyone, I'm afraid." Dr. Aldridge smiled warmly across her desk. "I know that your intentions were good this morning. And I understand that you want your son to take his meds so that he can be better. There's nothing wrong with that. You are both wonderful parents. I've seen that in you since the day I met you. But you're also human. And dealing with a complicated, emotionally charged situation."

"But I . . . but I forced him to. Literally."

"Did he take the medication?"

"Yes."

"Then that part of the story is good. Because Nate *does* need to keep taking them to get better. Sometimes, as parents, we need to do things our children don't like. In a tough situation, we need to prioritize what's best for them. You knew Nate needed to take his meds, and you had run out of options. I'm not saying that what you did is the best way to get Nate to take his meds, but it was what you knew to do in that moment. Moving forward, we can work together on better strategies for getting him to keep taking his medication. Ashley is also right in that Nate will only get better in an environment that's filled with trust and security."

Listening to Dr. Aldridge, Pete looked very small and frail. I could tell that he didn't want to be let off the hook so easily.

"Pete," I began.

"No, please Ash, let me start." For the first time since we'd entered Dr. Aldridge's office, my husband looked at me. "I feel horrible about what I did this morning. And I'm so sorry. I didn't know what else to do, and my fear took over."

I reached for his hand and squeezed. "I know. And it's okay. I don't know what to do with all of this either."

"Nate's just started to make so much progress lately. He can't go back there. *We* can't go back there. And all of the research I've looked at . . . all of the information Dr. Aldridge has given us to read, and anything else I can get my hands on . . . it all supports the fact that this disease is one that won't impact a person's ability to function normally in society — *as long as they take their meds*. It all comes down to that. And if he doesn't take them, I know it will destroy our family. So he needs to take them. For himself, and for all of us."

I nodded, and was somewhat surprised to hear him talk about reading so much information on Nate's disease. I couldn't remember the last time Pete had read an article or book to help our children. It wasn't that he didn't care, but normally I was the big reader, the one constantly shoving articles at him on raising children. Pete's research showed me in a big way how much he cared about what was going on.

Dr. Aldridge jumped into the conversation. "You're right, Pete. Nate does need to take his meds. It will be easier once we've found the best ones for him, but you have to realize this could be a lifelong battle, even when he's taking the right drugs.

"I've seen so many reasons why people don't take their meds. In Nate's case, and in so many others, it's the side effects that make them want to stop. But then there will be other things as well. Like when he feels better, and is convinced he's 'normal' and doesn't need them. Or when he becomes a teenager and struggles with his independence, and views his medication as a leash from you to him. A leash that he wants to rid himself of."

Dr. Aldridge's words made sense, but they made me feel sick to my stomach. I hadn't gotten past the side effects to realize the umpteen dozen other reasons that Nate might want to stop taking his meds.

"We'll work on all of this together, and take it as it comes. We never stop with the 'one day at a time' around here," Dr. Aldridge said to us, her voice softening. "Nate's a great kid. And you are wonderful parents. I'll work with both of you on the different strategies for keeping him on track. So he sticks with his recovery plan. And so he takes his meds. Not only for him, as you said, but also for you and Grace."

"What about today? What if he doesn't take them when we go home?" Pete asked. I could tell how anxious he was about living through another night of Nate refusing to take his pills.

"Why don't we all go and see Nate right now? He should be done his art therapy, and I'll spend some time with him to explain why the new meds will be better. Through all of our time together, I've gotten to know Nate quite well, and I'm confident I can get him to take his new meds before you leave here. Does that sound good?"

"Yes, definitely," Pete answered, his voice mirroring the relief I felt.

As we followed Dr. Aldridge down the hall to the elevator, I took Pete's hand and gave it three small squeezes. It was something we had done at work earlier when we were newlyweds and wanted to communicate something between just the two of us, and others were in the room.

Pete turned to look into my eyes. His were warm and compassionate. Mine welled. When our gaze broke and he pulled me in to kiss my forehead, I knew he wasn't upset with me for what I had told Dr. Aldridge.

The elevator arrived, shaking us from our moment. We stepped onto it, still hand in hand, to go and start over with our son.

54

At five-thirty I turned off my alarm and walked across our bedroom to the shower. It was Tuesday morning, the day after Nate's first day at Henry Lewis, and my first full day back at work. I was already dreading leaving my son.

I stepped into the shower and let the hot spray hit my face, thinking of my day ahead. Jack and my other colleagues were still unaware of what had taken me from work for so long, and I was nervous about what questions I'd get when I returned. I'd been in a few times since Nate had gone into the hospital, but had always managed to dodge any questions thrown my way.

"Why don't you just tell them?" Pete asked me when I came home from my first meeting with Jack. Jack had grilled me on what was keeping me away from work, practically demanding that I tell him everything. But I'd stuck to my position of it being a private family crisis about which I didn't want to share details.

"I don't know," I'd responded simply. And I didn't. It wasn't that I was embarrassed about Nate or what he was going through, but every instinct in my gut was forcing me to protect my son. To keep him safe from a world of judgement and stigma.

But I knew more questions would come that day. And at some point, the world would find out about Nate's illness. Whatever he was ultimately diagnosed with, it wasn't going to go away.

"You ready?" Pete asked sleepily when I emerged from our closet dressed for a full day at the office. It had been only about a month since I'd been away from work, yet I suddenly felt like I was wearing someone else's clothes. And as though I was going to someone else's job. Because mine wasn't in advertising any-more — it was taking care of my son.

"Ready as I'll ever be," I responded miserably. My heart felt differently, but my brain was kicking reasonable logic into play. Nate's drugs were expensive, and without benefits through my work, we wouldn't be able to afford them.

"Put your chin up, Ash," Pete said, pulling me in for a hug. "I know how tough it is for you to leave Nate. But he's doing great. He had a successful day at Henry Lewis yesterday, and seemed to really love it. And the Aripiprazole seems to be really working. He's adjusting well with no side effects. And he seems more and more like the Nate we used to know."

I nodded, wiping away a tear. Pete was right. I was ecstatic that Nate was doing so well, but I still didn't want to leave him. Nate might be ready for it, but I certainly wasn't.

"Plus you *love* your job. Don't you miss it?"

I snorted. "Miss what? The crazy late nights followed by seven o'clock breakfast meetings? Or perhaps it's the stress and anxiety that's so entrenched in every project I take on? Yeah, that's got to be it. Who wouldn't miss *that*?"

Pete smiled at me, tucking a lose strand of hair behind my ear. "Sweetie, the stress comes part and parcel with the thrill you experience every time you land the next big account. And the anxiety you feel comes directly before the excitement I see in your eyes when you burn the midnight oil only to *finally* come up with the perfect creative design."

I listened as my husband pointed out all of the things I loved about my job. I was surprised he had picked up on them; he wasn't usually a man for noticing details.

"Do you know how I can always tell when you've thought of the most amazing idea for one of your clients? You come home humming that song by Bob Marley, 'Three Little Birds.' You might not realize it, but on your best days at work you come home and hum it all night long."

"I do?" I chuckled outwardly.

"Yes. And I have to tell you, I hear it a lot." Pete smiled again, bringing me in for a hug. "It might not feel like it right now because of all that we just went through, but you wouldn't be you without your job. You love it too much. It makes you happy. And we all need you to be happy as much as we need Nate to be happy."

I wiped away tears, taking in what he was telling me. "I want to believe that. I really do. But trying to stay on top of my job with all that's been going on at home hasn't been fun. Or easy for that matter. And the whole work thing has started to feel, well, forced or something. Like I have to be there instead of *want* to be there."

"Try not to overthink it, Ash. Just take it day by day and we'll see what happens."

"One day at a time?" I asked with a half smile, referencing the advice we'd been given repeatedly.

"Exactly. Focus only on getting through today. It's your Day One that matters right now. That's it. You can worry about Day Two tomorrow."

I sighed, thinking that Pete was right. I had to at least try to get through one day.

"And don't worry about Nate at all. I'll be at the school all day again, and he's honestly doing great. And that school is fantastic! You told me yourself you loved everyone you met there yesterday, and so did I. And we can't forget about Nate's new friend there, Adam. I've never seen him so happy about meeting someone new."

"Yeah," I responded, smiling warmly. The two boys had both started at the school the day before, and I had talked to his mother, Olivia, for a long time when they were doing their play therapy assessment with the nurse. Olivia told me Adam had been diagnosed with Tourette Syndrome, and had been having a tough time adjusting in a regular classroom after his diagnosis.

"I'm so glad Nate seems to have found someone so quickly." I glanced at the clock on my bedside table and took a deep breath. I had to go if I was going to have some breakfast with the kids. "It's now or never. My first meeting is at nine."

When Pete and I got downstairs, Grace and Nate were sitting side by side, eating Cheerios. Nate looked up and grinned through his mouthful of cereal. It was the first truly genuine smile I'd seen since he had gotten home.

"Good morning," I said to both of them.

"Do I get to go to my new school again today?" Nate asked eagerly. "My new friend Adam said he wants to play superheroes again. We did that with one of the nurses. I was Batman. So can I go again? *Please*?"

"You bet, champ," Pete replied, tousling Nate's hair. "I'm going to drive you there right after I drop Grace off."

"Awesome!" Nate fist-pumped the air and returned to his cereal. His appetite had returned alongside his newfound zest for school. The twitching had stopped and he was no longer nauseated or dizzy.

I made some toast and we sat at the table eating breakfast

as a family. Pete handed me the business section of the paper, which I pretended to read while keeping my ears tuned into the conversation between my children. Grace was teasing Nate about how quickly his room had become a mess since returning home, and he was bugging her about spending too much time on the phone. Through their bickering, my heart soared. Life suddenly seemed normal again.

"Aren't you going to be late?" Pete said, nudging me. I glanced at the clock.

"I guess." I hesitated. I didn't want to leave my family moment.

"Sweetie, we'll be here when you get back. We'll have a nice steak dinner tonight, okay? Now, go kick some advertising butt."

55
Nate

Dad comes with me to the same room I was in yesterday. I look for Adam but he is not there.

"Where is Adam, Dad?" I ask.

"I'm not sure, champ. We'll keep an eye out for him, though. He should be here soon."

"Nate?" A lady wearing a bright green shirt walks over. "I'm Miss Monica, one of the teachers here at Henry Lewis. We're going to be doing some music this morning. Does that sound like fun to you?"

I stare at the teacher. I blink at her. I like music, but I feel nervous. I don't want to be laughed at by mean kids again. What if they want me to do something I can't do? What if they make fun of me?

Miss Monica continues talking to me. "We're going to play on the xylophone today. Do you know what a xylophone is?"

I nod. I played with one in my music class last year. I learned how to play "Mary Had a Little Lamb." I can play it really, really fast.

"I can play some stuff," I volunteer slowly. I like Miss Monica. She seems nice.

"That's wonderful!" Miss Monica replies. She smiles at me. She takes my hand and leads me down the hall, which has lots of colourful paintings. I can tell they were done by kids. Some of them are good. Others are just scribbles. My favourite one is of a thunderstorm. There is a big bolt of yellow lightning. I am going to paint one just like it.

I want to point out the paintings that I like to my dad. I look around to try to find him, but he is not there.

"Where did my dad go?" I ask Miss Monica.

"He is going to wait in the parents' room. He will be right around the corner if you need him. For our music class, it will be just you and me. But I promise we're going to have lots of fun. Does that sound okay to you?"

I shrug. I want Dad to stay with me. I want Mom too, but she told me she had to go to work again. Then I remember my friend. "Do I get to play with Adam?"

I cannot wait for her to answer. I really, really, really hope she says yes. I like Adam a lot.

"Well, as a matter of fact, you do. He's already in the class. Do you want to go and see him?"

I nod. I'm excited to see my new friend.

When we walk into the classroom, Adam is already there. He is sitting in the corner by himself, playing on a keyboard. His back is to me so I go and sit beside him.

"Hi Adam. What are you playing?" I ask. He looks up at me and grins. He does not say anything, but his eyes are blinking really fast. Sometimes his mouth twitches in a funny way. He points to the keyboard and bangs a song on the keyboard that does not sound good. Every once in a while, I think he might be singing, because he makes a funny noise in the back of his throat that sounds like hooting. But then he stops. It seems funny to me but I don't care about the twitching or the hooting. Because he is my friend.

When Adam is finished the song, he gives me a big grin. I know he is proud of his song. He thinks it sounded good. I won't tell him that it didn't.

"Adam? Nate?" Miss Monica calls out to us. "Can you come over here, please?"

We both stand up and walk over to where Miss Monica is standing by the window. "This is Miss Debbie. She is one of the nurses here and is going to stay with us while we play on the xylophones."

"Can I play my songs now?"

"Of course." Miss Monica gets two xylophones off the shelf and hands one to me. I play "Mary Had a Little Lamb" as fast as I can.

"That's great. Good job, Nate." Miss Monica gives me a high five. "Now, Adam, would you like to play something?"

He shakes his head. "I don't know how."

"I can teach him," I offer. It is easy and I know Adam will be able to play it soon. "Here, Adam. You can just use the colours. I will show you which ones to hit. The first part is red, blue, green, blue, red, red, red. " I bang out the first notes on the colours.

Adam tries next but screws up when he gets to green. He tries to hit it twice, even though you only hit it once. So I show him again. After five tries, he gets it right.

"Is that good?" I ask Miss Monica.

She smiles at me and brings me in for a hug. "Nate, you have no idea just how good that was. I can't wait to tell your parents."

Beside us, Adam starts hooting again.

I think that means he is happy too.

56
Ashley

"Everything okay today, Carty?" Jack asked me, popping into my office. "How's it going, being back into the swing of things?"

"Like I never left," I replied. I forced myself to grin at him.

"Good, good. Happy to hear it. We've missed you. This place has suffered since you've been gone."

"Well, then, I'm glad to be back so that I can be more involved."

"You won't . . . you won't be leaving again, will you?" Jack raised his right eyebrow and peered at me across my desk. He looked both skeptical and nervous, leaning in as he waited for my answer.

I forced myself to respond, pushing the image of Nate from my mind. "No. I'm back for good now."

"Good, good . . ." Jack said again, half smiling, but not looking convinced.

After a moment, he cleared his throat, and started to ask me another question, but then quickly stopped. I sensed it was about what had taken me away for so long.

"Jack, I don't mean to cut this short, but I've got a lot of catching up to do," I interrupted, redirecting the conversation. "And I've got a client meeting at eleven. Don't take this the wrong way, but can we catch up later?"

"Yeah, yeah. Of course. Plus, I'll see you at the client dinner tonight anyway."

"The client dinner?"

"Yes . . . didn't Emily tell you? We're having dinner with Brian, Mark, and Hannah," Jack's right eyebrow returned to its raised position, sensing my apprehension.

I shook my head. "I have a debrief meeting with her, but it isn't until three o'clock."

"Well, she'll tell you there. We're going to Sassafraz at seven. Don't be late." Jack stood to leave the room.

My pulse quickened, and I felt the innate need to please my boss begin to take over. It was one of the reasons I'd always had a tough time saying no, especially to Jack. And it was also why I was often away from my family at night.

I took a quick breath, and responded swiftly. "It's too bad that I didn't know about the dinner sooner. Unfortunately, I won't be able to go tonight as I have a previous commitment."

"Not go tonight? Of course you're going tonight. You're back, Carty. We need you. And it's a big client dinner. It's important that you be there." Jack started to leave the room.

"I'm sorry, Jack. But I can't. As I said, I have a previous commitment."

"To whom? What is more important than work?"

"My family," I responded clearly. I looked Jack straight in the eyes and my voice did not falter. "I'm here all day today. And I will be tomorrow and the next day and the day after that. And I'll work late and on weekends when a client needs me to deliver on creative. But tonight? I'll be home with my family. I didn't know about the dinner. If I had known earlier, I could have made other arrangements. But I didn't, and I've promised my family I will be home to eat with them. So you'll have to go ahead without me this time. It's only dinner, not working on their business, and I'll see them again soon enough."

Jack hesitated. He squinted his eyes, and I started to wonder if he'd had it with me and my absent ways. I was walking on thin ice, and I wondered if I'd gone too far.

"Fine. Whatever. Tell Ben he needs to be at the dinner." Jack practically grunted the words as he started to leave my office.

Then, just before he walked out of the door, he paused and turned to look at me. "Carty? Just promise me you won't leave us for good, okay? This place really isn't the same without you. No one's got the same talent or grit."

I nodded, grinning at my boss and relieved to see Jack show me his cards: he needed me. Even more than I needed him. And he was prepared to be flexible when I needed to put my family first.

"I promise, Jack. I'll be back in the office tomorrow at nine o'clock. Right after I've had breakfast with my kids."

"Fine. We'll catch up then." Jack waved his right hand in the air and was gone.

57

That night, the four of us sat around the dinner table as Nate talked eagerly about his time at school.

"So, really, Adam and I just got to play all day. Even though it was school! Can you believe that, Mom? Can you? We played all kinds of music and then played with Play-Doh. We made all kinds of stuff, and the nurse loved my elephant the most. I could tell. She asked all kinds of questions about it, and said that she liked that my elephant was laughing and having fun with the rhinoceros that Adam made."

Hearing of the elephant sculpture Nate had made at school, my mind flew to the picture that Nate had drawn before being admitted into the hospital. I looked up and glanced at the fridge;

the picture was no longer there. The angry elephant in the sky was gone.

I returned my eyes to my son, smiling at him and taking in his joy. The new medication was working, and he'd made a new friend. Life was good.

"That's really great, honey! I'm so glad you're happy. How about you, Grace? How was your day?"

"It was *awesome*. Because I got to start in my volleyball game again even though everyone else wanted to . . ." Grace launched into a full report of her game, with great detail around all the points she scored. According to her confident self, she'd practically won the game all on her own.

"How about you, Ash? How was being back to work?" Pete asked, grabbing more asparagus tips.

"It was good. Really good, actually. It was great to be involved again, and we had an amazing brainstorming session this afternoon. The team is going to be working tonight on the creative, and I'll circle back in the morning to see how far they've come. We'll get there . . ." I smiled at Pete. Both of us knew that if it had been a few months before, I would have stayed to ensure we reached the right solution.

But I hadn't been prepared to give up my family dinner for anything, or anyone. If the creative wasn't strong, we'd start again. We'd beg for an extension, if absolutely necessary. But we'd get there.

"How about some ice cream for dessert?" Pete asked, clearing the table and heading for the freezer. "A little birdie told me that you kids might like to have some Candy Cane Chocolate Fudge."

"Yeah!" both kids yelled at the same time. Nate whistled a five-note tune to show his glee. It was the second time he'd done it since I got home, and it was new for him. I wondered where he'd picked it up.

"Crazy to think Christmas is right around the corner,"

Pete continued as we all spooned up the minty sweetness of the ice cream. It was a long-standing family favourite that always appeared on the shelves of grocery stores in early December. Nate was licking his bowl.

"No kidding." I swallowed, feeling a slight sense of panic when I realized we had about two weeks until Christmas Eve. With all that we had gone through with Nate, it had come up so fast. We needed to get our tree and buy presents and decorate the house and hang lights . . . the list was endless.

"Can I get a xylophone?" Nate asked excitedly. His lips were outlined in chocolate. "Miss Monica says I'm really good at it. I want to practice at home, too."

"Put it in your letter to Santa," I said, laughing. I stood to help Pete clear the table. "Maybe he'll bring you one."

"I think it's going to be an awesome Christmas. With all we've been through, I'm really looking forward to it this year," Pete said as we loaded the dishwasher. He continued in a hushed voice so the kids wouldn't hear. "It's a new beginning for us, Ash. A new life. And maybe one that should include others we haven't seen in a long time."

I held the spoon I was about to load in mid-air and stared at my husband. I knew what he was alluding to, and I didn't want to talk about it.

"Your dad's stable now, Ashley. And the last time I talked to him he told me that he's desperate to see you again. To explain things. And to be in your life again. But, well . . . I don't think he knows what to say. If we invited him here . . . if we extended an olive branch, I think he'd come."

I began to protest, but Pete cut me off. "Don't answer now. Just think about it. We could invite him here for a few days over the holidays. I think it would be good for *everyone* in our family, not just you."

By everyone, I knew he meant Nate. Of course, Grace missed her grandfather as well, but Nate had been hit the hardest by my father no longer being in our lives. The two of them had always shared a special bond, and it was Nate who always brought up his name and asked when he was coming back. Nate had never stopped obsessing over every gift my dad had ever given him before we'd kicked him out on that awful Christmas Eve.

The more I thought about it, the more uncomfortable I felt. The anxiety was turning my neck into a mosaic of patchy red skin, and I didn't want to think about it for one minute more. I knew Pete had a point about reconnecting, but despite everything I had learned about my father, I still didn't know if I could handle reconciling with the parent who had practically abandoned his daughter when she had needed him the most.

"I don't know. We'll see," I said curtly, shutting down the conversation. Offering a "maybe" was all I could promise him at that moment. It was all I was ready for. The rest would have to wait.

58

The days leading up to Christmas flew by at the speed of Santa's sleigh as Pete and I scrambled to get ready. Nate continued to do well in school, adjusting to his new classroom at Henry Lewis more and more each day. We hadn't seen him so happy and well balanced in years. He continued to see Dr. Aldridge, although she had recently suggested that he could begin to see her less frequently. His response to the new meds fell well within the best-case scenario Dr. Aldridge had offered us, and even she was astounded by Nate's progress.

Pete didn't press the suggestion of inviting my father for Christmas again, and I was silently relieved to not have to think about it. Although we were both excited about the holidays and how well Nate was doing, every day was a new day, and we never knew what we would get. Dr. Aldridge had warned us repeatedly that something unexpected could trigger a setback, or even a really bad day. Regardless of my own feelings about reconnecting with my father, I didn't know how something as major as a visit with his grandfather would impact Nate's progress.

On the Friday night before Christmas, we invited Tay's family over for hot chocolate and Christmas cookies. It was the first social activity we'd engaged in with people outside of our immediate family since Nate had come home from the hospital. I was nervous about what could happen, but we needed to start somewhere. And Tay's family felt like an extension of our own, so they were the perfect choice.

"Why don't you want to tell anyone? What are you so worried about?" Tay asked me that night, taking a sip of her wine. We were sitting across from each other, next to the glowing fire that burned hot underneath a mantle of evergreen and white twinkly lights. Our husbands were downstairs with the kids, playing a game of Twister and eating gummy worms.

"Protecting Nate. He's suffered so much already. The kids in his old class were crueler than I could have ever imagined. Just because he wasn't acting 'normal.' And now that we know what we're dealing with, I don't know that it will stop, just because Nate's symptoms have. Mental illness isn't something the world accepts with open arms. The minute everyone knows . . . *really* knows, well, I'm worried about how they will treat him. If they will accept him, or if they will be malicious, just as they were before. As long as I protect the truth, I can protect my son."

"But Nate's at a new school now."

"I know. And it's been wonderful for him. I've never seen him so happy. But he can't stay there forever. Sooner or later we'll need to integrate him back into a regular classroom."

"Believe me, I absolutely understand the need to protect your children. And I know you have Nate's best interests at heart. But you can't keep the secret forever. If you do, Nate will start to think of it as just that. A secret. He'll think he shouldn't tell anyone either. Which will make him feel like it's a bad thing that he should be embarrassed about. And he shouldn't. Bipolar disorder is just like any other disease that any of us could suddenly be diagnosed with. It isn't anyone's fault, and it's certainly not something to be embarrassed about."

I took a big sip of my wine and thought about what Tay was saying. The last thing I wanted to do was make Nate feel embarrassed about the hand he'd been dealt. While he would need to come to terms with his disease, and I suspected that would happen in different ways as he grew older, I never, ever wanted him to feel embarrassed by it. Or, for one split second, think that I was.

"Ashley, you're his *mother*. If you're not the one standing by his side and acting one hundred percent committed to Nate and all that he's been dealt, who will? He's going to feed off your actions. If you don't tell anyone, he won't either. And over time he'll think that it's something he shouldn't talk about. I don't know what the future holds, or if Nate will suffer because some ignorant idiot doesn't fully understand mental illness, but you'll deal with that when it comes."

"I don't know . . ." I responded, taking another sip of wine. "I'm not sure he's ready for that."

"Just think about it. You don't need to do anything tomorrow, but soon the day will come. I think you should let Nate be proud of who he is. Mental illness and all. Good or bad, it's a part of him. And none of us should ever be ashamed of anything that is a part of us."

"You're right about that," I answered simply.

"Of course I'm right. As always," Tay said, laughing. She helped herself to the bottle of wine sitting in front of us, filling my glass first and then her own.

"Mommy?" A little voice behind me asked. "Can I go to my room for a bit?"

I turned to see Nate standing behind us. He looked like he was near tears. "Of course, honey. Is everything okay?"

Nate shook his head and ran up the stairs. I glanced at Tay, hoping he hadn't heard what we'd been talking about, and went up the stairs after him. He had crawled in bed and buried himself underneath his duvet and pillow.

"Nate?" I asked, peaking underneath his covers. "Everything okay?"

When he didn't respond, I crawled in with him and gave him a hug. I decided to wait until he was ready to talk to me and tell me what was on his mind. It was the first time since being in the hospital that he'd had a sudden mood shift, and I didn't want to push him.

After about five minutes, he said to me in a very quiet voice, "Mommy? What is bipoly disease?"

"Bipoly?" I asked. My heart screeched to a standstill. Pete and I still hadn't fully told Nate about his diagnosis. We felt he was too young. But he'd clearly heard something.

"Yeah. What you and Auntie Tay were talking about. I came up for some more hot chocolate and I heard you tell her that I have a disease. Bipoly disease. Am I going to die?"

"Oh sweetie, no!" I sat up and pulled Nate into my lap. His moment of truth was about to find him, whether I liked it or not.

"Then what's wrong with me? Everyone keeps pretending like everything is okay. But it isn't! I know it isn't. You don't stay in the hospital if everything's okay. Why can't you just tell me?" Nate looked up with eyes as round as saucers, full with tears.

I took a deep breath and knew what I had to do. I began the story, right from the very beginning. Right from the very first night Nate had left the house.

I left no details out. Dr. Aldridge had told me that Nate didn't remember the vast majority of the last two months. And he deserved to know. It was about him, after all, and the fate he'd been given. There was no reason to hide it. And absolutely nothing to be embarrassed about.

"So that's why I needed to start taking all of that medication? It's why I stayed in the hospital for so long?" Nate's memories had begun to kick in at around the point in my story when he'd come home. When the medication had started to work. Before that, memories were pretty foggy for him. Like a dream, he explained.

"Yes. And it's the medication that has made you better. And a whole bunch of other things, alongside it."

"Like what?"

"Well, like all of your conversations with Dr. Aldridge. And the art lessons you had with Payton. And your music lessons at Henry Lewis." I pulled my son in and kissed the top of his head. "A whole bunch of people have worked very hard to make you better. And you are doing so great! I'm very proud of you. You are making friends at your new school, and the teachers and nurses say you are doing so well and learning lots of new things."

"I know. I really am." Nate's response was confident and bold, and he smiled when he'd said it.

"Yes, you really are," I agreed. Behind me, I heard Pete quietly walk into the room. He sat on the bed. I suspected Tay had gone to get him so that he could join my conversation with our son, and she was probably downstairs entertaining Grace to keep her distracted.

"So now I have bipoly disease? And I have to keep taking my medication and going to my new school to stay better?"

"Bipolar disorder," I corrected. Beside me, I could feel Pete become rigid, still uncertain about whether telling Nate was the way to go. But I was tired of keeping everything a secret. I didn't want to give in to the disease we'd all been handed.

So I continued. "Yes, honey, we suspect you have something

called bipolar disorder. We don't know for sure yet, but Dr. Aldridge is pretty sure that's what's going on."

"When will we know?"

"Well, right now she's diagnosed you with something called Psychosis NOS. It basically means that we know you need to keep working with Dr. Aldridge, and that you need to stay on your new medication, but that we won't know for sure until Dr. Aldridge can provide her final answer in about six months. She wants to monitor you until then, just in case we find out other things or something different happens."

"Six months? How long is that?" Nate asked.

"Probably by next summer," Pete said.

"Whoa. That's a long time from now!" Nate exclaimed. "Does it mean I'll get to stay at my new school until then? Do I get to stay with Adam?"

I nodded. Despite learning everything I could tell him about his disorder, he was fine. There was no embarrassment. No stigma. No shame.

In that moment, something clicked, and I decided to bridge a very big gap between two worlds that suddenly seemed way too far away. "There's one other thing, buddy. One last thing you should know. It's about your grandpa."

"Grandpa?" Nate asked excitedly. It was the first time in three years that I'd mentioned my father to Nate.

"Yes. Grandpa. The biggest reason we think you have bipolar disorder is because your grandpa also has it. And it's genetic, which is a fancy word for something that runs in our family."

"Really? I'm the same as Grandpa?" Nate asked excitedly. I felt a sharp pang rip through my heart. My son missed his grandfather so much that he was overjoyed to hear about the disorder that bound them together, even through their years of separation.

"Yes, sweetie. We think you have the same disorder as Grandpa."

"Can I . . . can I talk to him about it?" Nate asked.

"I don't know, hon," I replied honestly. "Maybe we'll see if we can get together with him soon. But I don't know for sure that it will happen. We'll have to ask him first."

Beside me, I sensed that Pete was smiling. He pulled Nate and me in for a group hug and it was in that giant squeeze that I started to really feel like everything might be okay.

59

We invited my father to visit us, starting on New Year's Day. Pete called him at home in Florida, and my father eagerly accepted our invitation to come to Toronto. He found a last-minute flight and booked a room for three nights at a hotel close to our house. Even though we had the space, we both knew it would be far too uncomfortable to have him stay with us.

"Do I look okay?" I asked Pete nervously. The kids were upstairs cleaning up their rooms, and Pete and I were getting out cheese and crackers to offer my father when he arrived. I looked down, smoothing non-existent wrinkles from my winter grey dress. "Maybe I should have worn jeans. Do you think I should have worn jeans?"

"Honey, it's okay. Your father won't care how you're dressed. He's so excited to be coming here. Anything other than that won't matter to him."

"Yes, well, it will be good for him to see the kids," I said, checking my lip gloss again in the mirror.

"That's true. But he also wants to see *you*, Ash. You're his only child, sweetie. And I happen to know that he loves you very much."

At that moment, the doorbell rang. I froze where I was standing, a brick of old cheddar dangling from my right hand.

"It's okay. I'll get it. You stay here." Pete gave me a hug and walked towards the door.

"No!" I said, almost too forcefully. "I mean, no, thanks, honey. I will get it. I can let him in."

I held my head high and walked towards the door. When I opened it, I found my father standing on the step, looking as nervous as I felt.

He had lost a considerable amount of weight, and was far too skinny for his frame. His face was gaunt, filled with wrinkles that were new to me, and he looked much older than the man in my mind.

"Hi Ashley," my father said. He extended his arms to offer the big bouquet of purple freesia he was holding. I was touched that he'd brought them, that he'd even remembered they were my favourite. I accepted the flowers, inhaling deeply, and was instantly transported back to happy times with my mother. I loved purple freesia so much because they reminded me of her. They were her favourite too.

"Uh, hi. Thank you for the flowers. Please, come in." I held the door open for him. He awkwardly stepped in, and took off his shoes.

Pete shook my father's hand and offered to take his coat. My father's frail body became more exposed, and I realized just how emaciated and undernourished he looked. I couldn't even guess how much weight he'd lost.

"*Grandpa!*" Nate shrieked, interrupting my thoughts. He ran into the front hallway and ploughed into my father, giving him a giant hug. It was the happiest I'd seen Nate in a long time.

"Well, hello, young fellow," my father chuckled, returning Nate's hug. "Look how big you've gotten. You're huge! Practically a man yourself —"

"I've missed you!" Nate squirmed out of my father's grip and peeled off his sweatshirt to reveal his faded, orange shirt that read *Grandpa Loves Me.* It was about four sizes too small. "Look! I've still got the T-shirt you gave me. And I still love it! I haven't thrown it out, even though Mom wants me to."

My mind immediately flew back to the Christmas Eve when my father passed out the shirts, and I found myself getting flustered at the memory. I forced myself to focus on the present.

"Where's Grace?" my father asked.

"I'm here," Grace responded, walking into the hall and giving her grandfather a shy hug. "Hi Grandpa."

"I really can't believe this. You kids . . . you're . . . you're so *big!*" my father said, his eyes growing misty. The tear he wiped quickly from his right eye did not go unnoticed by me.

"Why don't we let Grandpa come in? We can go and sit in the family room. We've got some snacks we can put out, and then we can have a visit. Does that sound okay?"

We made our way into the family room, and settled into the couches. "Can I get you something to drink?" I asked my father.

"Just a water, thank you," he replied quickly. I breathed a sigh of relief, thankful for the non-alcoholic drink order. I had been so worried he was going to ask for his beloved single-malt Scotch.

I handed my father his water, and put out the cheese and crackers, noticing as I put the tray down that my hands were shaking. I wondered if everyone else felt as uncomfortable as I did. Stealing a quick glance at my father sitting awkwardly on the couch, I suspected that he did as well.

As I sat next to Pete on the couch opposite my father, who was sitting with a grandchild on either side of him, I realized it was only the adults who felt any sense of angst. Grace had launched into stories about all of her friends at school, and Nate was eagerly showing his grandpa all of the new toys he had gotten for Christmas. My father was nodding happily, alternating his attention between the kids. It was as if they had never been apart from each other.

I cleared my throat uneasily, trying to figure out a way to participate in the conversation. "How was your flight? Did you have any trouble getting here?"

"No, no. It was fine, actually. I'd been a bit worried about it because I haven't flown in a long time, but everything turned out okay. And it was worth it to be able to come here." My father smiled at me across the table, his new wrinkles deepening as his grin widened.

I was shocked to hear him say that he hadn't been on a plane. "You haven't flown in a while? But you love to travel." My father had been a consummate world traveller, continually hopping from continent to continent, visiting friends in each place. He was *the* global jetsetter whose bags were always packed for the next big adventure. I wondered what had happened to change things.

"I just . . . haven't. Things are different now." My father took a deep breath and looked straight at me. "A lot of things have changed in the last three years, Ashley. I'm not the same father you used to know."

I nodded, unsure of what to say next.

"Mom, can I have some chocolate milk?" Grace asked, standing from the couch and starting towards the kitchen.

"Oh! Me too!" Nate was quick on his sister's heels, leaving Pete and me alone with my father.

"Where do you live now?" I asked my dad, realizing I didn't even know where in Florida his house was.

"On the coast. A little town called Melbourne Beach. It's about a hundred miles from Orlando."

"Do you live in a condo?" After I said the sentence out loud, I realized how sad I was to have had to ask. It hurt my heart to fully realize that I had no idea where my own father lived, or anything about him. We had become completely estranged.

"A little house actually. It's very small. But it's right on the ocean. I love to go for walks up and down the beach. Early in the morning, and often again when the sun is setting. When I went through my uh . . . I mean . . . when I stopped to really learn a few things about myself a year or so ago, I realized that my favourite place to be is on the water. But I had to get out of Miami, which is where I'd lived previously. The place wasn't good for me. So I moved to Melbourne Beach."

"It sounds lovely," I responded. "Do you live with anyone there?"

"No. Just me. I have a few friends that I sometimes get together with to play afternoon bridge. And we always go for Sunday brunch after church. But it's just me in the house."

"You go to *church*?" We had gone all the time when my mother was alive, but after she died, my father claimed to have become an atheist and turned his back on the church. He had vowed to never return again.

"Yes. Every Sunday, in fact."

"When did you start going again?"

"About a year or so, I guess. It's a small little community chapel. It's Christian based, but non-denominational."

"I see."

An awkward pause took over the room, and I wished the kids would come back. "The kids are certainly happy to see you," I said, hoping they'd hear me from the kitchen and take it as a cue.

"And I'm so happy to see them. They really are wonderful kids, Ashley. You both should be very proud."

"We are," Pete said. He took my hand and gave me a squeeze, as if to say everything would be okay.

"When are we eating?" Grace called from the kitchen. "I'm *starving*!"

"Soon. Why don't you come out here and have more cheese and crackers if you're hungry?" I stood from my chair. "I'll go grab the kids and check on dinner. It's lasagna. Is that okay with you, Dad? I remembered how much you used to like it."

"It's great, thank you." My father looked pleased.

"Mom?" Grace whispered when I walked into the kitchen. "Why's he so *skinny*?"

"I don't know, sweetie. I guess he lost some weight." I brought my kids in for a hug. "It's so nice to have him here. We haven't seen him in a long time. Why don't you go and visit with him some more, and I'll finish getting dinner ready?"

I used dinner preparation as an excuse to escape, and puttered about the kitchen while my father talked to Pete and the kids. When we finally sat down to eat, the awkwardness I'd felt earlier followed us to the dining room table.

"Can you please pass the salad?" I asked, pointing to the big wooden bowl filled with Caesar-covered romaine and croutons.

My father lifted the bowl and passed it down the table. It looked heavy for him, almost as though he was struggling to lift it. He smiled sheepishly, realizing that I had noticed.

"How long are you on Christmas break for?" my father asked the kids. He took a sip of his milk, which he'd requested with his meal once we'd sat down.

"Twelve more days!" Grace replied gleefully. I raised an eyebrow at my daughter, finding it interesting that she was suddenly excited about being off. Just two days before she had begged to go back so she could see her friends.

"I go to a new school now," Nate said between bites of pie.

I'd made lemon meringue, as it was another one of my father's favourites. "It's awesome there. And my best friend Adam likes all the same things that I do. Especially superheroes!"

"That's wonderful. I'm glad you found a friend you like so well," my dad said. From across the table, I watched his response carefully, and tried to gauge whether or not he previously knew about Nate's new school. After Pete's confession in the hospital, he'd promised to not have any more contact with my father. Other than calling my dad to invite him to come, which I'd asked him to do, my husband had sworn up and down that he hadn't talked to my father again.

"What's your school called?" my father asked. The look in his eyes was so genuine that I knew wholeheartedly that he'd had no more contact with Pete. Which meant he also didn't know about what Nate had been through. Or that his grandson had followed in his bipolar footsteps.

"It's called the Henry Lewis School Hospital," Nate answered simply. "And I love it!"

"Hospital? I think you've got your words mixed up," my dad said, grinning at Nate before he took another bite of pie.

Nate shook his head. "Nope. I meant hospital, silly grandpa. Didn't Mommy tell you? I've got bipoly disease . . . just like you."

60

After dinner, my father and I stood side by side in silence while we finished the dishes. He washed the pots while I dried. Neither of us spoke.

I'd managed to quickly change the subject after Nate's confession about him being bipolar, but I knew neither my father nor I had stopped thinking about it since. And I was certain he had many questions for me, just as I had for him.

Pete had made a quick exit after helping clear the table, offering to help Nate with his new helicopter Lego set that he'd gotten in his stocking. Grace was upstairs talking on the phone.

"Ash," my father started, just as I cleared my throat to say something to him.

"You go first," I offered. I wasn't sure what I was going to say anyway.

"Is it true? What Nate said tonight . . . is he really bipolar?"

"We think so," I replied honestly. "He's been officially diagnosed with Psychosis NOS, which stands for —"

"Not otherwise specified," my father interrupted gently. "I know what it means."

"Yeah . . . sorry. I sometimes forget that you know a lot about all of this, too."

"Ashley," my father started. "Can we sit down? I've got some things I'd like to explain to you."

I nodded and pointed to the kitchen table. We sat across from each other in silence. His breathing became rapid, almost as though he couldn't get enough air. He was more nervous than I'd ever seen him.

Then, finally, after a breath so big I thought he wasn't going to exhale, my father began to talk.

After he'd left our house that Christmas Eve three years prior, it had been a fast and fierce downward spiral into the wild pit of uncontrollable blunder. He started drinking earlier and earlier, sometimes barely making it past breakfast before he poured his first Scotch, and didn't stop pouring until he'd passed out.

Most often, somewhere around the tenth or eleventh drink in my father's day, rage would slowly seep into his body, quite often metastasizing into vicious attacks on whoever happened to be with him. He alienated every acquaintance he had in one way or another, ultimately driving them all out of his life. Before long, he had no one left.

"So I moved to Miami," my father continued, fidgeting with his fingers. "Thought I'd start over and make new friends. But it turns out I got mixed up with the wrong crowd there, too . . . which I know sounds funny for a guy who's almost seventy years old." He chuckled lightly at his own expense, but I remained fixated on everything he was telling me. I was absorbing every word. It was the first time my father had been completely engaged. The first time since I was seven years old that we'd had an honest conversation filled with meaning.

"Pretty soon the booze wasn't enough. I have no idea when I got into the drugs . . . I actually don't even remember my first time . . . but I somehow got mixed up in cocaine. I was spiralling more and more out of control. I knew where I was headed, but there was nothing I could do to stop it."

"Why didn't you call someone? Didn't you want help?" I asked gently, trying to shake the guilt that suddenly over-whelmed me. If I had been a better daughter, and not kicked him out the way I had, he might have found the strength to call me.

"I don't know. I knew I *should* have wanted to get help, but for some reason I didn't. Or I couldn't. I'm not really sure which one it was." My father sighed, pain from long-ago days clouding his sober eyes. "It's tough to explain. You know that scene in *Titanic* . . . the one where they know the iceberg is right in front of them . . . and they *know* that they need to steer the ship. They even *know* exactly what they have to do to avoid smashing into that iceberg, yet . . ."

"Yet they just can't seem to get the ship to turn?" I finished. "No matter what they try."

"Exactly." My father looked down at his hands, which he was wringing together tightly. I could see how hard this conversa-tion was for him. "I knew I was going to smash into the iceberg. And I knew what I needed to do in order to avoid it. But for some reason, I just couldn't manage to do it."

I nodded. After seeing what Nate went through — how he had so little control over what he did — I could understand what my father was saying.

"And then that fateful night came. Too much blow. Or maybe it had nothing to do with the drugs. I don't know for sure, although my doctor is convinced the drugs were a trigger. The hypomania I'd been experiencing for years intensified, leading to extreme mania with psychosis. I turned into a full loony that night, thinking Russian spies were out to get me and a whole bunch of other crazy stuff."

"Yeah," I said gently. "Pete filled me in on what happened that night. I'm so sorry that you went through it." *Especially with me not being there for you*, I thought to myself.

"I was admitted into the psych ward. Stayed in the hospital for three months before they let me out. Can you believe that? I was locked up in a psych ward for three *months*."

"Why so long?"

"It took a while to diagnose. At first, they thought I might be schizophrenic. And then I had a hell of a time with meds. It seemed every side effect known to man had a thing for me. Nausea, rashes, hand tremors . . . you name it, I had it. So then they had to give me more drugs to help with the side effects. I wasn't suffering from psychosis any longer, but I was a walking zombie. It was awful." My father shuddered in his chair, remembering his hell on earth.

"I know how hard it can be. Nate . . . he, uh, he had trouble with his medication as well. He experienced wicked side effects. Thankfully, his psychiatrist quickly switched him to Aripiprazole and, well, so far it seems to be working well for him."

"That's good. I've heard good things about Aripiprazole. I tried it, but it didn't work so well for me, I'm afraid. I'm on Quetiapine. Seems to be working so far."

"Have you . . . have you had an episode since your first?"

My father shook his head. "No, after I got clean and finally found the right meds for me, I've been okay. And I count each day that I'm episode-free right along with my sobriety. My psychiatrist assures me that for every day I go without an episode, the less chance there is for a second or a third."

"That's great. I'm glad you're better."

"Yeah. It's been a long road, but I finally feel like I can at least see down the one I'm walking on now." My father smiled deeply, and I was immediately taken back to a time when I was a child. It was the last time I remembered seeing him genuinely laugh, and I forgot how good it made me feel to be with him when he was happy.

"Can you tell me what happened to Nate?" My father gently invited me to bring Nate into the conversation. And I knew what he was asking. Every bipolar person has a story.

So I started at the beginning, just as I had done with Nate himself, telling my father everything that had happened over the past year. Other than Tay, it was the first time I'd told someone absolutely everything, and it felt as though a pound of weight was being lifted from my shoulders with every word I said. My father did not take his eyes off me as I explained everything, and I watched them repeatedly fill with tears as I recounted the ride Nate had been on.

"Ashley . . . I'm so very, very sorry. About everything." The tears that had dampened his eyes while I was telling him Nate's story finally fell, coursing down his cheeks. "I was an awful father to you. I know that now. And I should have been there for you while you were dealing with all of this."

"But you didn't know! You didn't know what was causing you to act the way you were."

"The disease is not a complete excuse. After your mom died, you needed me. You were *seven years old*, for goodness' sake. I can't imagine dealing with losing a mother at that age. And you should have had me there to help you through it. But I wasn't. I wasn't there for you. And you will never know how sorry I am about it, or how much I regret it."

"This disease . . . it makes you do funny things," I said. "It takes over rational thinking. And judgement. You couldn't have known that at the time. You didn't know."

"You're right. I didn't. But the six-week bout of depression

I went through after your mother died wasn't normal. Even for a man who had just lost the love of his life. Deep down inside, I knew it. Even then. And if I had just listened to what my gut was telling me, maybe I could have gotten help sooner. So that you wouldn't have had to spend your childhood parentless."

"What was it like to go through? When you were so depressed, I mean." I'd wondered about it for years, and felt the closeness of our current conversation had opened the door to ask. As a child, I'd caught glimpses of my father in his darkened room. Never sleeping or talking or eating. Always staring, never seeing. A breathing corpse.

"It's tough to describe. To be honest, I don't know that anyone can fully understand it unless they've been through it. To call it depression is an understatement because, on the surface, it simply implies sadness. And that part is there, for sure. But it barely scratches the surface of what it's truly like. It's very different from sadness. Bipolar depression is much, much more than that. I mean, if you even step outside, the sun *physically* hurts your entire body. Which is why I kept the room so dark. You can't even see the sun or a light. The pain hurts too much. You just want to be dead. Because, in that moment, there is no reason to live."

I took my father's hand in my own. It felt like ice, and I realized as soon as I touched him that he was shaking like a leaf. "Are you cold?" I asked him. "I could get you a sweater. Or we could go by the fire?"

"No, no . . . I'm alright. It's the tremors. From the meds. It's the one side effect I haven't been able to shake. It gets worse when I'm nervous or upset." My father shrugged apologetically.

I squeezed my father's hand. The tremors seemed to lighten up a tiny bit, although I couldn't be sure if it was just my imagination.

"Can I ask you something? Do you . . . do you think Nate's going to be okay? I'm so afraid of the future. Every day when I wake up, I'm scared that Nate will slip back into an episode and I'll lose my son all over again. Do you think it will happen?" I'd wanted to ask someone since Nate had come home, but I'd been too frightened.

"I don't know," my father responded honestly. "But I do know that you are doing all of the right things for your son. He's very lucky to have you."

"But what if he has another episode? What if he goes crazy again?"

"Ashley, listen to me. This is an awful disease when it's at its worst. There's no doubt about that. But when it's properly treated, a person can be a fully functioning member of society. And Nate will continue to get stronger with each day that passes. The longer he goes without an episode, the less likely he is to have another. And there's no reason why Nate can't live a normal life. There are so many people walking around with bipolar disorder. Probably more than anyone knows."

"There are?" I asked, sniffling into the sleeve of my dress. I wanted to hear more about the success stories. About the people who had figured out a way to properly treat bipolar disorder and were living normal lives as a result. I was deathly afraid that Nate wouldn't be healthy. I was scared my whole family was going to spend a lifetime in fear of another horrific episode.

"Yes. I'm very sure about that. There are a ton of people out there who are leading healthy, happy lives. They're not scared of it . . . they've embraced it. They've accepted everything about it, and have created thriving lives for themselves. For example, one person in my support group is an absolutely amazing teacher. He teaches the fourth grade. And he's going to get married this summer to a fantastic woman who loves him wholeheartedly and unconditionally. And another person in my support group is a judge. He's been on the bench for twenty-five years."

"A judge? Really?"

"Yes." My father patted the top of my hand as if to comfort

me. A sprinkle of warmth shot straight to my heart. It was the first time in over thirty years that I felt I had a parent guiding me.

"These people that I'm telling you about . . . they aren't afraid. And they aren't ashamed. Because it is who they are and, in many cases, it has shaped who they've become. My very own ER doctor who admitted me when I first went into the hospital? She is also bipolar . . . and she's a *wonderful* doctor because of it. When I talked to her again about a year after I'd been diagnosed, she told me that it's the reason she went into medicine. That having the disease has made her more empathetic to her patients."

"So you really think Nate could be okay?"

"I believe bipolar disorder can be properly treated. If Nate stays on his meds, and continues any form of therapy that proves helpful for him, then he's got more than a fighting chance. Add in his tenacity and courage, and I have no doubt. My grandson has a long life ahead of him. One he should be looking forward to."

I nodded, thinking about the irony all around me. Bipolar disorder was a complicated disease that had taken my father away from me for too many years, and yet it was also what had brought him back to me.

"Ashley, listen to your father," he said, taking both of my hands in his. He was still trembling. "This tragedy that you've been through in the past few months? I know it's felt like hell . . . but, if you look harder, I think you'll see that it's actually been a blessing. It's really what gave Nate his life back."

"How so?"

"The greatest power we have in this world is knowledge. And we have that now. We know what we're dealing with. Which means a treatment plan with the ultimate goal of a healthy life. Without that, Nate would have been stuck in a dark box, struggling to come to terms with why he couldn't cope with life the way he was supposed to." My father sighed, looking straight into my eyes. "I know how this sounds, but unless you've been there, you can't fully understand how difficult that is. But I assure you, now that Nate is on the road to recovery, he's been given his life back. And that's a gift. If Nate hadn't gone through his first episode, he wouldn't have been diagnosed. And he would have been trapped in what feels like never-ending purgatory."

I took in all that he was telling me, believing for the first time that things would be all right. No matter what.

Having the father that I'd missed for a lifetime comfort me in the way that all parents should made me weep. I couldn't hold back any longer. I fell into his arms, crying openly, and let my dad wipe away my tears as if I were seven years old again.

61
Nate

"Grace? Grace! Wait for me, would you? Stop!" My heart is racing, and I struggle to keep up with my sister. She is practically running across the swinging planks that are hanging so high up in the air they are part of the tops of the palm trees that surround us.

I feel like we are towering above the whole world. Because we actually are. We are so high up in the air that we are actually in the fronds. That is a very big word for palm tree leaves. I know that because learned it in my science class at my new school.

"Please, Grace! Wait up!" I'm breathing hard. I'm very scared. But I know I need to keep going. I have to finish walking over the swinging planks so that I can get to what's next: the big long rope that I have to walk across. All by myself. Way up in the air. But I will. Because I know I have to do it. I know I have to just keep going.

Grace laughs as I call after her again. She shrugs her shoulders, like she is trying to tell me that she doesn't care. She won't wait for me. She starts skipping across the wobbly planks that are so high up in the air.

I stop for a minute. I try to wipe my hands on my shirt. It is really hard for me to do. I can't do it very well because the plank I am standing on is so wobbly that it is knocking me off balance when I let go with two hands. So I try and only let go with one hand at a time. I wipe my right hand first. Then my left.

In front of me, Grace throws her head back, still laughing, and lets her hair float all around her. The sky that surrounds her is bright blue. She is getting farther and farther ahead of me.

I am too scared to run after her. Too scared to catch up.

We are at Treetop Trek in Melbourne Beach, and my grandpa has brought my whole family here for the day so we can try out the obstacle course challenge. Behind me, I can hear my mother's calm voice, encouraging me to move forward.

"Go on, Nate. You can do it . . . I'm right behind you. You won't fall." Something in my mom's voice reminds me of when I was little. It is quiet, only a bit louder than a whisper, and makes me feel instantly better.

It is the second day of our March Break vacation. When we woke up that morning, Grandpa said he wanted to kick it off with a special surprise for our whole family. So we piled into his car, and he drove us to what he said was the best thing in Melbourne Beach.

"Grandpa!? Are you serious?" Grace yelled when Grandpa pulled up to the front of the park. "Julian, a boy in my class who I absolutely adore, was just telling me about zip lining. I've been absolutely dying to try it! How did you know?"

Grandpa laughed quietly from the front seat. "I didn't actually."

"Uh, Dad?" my mom said to Grandpa. "Have you forgotten that both Nate and I don't like heights?"

Grandpa turned his head around to look at my mom. He smiled and winked. "No, Ash, I haven't forgotten that part at all. In fact, it's exactly why I brought you here."

Sitting in the car, the whole thing seemed a bit mean to me. And I felt bad for my mom when we were all on the ground, looking up at the longest zip line. She was breathing quickly, and kept squeezing her lips together. I could tell she was very, very scared.

"It's okay, Mom," I whispered to her. My heart was pounding — big time — just thinking about going up in the air. But I didn't want to hurt my grandpa's feelings. He seemed so excited to bring us there. "I'm scared, too, Mom. Maybe we should do it together. I think it would make Grandpa happy."

"I don't know, Bean. I'm not sure I can go that high up . . ." my mom said. I watched her take a big breath of air as she put up her hand to block the sun from her eyes and looked up to the obstacle course that was so far up in the sky.

"I think you can do it. We both can." I was surprised to hear myself trying to convince her to do something that I didn't want to do myself.

Mom shook her head. She pursed her lips and took a deep breath through her nose. "Honestly, Dad? This wasn't really what I had in mind when we brought the family to Florida. Couldn't we have just gone to the beach or something?"

"Tomorrow, Ash. And the day after that. Today it's all about overcoming fear." I watched Grandpa and Mom exchange a look. I could tell they were both thinking of something that they weren't going to share with the rest of us.

"Okay . . . I guess I'll do it. If Nate will too. What do you say, Bean? Are you still ready to go up there with your mom?"

I nodded. I was suddenly not as brave as I was when I was trying to convince her to go. But I didn't want to disappoint my grandpa.

"You coming too, Dad?" my mom asked, laughing. I could tell she didn't think he would.

"In fact, I am. It will be my fourth time. The strength trainer I've been working with is the one who recommended it. Said I've become strong enough to do the whole thing. And, what d'you know? He was right." Grandpa grinned. He looked very proud of himself.

Once we all agreed to start, the people who worked there helped us into our harnesses. Then we started the climb up the ladder to the beginning of the course. My dad and Grace went first, followed by my grandpa. Then me. Then Mom.

Now I am walking across the bridge, which only has hanging planks. It is kind of like a ladder but it is a bridge. A very wobbly bridge.

"You can do it, Nate. Keep going. I'm right behind you." There it is again. Mom's soft voice that is gentle but also strong. It makes me feel better. So I keep going.

My legs are shaking underneath me, making the planks shake from side to side. I take a big breath. Try to make myself balanced. Then I start walking again.

With each step I take, I become less and less scared.

By the time we all reach the first zip line, we are laughing and having so much fun. I am loving every minute of it. And so is my mom.

At the zip line, a man helps attach a thing they call a caribiner to the wheel that is on the cable. I stand on the platform and look out in front of me. All I can see is a big open field in the far distance, with lots of palm trees surrounding the rope. If I follow the rope with my eyes, I can see another platform that looks like it is very far away. My dad and Grace have already taken their turns. My sister screamed the whole way across.

319

"Your turn, Dad," my mom says, laughing, and Grandpa makes us both promise that if he goes first, we'll follow him. He whoops and laughs as he flies through the air. I stand next to Mom and we're both laughing as Grandpa is waving one of his arms and looking goofy. I laugh and say to Mom that he looks like a wild bird.

"A seagull?" she laughs.

"More like a pelican," I say, and soon we're both giggling hysterically. I can hear in our laughs that we are both still nervous. I feel very jumpy.

I go next. I want to show her that I can do it. I want to show my mom so that she won't be scared.

I start to feel even more nervous. Mom is standing beside me. "You can do this, Bean. I know you can." Her voice sounds reassuring, but also nervous.

"You can too, Mom. You promise you'll do it too?" She nods. They move me up to the platform and I can feel the belly bubbles start. But they're different than the belly bubbles I used to feel. "I'm not scared, Mom. I'm not scared anymore."

And suddenly, I'm flying.

62
Ashley

I watched my son soar through the air. As soon as he pushed off, his face looked terrified, like he'd realized he'd made a huge mistake. My heart leapt, and I just wanted to grab him and hold him back, but it was too late for both of us. And before I knew it, he was shrieking with joy the entire way across.

I stepped up to the platform. I'd never done anything like this. Everything in my body was screaming for me not to do this. But if Nate could find the strength, then I could too. I looked down and my stomach clenched. It was so far down. This was crazy. What if something happened? What if the rope broke? What if the handbrake faltered and I crashed into everyone on the other side?

I looked across and saw Nate and my dad on the other platform, motioning for me to follow them. Grace hopped up and down, and Pete waved happily.

The angry elephants were gone. In their place was my family of goofy pelicans. And I wanted nothing more than to join them on the other side. I could do this.

I took a deep breath, and jumped.

Acknowledgements

Sadly, I know too many people who have struggled, or are struggling, with mental illness. Many of them are acquaintances.
Some are within my family. And one person, in particular, is an
extremely close friend.

And I've watched, often helpless, as he's had to brave a scary
world that has been filled with demons of his own making — and
then, later, a scary world filled with judgement and stigma. Yet,
despite all of these obstacles, he has risen above. And today, he
is healthy. Thriving. Happily married, in a job that he loves, and
surrounded by family and friends who adore him. Many people
don't have a clue what he has been through. I'm quite certain

new friends would be in complete disbelief if they knew what actually happened so many years ago.

Elephant in the Sky is inspired by him. And a lot of what happens in this book took place in his real life. He told me that I could write his name in these acknowledgements. And, while I am so very proud of his courage, I realized that I simply couldn't do that to him when it came time to put pen to paper. Because I know that, despite his strength, there is too great a chance that others would come to false conclusions. Despite the fact that he *is* now living a healthy and happy life, some people would likely judge. As a nation, we are getting better. But the stigma still exists.

So my inspiration for this book shall remain nameless. But he knows who he is. I just hope he also knows that his unfaltering determination and relentless tenacity makes many of us extremely proud. He is an absolute pillar of strength and I am in awe of all that he has conquered and accomplished throughout the years.

Although it sounds clichéd, it is true that this book wouldn't have been finished without the help of many people. And I am grateful, first and foremost, to Brian — my husband and all-around rock. He not only constantly reassured me that I could write this book and encouraged me to keep going, but the father of our three wonderful children took on extra bath, bedtime, and clean-up duties to give me the extra time I needed to write. Brian, our life is filled with a whole lot of chaos, a ton of hard work, and even more happiness and joy, and I can't begin to imagine sharing it with anyone other than you.

To the first readers for their encouragement and insight: Ann Clark, Kathy Vucic, Ines Colucci, Wendy Gardham, Anthony Iantorno, Steven Clark, Jessica Belaire, Ian Clark, Donna Rawbone, John Rawbone, Brooke Allen, and Penny Hicks. Thank you for reading such an early draft of the manuscript, for your thoughts and perspective, and for loving the story enough to help me make it better.

I'm lucky to be surrounded by teachers and thankful that I'm able to turn to them when I have questions. Thank you, Steve Clark, Jessica Belaire, Katie Freure, and Tom Freure for always being so willing to answer questions about teaching elementary school and kids in a classroom.

To Dr. Jane Aldridge, who always lets me ask her endless questions about the medical field. Thank you for emailing back and forth with me about hospital visits, walking me through various medical procedures, and pointing me in the direction of thorough research when I needed detailed information.

And to Dr. Tonia Seli, who went above and beyond to help me better understand both psychiatry and mental illness. Dr. Seli, you really helped me a lot by taking so much time to explain the things that I needed to know. I had fun during our Starbucks chats, and I really appreciated that you would read through the manuscript with me to help ensure I got everything right. Thank you very much!

I'd also like to thank the parents, whether close friends or Facebook and Twitter acquaintances, who helped me see the world through the eyes of a nine-year-old. Thank you, Kathy Vucic and TJ Parass for sharing Oliver's writing samples, and Tom and Katie Freure for all of your kid-writing tips. And also to Andrew Selluski, Chantal Barlow, Marina Campbell-Matthews, Diana Flumian, Theresa Harding Gilligan, and Joanne Tenyenhuis.

To Dan Erenburg, one of my favourite New Yorkers, for giving me the answers to all of my Manhattan questions.

Thank you to the amazingly talented Negin Sairafi for the picture on the back of this book. I always have so much fun at our photo shoots, and she is a genius behind the camera.

And a big thanks to Constable Matt Baker, a dear friend and fantastic police officer, who let me ask him endless questions about his work. Whether it was a silly question sent over text message about whether or not a cop would take their shoes off when walking into a person's home, or a bigger discussion around protocol when dealing with missing children, Matt was always willing to help.

Helen Keller once said, "Alone we can do so little, together we can do so much." These words took on new meaning to me when I published my first book, and realized how many people (and how much work!) goes into each one. I'd like to thank all of the many people at ECW Press who have touched *Elephant in the Sky* along the way.

First, to my amazingly talented editor, Jen Hale, who has the ability to seamlessly move from lighthearted chatter about what a nine-year-old might call his parents to intense conversations about the impact of mental illness on a family. I know how lucky I am to be able to work with someone who edits the words on the page while also brilliantly reading between the lines of the story. Jen, you not only turn me into a better writer, but you are also a treasured friend.

To Erin Creasey, whose early and avid endorsement helped open so many doors. Thank you for being in my corner and for helping me in so many ways since the very beginning.

To Crissy Calhoun for all of her hard work and guidance. (And for always letting me have "a few extra days" whenever I needed it. You have no idea how much it helped!)

Thank you to my publicist, Sarah Dunn, for helping me get the message out about *Elephant in the Sky* and for always being there to help in whatever way is needed.

To David Gee, who kept designing until we got to the cover on the front of this book. I think it's amazing. You are so talented!

Thank you to Laura Pastore for proofreading the manuscript, Rachel Ironstone for the typesetting and production, and all of the amazing sales reps at Manda and Legato for keeping *Elephant in the Sky* on the right peoples' radars.

And to Jack David and David Caron, the publishers of ECW

Press, for having the faith in me to write a second book. Jack and David, you have built an amazing company and I've loved working with everyone throughout the entire process.

And thank you always and forever to my family, both immediate and extended . . .

To our amazing nanny, Chelsea Bradshaw, who uses her imagination to create magical worlds of discovery for my favourite three wee ones, while also taking amazing care of them in every possible way. I love how you love our kids and am so appreciative of all that you do for our whole family.

To Viola Burr, and in loving memory of Great Nana, who read *Chai Tea Sunday* out loud multiple times. Your support means the world to me.

To my big and happy family that I am so blessed to have married into: John and Donna Rawbone, Carolyn and Ivano Tonin, David and Karen Rawbone, Leanne and Mike Rafter . . . and for the ten grandchildren (ages five and under!) who fill our family functions with so much happy chaos. I have the sweetest nieces and nephews in the world — and I love them so much I couldn't help but borrow their names for some of the characters in this book.

To my brothers, Ian Clark and Steven Clark, who continue to fill my world with endless laughter and unhinged adventures. You guys are the best brothers a girl could ask for.

To Jessica Belaire, who not only rocks as a sister-in-law, but also helped me so much throughout the writing of this book, including helping me think of the perfect title.

And to Dale Mosser for always opening the doors to his cottage so I could write in the most beautiful place in the world. Dale, your kindness is never-ending.

To the two people who first taught me about unconditional love. Thank you to my mom, Ann Clark, for believing that I could do this before anyone else did. And to my dad, Bill Clark, for teaching me that dreams come true through determination and hard work. We don't get to pick our parents, but if we did, I'd still pick mine. I love you lots.

And finally, thank you to the great loves of my life: my husband (who is so wonderful he deserves two mentions) and my children, Avary, Jacob, and Emerson.

artbund
WHERE ART DOES GOOD

A portion of the proceeds from the sale of *Elephant in the Sky* will be donated to Artbound, a non-profit volunteer initiative that harnesses the power of the arts to ensure that underprivileged children live better lives.

Partnering with artists and those passionate about the arts, Artbound raises funds to build schools in developing nations to provide children with a full education, including art schools and programming. Their programs are designed to empower children through leadership training and the development of skills that will improve their living conditions and generate sustainable income to help break the cycle of poverty. In addition to arts programming, Artbound also raises funds for clean water facilities, medical care and alternative income programs — all working in unison to allow children to learn and develop in a healthy and safe environment.

Still, many more children are left behind, struggling with debilitating poverty and lack of education. Artbound will continue to raise funds to build new and fully sustainable infrastructures in communities most in need across the globe.

The Artbound team is comprised of young Canadian leaders from various industries who are dedicated to engaging a global community in volunteer, school building and mentorship. Please visit artbound.ca to learn more.

Invite Heather to Join Your Book Club

Heather loves to join in on the conversation. If your book club has selected *Chai Tea Sunday* or *Elephant in the Sky* and would like her to attend your meeting, just ask and she will meet you there! If distance is a challenge, Heather will video call your group using Skype or FaceTime, or call into the book club over the phone.

Simply go to HeatherAClark.com to contact Heather with the date and time, and she will do her best to schedule a visit.

GET THE EBOOK FREE!

At ECW Press, we want you to enjoy this book in whatever format you like, whenever you like. Leave your print book at home and take the eBook to go! Purchase the print edition and receive the eBook free. Just send an email to ebook@ecwpress.com and include:

- the book title
- the name of the store where you purchased it
- your receipt number
- your preference of file type: PDF or ePub?

A real person will respond to your email with your eBook attached. Thank you for supporting an independently owned Canadian publisher with your purchase!